The Bloodshed of the Betrayed

Written & Illustrated by

A. L. Slade

This is a work of fiction. Names, characters, places, and incidents are either the product of the author's imagination or are used fictitiously. Any resemblance to actual persons, living or dead, events, or locales is entirely coincidental.

Publication Data
Anthony, Amy.
The Bloodshed of the Betrayed / A. L. Slade
Series: The Mercy Chronicles; Book 1
Summary: "Upon falling in love with a human, angel Laramie sets off a series of events that changes both of their lives for the worse with malicious interference from Lucifer himself."

www.alslade.com

—TABLE OF CONTENTS—

The contents in this book are purely fictitious; however, some elements may be triggering to certain individuals. Mentions of self-harm, assault, parental abuse, blood, suicide, death, insomnia, eating disorders/mental illnesses, domestic abuse, sexual assault, and rape. If any of these topics are triggering to you, I encourage you to continue fastidiously. Reader discretion is strongly advised.

This is for Jennica Comley,
The first true fan of my work.

Prologue

aramie shuffles into the Fulfillment Room once the angel ahead ducks out and leaves. She glides forward and stops in the center of the room, her body language reserved and submissive. A circular halo protrudes from the top of her scalp into a vertical ring of blazing light, the manacle that binds all angels as God's followers by forcing them to rely on God for their sight.

'There is a task awaiting your… prowess which pertains to the happenings of Earth.' Laramie's designated Authoritarian Razael barks, one of Heaven's many regulators who assign responsibilities and dole out consequences.

Heaven's hierarchy classifies each angelic rank within the Angelic Choirs. The First Triad comprises Authoritarians, Seraphim—God's immediate attendants who oversee their throne—and Elders—the living symbols of God's justice and authority. The Second Triad consists of Dominions—those who regulate the duties of lower angels—Virtues—those who embark upon Earth to dole out signs and miracles—and Powers—those who supervise angels' affairs. The Final Triad consists of Scribes—the educators and monitors of Earth who control what knowledge Humans possess of Heaven and God's existence—Archangels—those entrusted with tasks within Heaven—and finally, Angels—

the lowest order of celestial beings most concerned with the affairs of Heaven.

When Razael speaks, Laramie raises her head ever so slightly, the tawny amber wings protruding from her back resting carefully around her shoulders. 'A disturbance has been sensed at 43.013000, -81.218900 and requires surveillance. You have been enlisted to go there and record any irregular behaviour. You will be issued a Conversion Clock and are to record your findings and meet with Scribe Batair to ensure they are transcribed properly.'

Laramie lifts her head, inky black hair parting around her face, to find a familiar gold stopwatch, a furled parchment strip, and an ornate quill-like pen placed atop the cardinal pedestal in the center of the room. She nods her head solemnly. "I will not disappoint."

The air thins and she can feel Razael glowering. 'I should expect not. Go now.'

Laramie swipes the pedestal's contents to proceed to the exit when a sudden sensation develops in her previously emotionless interior. She falters, the impossibility of the foreign feeling leaving her momentarily stunned. She stiffens in place, unsure how to proceed when she *feels*. What does she do? Why does she feel? What does it mean? Has she done something wrong?

A hollow emptiness overwhelms her system, reverting it to its rudimentary state. For the first time since she was appointed and inured to her responsibilities as a Virtue, Laramie doesn't know what to do.

She feebly glances up at Razael, desperately seeking guidance. His expression remains the way it always is when he regards her, scrutinizing and cold. However, something new flickers behind his eyes—something Laramie fails to notice, too preoccupied with her sudden affliction.

'Go now.' Razael repeats, his tone sharp and booming. Quickly returning to her senses, Laramie elects to ignore her conundrum in favour of focusing on her assignment, taking a moment to recall what it is before clambering out of the room, hasty to leave Razael's presence.

The tension instantly seeps from her body as soon as she is outside Razael's range. Carefully pocketing her instruments with trembling hands, Laramie soars towards the portal that separates Heaven's and Earth's domains, also known as, The Passage.

Landing gracefully just in front of the sealed rift, Laramie idly watches as the Power stationed a few feet away steps forward to unlock the apertures mechanisms—the entryway expands in a current of swirling cloud-like light to delineate her silhouette. Gentle splashes and whistling winds accumulate a modest breeze that disrupts the indifferent air.

Laramie flexes her wings and momentarily hesitates, allowing herself to consider her affliction without Razael looming over her. It's unlike anything she's encountered to date; emotions, they're forbidden. Perhaps by ignoring it, they will cede, and she may never think or speak of this again.

Confident in her plan, Laramie focuses on suppressing the emotions whirling around her body in a frenzy. She valiantly crosses The Passage and begins her descent to Earth.

MAGDA

I return to my dorm with a heavy sigh, closing and locking the door behind me. After an hour-long lecture, the only thing I can focus on is taking a nice long nap, preferably one I can wake up from after exams are over and I already have my degree, but that's neither here nor there.

Despite being only twenty-three years old, my body feels like it's waning already. There are only two reasonable explanations: either I'm severely out of shape and practice detrimentally poor posture, or I'm a twenty-year-old university student trapped in the body of an eighty-year-old. Both are equally likely, so I may never know the answer.

Shrugging my backpack off my shoulders, I kick off my shoes and unpack my books to study. Just what I need after almost falling asleep during an exhausting hour-long lecture; mindless studying for another six hours or so. I shuffle my music playlist and turn the volume on low while sorting my textbooks by which ones I need. Finally pulling my notebook from my backpack, I rub my eyes a bit too aggressively before begrudgingly beginning my studies.

Since I'm essentially another broke college student, it'd be accurate to assume my dorm isn't very nice. It's small, and I've procrastinated properly furnishing it since I initially moved in (not that I even own that much stuff anyway), which means I've got a few stacks of partially unpacked boxes scattered around the room. It's got everything a basic room needs, though; a bed, a desk, a bathroom, and a dresser, but nothing more really. The only thing I bothered to install in my room is a painting my younger brother got me for my sixteenth birthday, truly a testament to his adoration; a grey canvas with 'WORLD'S OKAYEST SISTER' written in bold black letters.

When my phone suddenly rings, startling me, I almost throw my textbook across the room. I manage to stop myself before chucking the stupidly expensive hunch of tree and ink at the wall, and instead, I gently drop it on my desk with a solid *thump*. After checking the caller, I eagerly accept the video-chat request, propping my phone against the stack of books on my desk.

"Finally figuring out technology, are we?" I joke with a grin. "Hey, Dad."

Dad's smile seems forced—feigning happiness. "Hi, Magda. Just calling to check up on you. How are things?"

I nod. "Pretty good. Where's Mom?"

"What, you can't stand to have a nice conversation with your dear old dad for once without your mother?"

"You hit the nail right on the head, old man."

Dad smiles. Luckily, it's more genuine this time. "She's in the bathroom right now. So what's going on with you?"

"Well, I just got back from class like, ten minutes ago. I'm doing some studying now since I have another class in a few hours."

"Oh, sorry, dear, I didn't mean to interrupt."

"Nah, it's cool. I'm always happy to hear from you."

He glances around, nervous and distracted. His expression is far from his usual happy-go-lucky grin; instead, his eyes are downcast, and his lips are pressed into a disingenuous smile. It spikes my anxiety. "Is everything okay?"

He nods quickly—too quickly. Something's up. "Of course! Everything's just fine with us. How's university treating you?"

"Pretty good, actually," I'm unconvinced but decide against prying, instead, hoping I can at least distract him from whatever's on his mind. "It's a lot of work, and I've been pretty exhausted lately, but I'd say I'm enjoying it, I think. It's school, so I can't say for certain yet."

Dad smiles and exhales shakily, glancing away from the screen in silence for a few moments. I open my mouth to say something when he bobs his head and turns back to the camera with another fake smile. "Well, sweetie, I just wanted to see how things were with you."

I nod slowly, suspicious. "Yeah, okay. You're acting kind of weird, Dad. Well, weirder than usual. You sure everything's okay?"

"Of course! Never been better. Feeling spiffy."

"Dad, I love you, but I'm pretty sure you're the first person to use the word 'spiffy' since the eighteen hundreds."

I flinch when Dad barks out a laugh, throwing his head back in a hearty guffaw. It isn't until I feel myself smiling and my shoulders sagging that I realize just how uneasy Dad's behaviour made me. It's a huge relief to see him laughing like this and to know he's capable of it, at least.

"Oh, sweetie, I needed that laugh. But, I should go now. I love you, Maggie."

"Oh, okay. Bye, I love you too."

"I hope we'll get to see you soon," His trembling lips catch on his words, almost like he's choking on them. He sounds like he's in pain, if only from the soft sobs barely suppressed in his throat.

"Me too," I answer with as much deliberation as I can manage. I don't want to force Dad to talk if he doesn't want to, but seeing him so distressed is unnerving enough that I have to stop myself from prodding him.

I try not to let my smile falter, focused on providing as much comfort as I can to ease his worries. I wave before Dad ends the call, his parting words of, "I hope we'll get to see you soon," echoing like claps of thunder in my head. I lean back in my chair for a few long moments, wracking my brain for anything I may have said that upset Dad, but a part of me knows with complete conviction that whatever is bothering him precedes our conversation. Still, I can't help but gnaw on the possibility that I did something wrong.

I chuckle humourlessly. My tendency to overthink, while typically unhelpful, is one of the main reasons Mom and Dad seem to think I'll be a good doctor. I don't disregard any possibilities; instead, I consider them all before making a decision. Again, this doesn't always work in anyone's favour (especially mine) since I tend to needlessly plague myself with every worst-case scenario, no matter how unrealistic or down-right impossible they may be.

Despite knowing it won't absolve me of my nervous paranoia, I attempt to concentrate back on my studies, if at least as a momentary distraction from my newfound worries.

LARAMIE

Laramie lands gracefully, shrugging her shoulders to adjust her dishevelled feathers as she pulls the Conversion Clock from her robe and clicks it open. The gold surface of the device shines brilliantly, bathed in sunlight—the left panel indicates mortal time while the right converts it into angelic terms.

Friday, October 1st, 2021, at 11:26 am, becomes "Medaen," meaning "noon." Glancing briefly at the time, Laramie snaps the device shut and pockets it with a calculated swiftness. Lifting her head, the Virtue scans her surroundings for her destination, eyes darting over the encompassing expanse. She regards the pale blue sky with newfound fondness and watches the fresh snowflakes raining in a shower of sparkling white fractals. When one lands on her forehead, she flinches, reaching up to feel the moisture gathering on her skin. A flurry of emotion that she can't even identify sweeps her; giddiness, excitement, fascination, overwhelm, tranquillity. It's as though she only recognizes the empty pit her chest used to comprise now that it's been filled.

The angel smiles coolly and squeezes her eyes shut to face the sky. Snowflakes dust her face in an intense burst of feeling where everything is so new, raw, and pure.

She feels *everything,* and it's indescribable.

Wiping the flakes from her face, Laramie composes herself to the best of her abilities and peers around the frosty terrain. She instantly recognizes the sidewalk to her left that branches off towards the small town of Lauder, Ontario, the district she's been delegated.

Shaking her feathers to rid them of their accumulated snow, she fares the biting Whynthal air and soars above the rooftops, laughing freely at the snow falling all around her. She slows only when she determines her coordinates, a large building bustling with commotion none other than Salcombe University.

Gliding just above the main entrance, Laramie perches atop a concrete awning, allowing her legs to dangle over the edge. She swings them once, twice, three times before retrieving the scroll and pen from her pocket to begin her assignment.

Determined to transcend her commission to prove Razael wrong with his constant expectation that she'll fail, Laramie immerses herself in the routine practice of observing and recording. Her eyes dart methodically across the landscape, inquisitive as she unfurls her blank scripture.

As dozens of humans spill in and out of the University, Laramie takes a particular interest in watching how their bodies move. She clings to the way their chests rise and fall with each intake of breath and the shift of their body as they walk. She watches as their hair billows in the whipping wind and the way their face enlivens if they see someone they recognize. She's captivated by the subtle shift of their face as their emotions fluctuate and the way their eyes narrow fractionally.

Laramie eases herself into the familiar routine of identifying aspects of interest and filtering it by importance in her head. No movement nor glance goes unnoticed by her; her eyes flit around the campus at a speed that should be impossible as her hand moves autonomously to record her observations as she makes them.

Turning her attention back towards the humans mulling

around, Laramie takes note of the slight limp in human #58's steps. She records the way human #23 listlessly cards his fingers through his dishevelled hair and human #12's hunched posture and ceaseless trembling as she staggers inside the building, teeth audibly chattering. The angel chronicles human #4's abnormal attire; instead of her usual black pants and blue winter jacket, she now wears a knee-length sleek blue dress with tall boots to match. Her hair is styled in an intricate braid that has Laramie mesmerized, her nose, cheeks, and ears dipped in a rosy red from the cold, her features enhanced with a fine layer of cosmetics. She's trembling intensely, her pace hurried and swift. Laramie accounts for the woman's unusual attire with a quick flick of the wrist before proceeding to the next point of interest.

She pours herself into her task, prepared to detect any disturbances, whether unassuming or explicit. Everything feels relatively normal enough, and nothing strikes her even remotely wrong, as Razael had implied, yet she can't help but anticipate something consequential approaches. Why else would she, of all her peers, be asked to supersede its notation?

Her concentration is seized by a sliver of movement beneath a nearby tree. She immediately whirls in the direction of the disturbance, following it with inquisitive eyes. She's able to determine its source when a dark figure stoops beneath the topiary with his back facing her. All Laramie can identify is his blond, ruffled hair, dark robes, and what looks like the contour of armour outfitted on top. Cocking her head to the side in speculation, the Virtue's jaw tenses, and she squints at the distinct sight of long, pale wings folded behind him.

Leaning forward, Laramie grips her quill tightly as she stares at the figure. Their head slowly turns to face her, and as soon as his face is visible, his malicious smirk paralyzes her in place.

Shaking her head, she scrambles to gather her thoughts while viciously scrawling on her parchment, gaze fixated on the figure. Her eyes momentarily scan his surroundings for anything explanative of his presence when she's captivated by a young woman heading into the university.

—ONE—

The Beginning Of The End

LARAMIE

ow.

She is *ineffable.*

I can't even begin to comprehend the sensation that imbues my chest when I see her. As soon as I catch her in my periphery, I can't bring myself to look away—when I regard her, I'm struck by the sight of her soul.

Even if it is merely for a second, I become transfixed by it; its colour is indescribable, one not yet seen nor termed by humans. Her presence encapsulates a warm hug promising comfort and safety, the burst of uncontrolled laughter in a spontaneous moment of jubilation, and the purest intimacy one could experience with their most trusted partner, and tethers them to a word I've never known before; home.

She has determined almond irises focused forward intently. Her long silky brown hair shimmers in the sun and sways in the wind with every bouncing step. There's a persistent eagerness in her gait, toned legs visible through the fabric of her pants, sliding across the concrete with confidence and calculation. She has pronounced Aboriginal features; a chiselled aquiline nose and taupe skin speckled with a constellation of acne across her face.

Something stirs within my very being, an ache that settles deep within my chest. It tugs, beckoning me to follow the human. The cajole of home, of following her and feeling like I've found where I need to be, tempts me, unlike anything I've ever experienced. It impacts me with such force that I feel tears blur my vision.

The only thing that keeps me from pursuing the human is the steady fear thrumming through my body, holding me in place. I hesitate, forcing myself to glance back at the figure under the tree as his eyes meet mine. A chill ripples through me, and I fight the urge to look away. His expression darkens, and the faintest ghost of a smirk dances across his lips before he suddenly flees. My immediate instinct is to give chase, however, I can't seem to leave the human when I turn back to face her. Something about her lures me from the only life I've ever known towards the possibility of experiencing the indescribable feeling of belonging.

Of being home.

Unable to fight the compulsion, I absentmindedly drift behind her on the sidewalk.

Razael's cold, stern voice shatters my stupor, reverberating in my mind as soon as I begin my contradictory pursuit. 'Do not discontinue your task. You have one chance not to abscond, or the consequences will be dire. Return to your post and continue recording irregular behaviour.'

Despite his warning against it, I can tell that what Razael wants is for me to abandon my post; the most diminutive form of infraction of his rules will goad him into banishing me for good, something I don't doubt he's wanted to do since The Dawn.

Something worrisome and thick accumulates into a thick

mass that lodges in my throat. Despite understanding that my fate depends on my fidelity to God, I know now with a certainty embedded in my very core that I must follow the human. It is my new purpose, not subjugated by God but bestowed by fate, by the very foundations of reality.

As much as I know I am only doing what Razael wants me to do, I don't care. I know I'm not doing this for Razael or anyone else. For the first time since my conception, I am doing something for myself.

I ignore Razael's warning and resume my pace in pursuit of the human. As compelled as I feel to her, I'm careful not to come close enough that I may come in contact with her, the knowledge that even the mere brush of my fingertips against her skin would have me petrified as stone, keeping at an arm's length.

To dissuade angels from fraternizing with humans (and thereby disobeying God), God has enforced penance when contact ensues between an angel and a human; the angel will, thereby, turn to stone. It has proved effective as a deterrent to more and more angels from even venturing to Earth, lest one misstep condemns them eternally.

Understanding I cannot embrace her to any degree, I instead allow myself to entertain the possibility that I may be authorized to reveal my corporeality to her; a burst of hope ignites within me when I realize that I may still interact with the human despite its improbability, granted I receive permission from a superior. As unlikely as it may be that I could somehow convince Razael to allow me to brandish my ubiquity, I cling to the knowledge that it's not yet unattainable.

Nothing would please me more than to know she can see me. That I no longer must glide unseen by her. That she may gaze upon my being and bask in my essence—what we call our Grace (that inhabits a mortal-looking form), the pure unrefined light that is what flows as blood beneath our skin and administers us our celestial abilities.

I know Razael and God will not approve of my fascination, but the way I feel—and the fact that I do—is unexplainable. And what an absolute bliss it is to *feel.*

Until now, angels have maintained emotionlessness, our interminable compliance the price we pay for existence. Emotions are a hindrance we lack that emboldens our fidelity to God; it has never been a requirement (or pertinent) to learn what emotions are and what they mean. Because of this, I cannot determine the emotion I feel with any level of conviction, as there is nothing I may compare to it. Is what I feel lust? Infatuation? Obsession? Adoration? There's no way for me to tell.

Besides, where have these emotions originated? Why have I begun to feel now? What has changed? Have I been tainted somehow, beguiled by a temptress human?

Something heavy and uncomfortable settles over me. My arms fall limp at my sides, and my hand brushes against the Conversion Clock in my pocket, the sudden realization of my long-abandoned task hitting me. What am I to do? How may I face Razael after abandoning his assigned task in lieu of my newfound fixation for a human?

It pains me to do so, but deep within, I know I must return to Heaven despite how badly I yearn to remain here, on Earth, with the human, never to face Razael again. How may I confront Razael—how may I face *Heaven* while I'm in a state of complete disarray? And… I feel. I *feel* and I *shouldn't.* I need help, I need to know what's happening to me, but the answers are not on Earth. If there even are answers, they will be in Heaven, stored safely in The Athenaeum, an incomparable book repository that contains unanimous worldly and otherworldly expertise.

At this point, it's my only hope.

Before making the difficult decision to leave the human, I manage to catch a glimpse of the keycard in her hand for her name: "Magda Mercy." Those two words provide satisfaction I've never felt before, a feeling of predestined affinity.

Refusing to look back, I turn away from my beloved Magda and allow my wings to spread behind me in their entirety. I ascend, soaring through the sky, approaching the mass of clouds hiding The Passage of Heaven.

The rift opens slowly, granting me ratification. I fold my wings as I land, my head cast down while I hastily rush to The Athenaeum in search of Scribe Batair; as she is expecting my presence, the probability that she may help me dramatically exceeds the likelihood of anyone else doing so.

I quickly locate the Scribe most frequently assigned to me in my periphery and hurriedly approach, admiring her from afar. She has gorgeous ebony skin, her halo and wings correspondent of her complexion. Her inky black dreads flow down to her waist, the reflection of a Stillfall sky cast across a murky waterfall. The only blemish she bears is the deliberate designs engraved onto her halo, symbolic of her status as a Scribe.

"Batair," I greet.

The Scribe looks up and turns to me with a curt nod, a simple acknowledgment of my presence. 'Virtue Laramie, I welcome you from your excursion. Shall I begin my transcription?'

I shake my head. "I need to speak with you about something first. It's imperative."

She regards me carefully, calculating. 'I… don't understand. You are amidst an unfinished task and have not been permitted to infringe upon it. It would be unwise to interrupt for something unrelated.'

I don't bother to hide my desperation, freely begging. *"Please,*

Batair. I need your help. It will take no time at all, I promise."

Something flashes behind her eyes, and she hesitates, silent for a few long moments. Finally, she nods and says, 'All right. What is it you need from me?'

Relief hits me harder than I'd anticipated in a euphoric wave. "I need your help identifying an… emotion."

She looks down for a moment before meeting my gaze again. 'That's… it's impossible that you are… that you feel.'

"As is what I thought as well. But I… I cannot say I've ever felt like I have now. I know I am feeling, I know something is wrong, but please, I need to know what it is. Maybe then I can gauge what it means and how I may… fix myself."

This time Batair stays silent much longer. Apprehension rushes through me as I await her response, suddenly terrified upon realizing she could warn Razael of my disobedience before I have a chance to explain.

'Okay,' She finally acquiesces. 'I will help.'

"Thank you. Thank you, Batair." I compose my thoughts before ultimately confessing to the worst act of treason I could commit as an angel—its severity just beneath directly revolting against God's authority. "It's… I've felt… I've gravitated towards a human. Involuntarily. She's captivated me; I cannot seem to resist her influence. The only way I can explain it is for the first time in my existence, I've been given a chance to choose my purpose, one that is not mandated by another but offered by my own volition. This human has allowed me to devote my entire being to her existence, to love her like no other may. The only other option I have is demise, something I will gladly choose if it guarantees her happiness and safety."

Despite knowing she does not feel emotions as I do, I cannot help but sense the shock emanating from Batair when I finish.

She stands silently as I reconsider every word I said, lest I'd accidentally admitted something I shouldn't have.

'Well, I cannot say I've known any angel to… to feel as you do, and as unsure as I am that you are capable of feeling this so soon, I surmise the emotion you are experiencing is love.'

Love.

While it may be nothing more than a potential explanation of what I've begun to feel, certainty solidifies any doubt I had within me, and I know now, without question, that what I'm feeling *is* love. I love her.

I *love* Magda.

'You should speak with Razael,' suggests Batair. 'There is no more I can do for you. If you are truly feeling emotions, you should speak with him so you may understand further what has become of you.'

I nod, mindlessly filtering her words, unable to focus on what she's saying as all the tension I've undergone suddenly dissipates from my body. Euphoria suffuses me with the overwhelming epiphany that if I have the ability to feel something so sanguine and remedial, I am not blighted but blessed.

An atmosphere of trepidation wrests me from my thoughts when I realize Razael's admonition weighs heavily in the air, concentrating around my being.

-TWO-

Here I Fall

LARAMIE

I turn around sedately, almost immediately paralyzed in anticipation of what may befall facing an irate Razael. While it startles me that he's chosen to confront me before I could approach the Fulfillment Room, ultimately, it reminds me of the severity of my negligence, and with it comes the sickly premonition that this will decidedly not end well.

'Face me, Apostate,' he spits. 'I entrust you, the most... *proficient* Virtue, with a time-sensitive task relative to a dangerous disturbance God sensed, and not only do you vacate your post, allowing it to go undocumented, but you willingly ignore my reminder of your task to frolic amongst a human, whose mere presence can slaughter you if you misstep. You have gone against my direct orders, and for what? What could possibly warrant such blatant disrespect and excuse your selfish behaviour? What could your human possibly possess that could necessitate banishment?'

The word alone makes me shiver, the weight it carries palpable even to the others all around me. Once exiled, banished angels become foredoomed to spend the rest of their time amongst humans on Earth, losing the ability to interact to any degree and perform miracles. They can do nothing but create torrential downpours and fatal storms with their weeps, the length of their deterioration conditional on their crime.

I'm subtly aware of Powers beginning to surround me, their accumulation threatening and potent. To my dismay, I sense Batair's absence alongside the glint of the swords each Power wields; Elyspiennes—weapons forged by God that boast the ability to sever any surface with its blade.

I stumble back a step without realizing, the metal of the nearest Elyspienne shining a hypnotic off-white blaze.

"Forgive me," I nervously stumble over my words as I force myself to face Razael. I shift my gaze enough that I can still see the nearest Elyspienne in my periphery, vibrating with ill-conceived intimidation and apprehension. "I humbly repent for disobeying your orders. I did not mean any disrespect. I…" I hesitate, choosing my words carefully. "I have a confession. I have… felt things on Earth. Emotions. A mortal—her name is Magda—has provoked them."

My voice dies in my throat when I feel the air darkening, a dangerous ire radiating from Razael's Grace. 'You have put us all at risk with your insubordination. We've come to discover it was Lucifer who had been sensed. The severity of this occasion required your immediate transmission of his location and any cues that may indicate how he managed to escape Hell.'

"I saw him."

'And what? You allowed him to flee? You failed to notify me immediately. Your negligence and selfishness could very well result in the avoidable carnage of our angels, the bloodshed of the betrayed, and defilement of Heaven. All for one human. Is that correct?'

The reality of what I've done alongside the scrutinizing gazes of my choiren is humiliating beyond remission.

"Yes," I whisper.

'And, alas, I tried to warn God not to send you on this quest, as I knew you would succumb to human feelings; your newfound emotions were a test, one to determine whether or not angels are prepared to feel again. God instructed me to give you emotions, and, as I expected, it's clear now that *you* are not. You have proven willing to bypass obvious danger in the name of affection towards another kind. As this human clearly means more to you than Heaven and our choiren, you may keep your feelings and your precious human. No greater punishment befits you than banishment.'

Dismay and dread consume me. My voice starts working before I even think to speak. "Razael, please, I'm sorry. Please, I will do better. I know I have sinned, but have mercy on me. Please, forgive me. *Please,* Razael…" I falter as two Powers yank me to my feet by my armpits, firmly steeling me in place. I'm easily overpowered yet struggle against them still, even as my body is pinned in place without any exemption.

"Please!" I plead, desperation clinging to my voice. "Razael, I'm begging you, please don't do this to me. I repent, I-I'm sorry, *please.* Mercy! MERCY!" My shrill cries are ignored as I'm stripped of my armour and forced onto my stomach. An angel's foot presses down into the small of my back, preventing me from escaping.

"MERCY!" I flail my arms to dislodge my combatants, but they don't even seem to notice. Only when rough hands seek purchase wherever they may find to outstretch my wingspan to its breaking point, do I start weeping. I arch my back to ease the pressure when they're pulled taut, but the foot digging into my back presses me harder to the ground. I cry and scream, but not one angel from the crowd watching my persecution unfold seems to care. I suppose I shouldn't blame them, as they lack the authority to intervene and would only face the same punishment if they even dared to indicate that Razael is misguided.

I brace myself for the pain, craning my neck against my better judgement to see the Powers' behind me. I watch in muted horror as one of them raises his Elyspienne, the blade swinging through the air above me. I turn away seconds before the surge of pain washes over my right wing, white-hot agony overtaking my back synchronously with a similar piercing sting in my halo.

I scream, desperately squirming beneath the pressure of the angel's foot. Wet, hot blood pours from my back, drenching my torso and sides as it soaks through my robe, pasting the fabric against my skin. The bright red hue of my Grace begins to darken in front of my very eyes as I'm forced to watch the angelic power drain from my being.

Weak and tired, I allow myself to sag fully against the ground, too tired to bolster myself any longer. Opaque blood drips down my neck, forming a puddle beneath my chin. My entire body benumbs in pain and exhaustion. I try speaking, managing a hoarse, "Please…" despite knowing Razael will choose to overlook my pleas. There's nothing I can say that may change the course of my fate, no matter how willing I am to reverse it.

Another slashing pain rips through my wings and back. I barely have time to cry out when my wings are brutally ripped from my shoulders concurrently as my halo shatters. I can feel pieces fracture and shower the ground in front of me, severing my connection to God—my holy bond into two broken horns. My eyes throb from the sudden loss of light, and I blink, squeezing my eyes shut as I'm overcome with an icy chill.

As soon as the weight of the angel's foot shifts from my back, my shuddering increases almost tenfold. I move to wrap my back with my robe to stop the bleeding further, but my limbs are so weak I can barely move my hands. The humiliation of feeling every angel's gaze on me has me meekly burying my face into the ground, ignoring the blood smeared across my forehead and nose.

I hear Razael's voice as though beneath a lake, unable to distinguish his words. Had I the energy to look up at him, I expect I would've seen a smug smirk leering down at me—all the more incentive for me not to look up.

When the Powers grab me by the armpits again, the sudden movement jostles my fresh wound with an abrasive burn. They callously drag me to The Passage, severed open by a bleary figure I barely recognize as Razael himself. A gust of cold wind strikes me in the face, and I manage to desperately claw at the Power's holding me despite my exhaustion. My exile is finalized when I'm mercilessly thrust from Heaven, the force of which is stagnant as though time decelerates with a fictitious ambience.

The world around me warps as I fall, glimpses of what I once knew as Heaven concealed behind a thick mass of white clouds rippling in front of my eyes. I plummet to the ground, the impact stinging my body stings as I tense and choke on another scream, my ears ringing loudly in my head.

The weather changes instantaneously; the sun grows dim as thick, grey clouds consume the once bright blue sky. Heavy rain begins to pour as thunder crashes from above me. Any hint of the sun is gone, and with the day's death rises the start of my new life, welcomed by an eerie, empty night.

This is it.

I'm officially banished.

I feel my chest slowly expanding, a burst of air pressing against it that has my neck and chest synchronously tightening and inflating. I gape, my throat constricting painfully until the pocket of air pocket from my mouth in a thick hack that mitigates my convulsing chest. Stunned, I stand there for a few moments as I cope with the abnormality of breathing.

It's almost excruciating to draw air in and out of my system when it's never had to before. Everything overwhelms me—the newfound need to breathe alongside the foreign beating in my chest. Is this what they call a… heartbeat? Am I generating a heart to produce heat? The sickening realization of what I've become plagues me; a demon.

I am no different to Lucifer's Fallen Angels—those misled by Lucifer whose wings were never stripped from their bodies and halos were never broken. They broke their halos as an act of rebellion, severing all ties to their creator and subsequently their one access to heat. While they can finally see, they may no longer communicate with God for guidance; the light they once gave to Heaven now belongs to them. Therefore, they developed hearts and blood circulation to survive and learned to breathe and adapt to the sensation of a heartbeat.

As if on cue, warmth spreads from the thumping in my chest and flows steadily through my whole body until I no longer feel the striking bite of cold. It replenishes the heat my halo provides, and I can't help but sigh comfortably at the sensation.

Was it worth it? A voice in my head taunts. *Was* she *really worth this?*

A small voice silences the other. *She was worth it.* Feeling *was worth this. This was worth it.*

Lightning strikes the ground in uneven bolts, and thunder clashes in the sky, lighting the clouds in luminescent blue and yellow hues. The thunder causes pedestrians to scatter as they use whatever they can find to keep themselves dry. I flinch at the deafening roar, the beating in my chest only heightening from the commotion that surrounds me.

I focus on occupying my mind with Magda to avoid drowning myself in my newfound sorrows. Glancing around me, I realize I'm in a damp alleyway where bright lights shine from the street ahead, sharper and more colourful than I'm used to. Upon seeing the glaring lights, I realize that the world around me has become substantially brighter, allowing me to see things as humans do.

My fascination is short-lived as the horror that any previously possessed abilities are gone settles over me. I focus on the Grace running through my body and attempt to grasp it and hold its power in the palm of my hand, but all I feel is a disconcerting emptiness.

With a huff, I stagger from the outdoor corridor and begin my search for anything of familiarity. The street I emerge to runs through a bustling city, and by following the sidewalk, I manage to find Salcombe University in my periphery, relieved beyond belief that I am, in fact, in Lauder.

Hope sparks within my empty chest; with a sudden burst of adrenaline, I rush towards the building, desperate for any indication of Magda. I briefly catch sight of the human leaving the building as she pulls her hood up over her head. Shivering, she zips her sweater up and begins to make her way down the sidewalk, movements light and habitual.

I carefully drift behind.

THREE

I Stand With You

MAGDA

auling myself outside after attending my last class of the day, I greedily inhale the scent of rainfall, fortuitous for a snowy October day. As tempted as I become to shed my sweater and stand in the rain for the rest of the night, the iciness of winter leaches through my layers, immediately dissuading me from doing so. I keep my hood up but face the sky and sigh into the comforting sensation of cold raindrops spilling down my cheeks.

There's a skip in my step as I bounce on my heels; with each hop, water splashes against the cuffs of my pants. The rainfall slows to a drizzle as I stop at the crosswalk and absentmindedly glance over at the group of people waiting to cross the street ahead. I suddenly wonder if I'm dreaming when I recognize a face in the crowd, his militarily uniform and dark brown braids distinct from the colloquial rest.

I vigorously blink the rain from my eyes as I brace myself for the disorienting feeling of awakening in my bed. When that doesn't happen after a few long seconds, I allow myself to entertain the prospect that it's real.

I start sprinting towards the man, the only warning I provide is my overexcited shout of, "OSCAR!" before leaping into his arms and nearly tackling him into traffic.

We plummet to the ground, Oscar landing unceremoniously on his ass. I throw my arms around him with all the strength I can muster in my moderately sleep-deprived system. I almost can't believe he's here, suddenly terrified that any second I'll snap out of whatever daze I'm in to realize I've just tackled a complete stranger, almost into traffic, instead of who I thought was my brother. I would probably die if I managed to do that; I wouldn't be too surprised, but I would definitely plan to launch myself off a cliff if I did.

"Oscar," I murmur, my trembling voice muffled from pressing my face into his shoulder. I don't know whether I'm shaking with excitement or from the cold at this point. "Oh my God, Oscar."

I can almost feel his grin against me. "Mags."

The sound of his voice and the tangible confirmation that he's here wrenches a sob from my throat. Oscar holds me back, gentler than my bone-crushing hold on him, but still with the same amount of desperation. As much as I'd love to maintain an indifferent veneer whenever he visits and act like I don't miss him, I can't, not when the last time I saw him was just over a year ago. Because he enlisted in the Canadian Military fresh at eighteen right after graduating, I see him so seldom that I don't have it in me to pretend I don't care when I get to see him.

Oscar somehow manages to pry me off him after a few more seconds. I let go of my crushing grip only when I realize he's started wheezing slightly, and I pull away to peer at him through damp lashes, the tears rolling down my cheeks combining with rainwater. The familiarity of his warm smile brings more tears to my eyes, and I can't help myself from leaning back into him and burying my face into his chest with a wide grin. I can even smell the stupid baby shampoo he insists on using to "properly hydrate" his hair. God, I've missed him so much.

"I haven't seen you in forever," Oscar says as we untangle ourselves from the hug. He begins wringing the moisture from his braids as I wipe my cheeks and straighten my posture.

"You're telling me," I reply, looking down. "It's been so long, Ossy. I've missed you so much. Do Mom and Dad know you're back? Why didn't you call to tell me you're here?"

"I wanted it to be a surprise…" he says hesitantly. His expression changes, but I can't quite pinpoint how exactly. "I just came from Mom and Dads, actually."

"Ohhh, that's why."

Oscar cocks his head, and I climb off his lap, uncaring if I accidentally kick him a few times before standing and offering my hand to him. He takes it, and I help him to his feet. "What's why?"

"Dad called me earlier, and he was acting weird."

Oscar blinks. "So?"

"He was hiding the fact that you're back, dumbass," I say with a laugh, exaggerating my eye roll. "He was acting all sad to throw me off. I mean, it worked and all, but he didn't have to act so constipated and save us both the worry."

"Can we… can we go somewhere?" Oscar asks with a nervous smile, flattening his uniform. "To catch up?"

"Yeah, of course. Do you wanna grab something to eat? There's this amazing coffee shop within walking distance we can go to. I just got out of a seminar so I could have a bite to eat."

"Sounds good to me," He flashes me a toothy grin and bows dramatically. "After you, m'lady." I giggle, playfully shoving him as we take a moment to shake off the rain. I can't help but laugh when I see the comically wide wet patch on his ass, unable to stifle myself in time. He looks over his shoulder, craning his neck to see what I'm laughing at, and I watch as his eyes narrow, and he shoots me a glare. I pretend not to be looking, whistling innocently as he flips me off and shakes his head like an exasperated parent. I hook my arm around his neck, pulling him down so I can ruffle his hair before sprinting in the direction of the coffee shop, grinning nervously when I hear the slap of footsteps following me close behind.

I manage to beat Oscar to the coffee shop solely because he doesn't know where he's going and is forced to follow me. Still, I rub it in his face when we get to the door, but he just rolls his eyes and sneers playfully. He even opens the door for me, only to thrust his shoulder out at the last minute, butting ahead of me when I make a move to enter. He doesn't even turn to face me, flipping me off for the second time in under ten minutes over his shoulder.

Refusing to be bothered, I follow Oscar inside and unzip my hoodie as we step in line to order our food. I order a Mocha coffee and a grilled cheese while Oscar gets a large hot chocolate with extra whipped cream and one of every type of muffin they offer, which ends up being eight. We pay, take our food when it's ready, and sit down to eat at a table overlooking the street.

"What are you doing?" I ask, watching in mild fascination as Oscar begins stacking his muffins in front of himself.

"I'm building a muffin wall. Duh."

"Of course, my mistake." I casually take a sip of my coffee, relishing the familiarity of our dynamic; I hadn't realized how much I'd missed Oscar until now. "So. What's up?"

Oscar's smile falters, and he looks down at the table, dejected as he begins disassembling his muffin wall. "Yeah, um, there's some stuff going on with Mom and Dad, and I kinda caught them right in the thick of it. They contacted me while I was at the base and planned to call you afterwards, but I told them not to. I just think it's best if I'm the one to tell you in person what's going on, instead of over the phone."

I laugh nervously, swallowing the panic that bubbles in my throat. "What are you talking about? You're scaring me."

"Well… if I'm being honest, Mom and Dad aren't doing too well. Dad lost his job. The company let some people go, and, unfortunately, he was one of them. Mom's sick, too, and they aren't in a place to afford proper treatment while they're living off Dad's unemployment. I sent them some money, but it's not enough. It's kind of why I've taken an emergency medical leave."

I hold my breath, looking up to meet Oscar's eyes while he avoids mine. My appetite is suddenly long forgotten as the anticipation of what's going on digs under my skin. I nervously bring the coffee cup to my lips.

What he says next staggers my awareness of the passing of time. "Mom… she has lung cancer."

Instantly I freeze, dropping my coffee without even realizing it. I'm too stunned to even process the scalding liquid that spills across the table and pools in my lap while my arm dangles at my side, my senses overwhelmed by a sudden engulfing numbness.

My mouth goes dry, my ears start ringing, and my vision blurs. I feel like I'm on the verge of passing out, tears forming as my whole body shuts down. I'm only distantly aware of the hot coffee seeping through my pants and burning my skin. I don't even realize I'm standing until I feel Oscar shaking my shoulders and calling out to me with a voice so distant it sounds like he's a mile away.

"Maggie! Maggie, talk to me. Mags!" His voice grows louder and more intelligible as the fog in my head clears. I look up at him with wide eyes, too stunned to speak. I open my mouth to say something, but I can't form any words. I realize I'm shaking when the sound of my teeth chattering reverberates in my ears.

"Maggie, say something," Oscar pleads, panic-stricken as he grabs a handful of napkins and begins vigorously wiping at my pants. I don't have the energy to do it myself or push him away. "Did it burn you? Are you hurt?"

Unable to say anything, I wordlessly shake my head, noting the relief in Oscar's expression when I answer him.

"Mags? Talk to me, are you okay?" His firm hands on my shoulders ground me. I look up at him with unfocused eyes, my head still swimming. It comes out as a quiet croak when I finally manage to say, "What… what kind?"

His breath hitches in his throat, and he nervously swallows. "Small cell carcinoma. Late-stage two, early-stage three."

My voice dies in my throat as my legs buckle beneath me, and I fall to the ground. Oscar seems to have predicted this as he effortlessly catches me before I hit the ground and guides me towards an unsoiled table.

"I don't have any money," I manage, holding my head in my hands as Oscar helps me sit down. "I don't have anything. What are we gonna do? How…"

He sighs and scrubs a hand over his face before taking a deep breath. "I don't know. We'll do whatever we can. I'm on leave, so I'll be here for a month, and I'll get a job. We'll send all the money we get back to Mom and Dad, and we'll figure everything out. Okay?"

I nod, doubtful of Oscar's certainty. How can he still have so much hope when Mom's so sick? It's… she has cancer—early-stage three lung cancer; literally an incurable disease. Even if we *can* get her the treatment she needs, who's to say it'll work? Any treatment we can get for Mom isn't guaranteed to prevent death.

No, I can't afford to be thinking like that—Oscar's right, he has to be. We can do this. We can figure everything out. It's just a matter of getting Mom the treatment she needs before it's too late.

LARAMIE

All I see when I close my eyes is the devastating look on Magda's face when Oscar tells her their mother has cancer; the look of haunted horror, of shock and denial and grief, the glassiness of her eyes and the way she immediately goes flush, complexion worryingly pale. The sight of her distress ignites a stinging sensation in my throat that spreads through my body like a blanket of irritation; it claws through my skin and into my very being. The feeling remains even as I watch the two cheerlessly return to Magda's dormitory.

The only peace I may now know will derive only from the one thing I'm unable to do since my banishment; curing Magda's mother. Somewhere in Heaven, Razael looks down on me in whatever form of satisfaction he may derive from my agony.

Oscar and Magda walk in silence. Dried tear tracks glisten on Magda's cheeks in the dull light, and the sight bores a substantial weight on my chest. If I could do anything that would make her feel if only slightly better, I would give everything I have left to without hesitation.

Oscar helps get Magda comfortable once they arrive before leaving momentarily. I remain by Magda's side, watching with a heavy heart as she curls up on her thin mattress like a weakened infant, struggling to pull an old blue, pink and purple blanket around her shoulders. She meekly clutches a wad of tissue against her face, and my heart physically aches to see her so distraught, pain that's worse than my own upon having my wings severed. At least then, I knew only I was feeling such profound pain; now I experience it because I know it's what she's feeling.

My hand instinctively extends to ease the sobs that wrack Magda's body, but I catch myself just before touching her, jerking my hand back to my chest as if burned.

I hang my head defeatedly, releasing a pitiful huff of air. As my eyes drift to the floor, they linger on the arm Magda uses to hold her tissues, to notice faint white and pink scars crisscrossing the skin that I hadn't seen before. My gut twists, a sickly feeling brewing uncomfortably in my stomach when I realize what they are.

She'd done this to herself.

-FOUR-

Lie Ability

MAGDA

hile I haven't relapsed in, what, four, five years? I find I've absently started scratching the scars I brandish along my arm, a nervous habit I adopted shortly after I first began self-harming at what would've been the tender age of eleven.

The urge to cut hasn't reared its ugly head in a few blissful months, during which I've managed to find some semblance of stability and well-being that has truthfully distracted me from even considering it again.

Still, looking down at the scars marring my skin, I remember precisely how I'd felt when I'd made them. I vividly remember the all too familiar sinking pit of overwhelming hopelessness in my stomach that would always precede the voice in my head that concentrates on my flaws and exacerbates them one by one. The only thing that would come next was the act of self-harming itself.

I'd scramble in search of whatever knife or razor-blade I could find, desperate to obtain the only means I had to satisfy the voice. I wouldn't stop cutting until the rush of blood in my ears would overwhelm it, granting me brief respite before the cycle eventually repeats itself.

"I brought snacks," Oscar cheerfully announces, snapping me from my thoughts. A timid smile hovers over his lips as he awaits my response. I don't have the energy to fake an optimistic reply, and I know what he's looking for isn't, "What's even the point of life anymore?" So I settle for simply nodding and looking down.

"Hey, Mags, it'll be all right," The mattress dips under his weight.

I look up at Oscar, reluctantly meeting his eyes; I can almost see the reflection of my skepticism in them. "How come it feels like this is my fault? Before you say anything, yes, I know I didn't give Mom cancer, but it's not fair that I'm spending Mom and Dad's money to go to University when that same money could be used to pay for her treatment."

"None of this is your fault," Oscar recites mechanically, the empty words used only to abate my insecurities. "There's no way you could've known this would happen. You decided to go to University, and Mom and Dad wanted to help pay for it, so they did. Hell, I remember you arguing with them that they shouldn't have to pay, and you could just take out a fuck ton of student loans. This wasn't your choice, and I know it's hard right now—"

"That's what she said," I blurt without thinking. I don't even realize I've said it until I hear it come out of my mouth. Giggling to myself, I glance over at Oscar to see him beaming with pride, offering me a high five with an extended arm.

"Nice," He praises when I accept. "As I was saying, all we can do in the meantime is relax and keep each other sane. We'll come up with the money somehow."

"We'd need to win the lottery to be able to afford treatment."

"You don't know that."

I raise a brow. "How much did Mom say chemotherapy costs, hmm? Or radiation therapy? Tell me."

Oscar flushes and scratches his neck, hanging his head in silence for a few seconds before finally muttering, "Twenty kay."

"My point exactly," I throw my arms up in exasperation. I nervously thread them through my hair, and I start tugging at the tufts, the urge to rip them from my scalp hard to resist. "If we're somehow gonna come up with *twenty thousand dollars,* then I need to be out there working, too. I can't spend Mom and Dad's money for my education when Mom… when she's dying. "

"Hey, don't say that."

"Well, it's true," Frustration and disappointment cut deeper than ever before. "I need to drop out and find a job. There should be a few I can get with a high school diploma. Can't be too picky, after all."

"But, Mags—"

"I have to. I don't want to do this, but I don't have any other choice here. With Mom this sick, a part-time job while I'm still in school won't cut it. Plus, this is *Mom and Dad's money* going toward my tuition. Hell, if I'd never gone to uni in the first place…" I falter, taking a deep breath. "I couldn't live with myself if I didn't do this. You'd do the same if you were me, and you know it. So don't even try to deny it."

"I know," He concedes, shoulders tense as he grasps his hands in his lap, elbows braced on his legs to hang his head defeatedly. "It's just… you're in your final year, and I want you to graduate after all the work you've put in so far. To get your Bachelor's degree, to finally get to do what you love. But if you drop out now…" He sighs. "Just because I can't do what I love doesn't mean you deserve the same.

"Truth is, I was stupid and didn't take school or life seriously. When I graduated, I needed a job… and joining the military meant I'd have a roof over my head. I'd have food, clothes, and an income, and most importantly, I'd be *doing* something with my life. I wouldn't have to rely on Mom and Dad when it was my fault I had nowhere to go."

I remember the day Oscar called to enthuse his dream of joining the military like it was yesterday. He'd been nearly hysterical with excitement, and it'd absolutely devastated me to find out his dream career would send him hundreds of miles away from us for years at a time. I kept my disapproval to myself and instead pretended to be just as excited as he was—he just sounded *so* passionate, and… now I know it was all a lie.

"Truthfully, I didn't want to," Oscar continues. "That was total bs. I didn't want you to know how irresponsible and careless I'd been with my future or how pathetic I am. I didn't want to disappoint Mom or Dad or… you. But, there's still hope for you; you can still be happy and pursue your dreams. I've made my bed, but I don't wanna lie in it."

I can't think of anything I can say that'll make a difference, so I settle for a hug to console Oscar with my actions when I can't find the words. I whisper an "I love you" into his shoulder, and he mutters the same back to me, his voice thick and wavering. "I'm sorry."

I pull away and force Oscar to look me in the eyes. "What on Earth could you possibly have to be sorry about?"

"For flipping you off earlier. I guess you're okay sometimes."

I laugh and lean back into him, shaking my head. "You're such an idiot."

"Can't spell idiot without 'i'. Wait, no, 'u.'"

"There's no 'u' in idiot, dumbass."

Oscar none-too-subtly changes the subject. "So, are you thinking about dropping out or just taking a leave of absence?"

"A what?"

"A leave of absence. It means you can leave for up to a year and then come back without needing to re-enroll. I did some research since I predicted you'd be too stubborn to be reasoned with, and would you look at that, I was right."

"That's a first."

He pouts. "Meanie."

"Oh, you'll live."

"Not to keep interfering with your targeted harassment of me, but I talked to Mom and Dad, and we all agreed it'd be best if you and I stayed with them for a while. I'll be staying with them anyways since your dorm doesn't allow guests and all, but you can stay longer than me if you need to."

"Good idea," All of this is irrefutable proof that bad things happen to good people. Mom is more than a good mother; she's a good wife, a good friend, and a good *person*. She always makes time for me whenever I need her. Even if it's after a particularly long day, she's always there to welcome me home with open arms.

I can't imagine not having someone to confide in and talk to, having no one to come to when I'm sad and cry on their shoulder, no one to sing and dance with, no one to listen to and love. Mom's always been that person for me, and I don't want to see a world where I don't have that anymore.

Oscar seems to read my mind with the way he leans in and presses a gentle kiss on my forehead. When he protectively wraps his arm around my shoulders, I close my eyes and lean my head against him.

"Thanks, Ossy," I mutter.

"No problem. Do you feel up to giving Mom and Dad a call to let them know we'll be staying with them?"

I open my eyes and nod, swallowing nervously as I sit up, my head spinning with horrific images of Mom, pale as a ghost with sunken eyes and a voice rougher than sandpaper, decrepit and frail, coughing, wheezing, and choking on her own tongue, shaking and seizing and *dying* and—

"You okay?" When Oscar's voice jerks me from my thoughts, I realize I've begun hyperventilating and struggle to slow my breathing with exaggerated breaths, my heart hammering against my chest like it's trying to pummel its way out.

I turn to Oscar and nod, watching as he pulls his phone out of his pocket and dials Mom's number. It rings for a minute before it's answered, and when it is, I gesture for the phone, and Oscar passes it to me.

"Hello?" Mom's voice is croaky and broken. I cringe at the sound, and my eyes instinctively water when she barks out a dry cough. She sounds so much worse than I'd anticipated.

"Mom?" I grimace at the tremble in my voice. "It's Maggie."

The phone goes silent for a long moment. "Maggie, sweetie. Has-has Oscar told you?"

I nod before remembering she can't see me. "Y-yeah. Yeah, he has."

Silence. "I'm sorry I wasn't the one to tell you. Oscar… well, he insisted and… and I don't know if I would've had it in me to break the news to you."

I squeeze my eyes shut, and my eyebrows furrow as my lip steadily trembles. "I… it's fine, Mom. I get it. I'm just… I think I'm still in shock. I-I can't believe it."

"Me too. Me too." She takes a shaky breath. "How-how are you both?"

I laugh weakly, void of any joy. Before any of this, I would've said tired but good; overall relatively satisfied with my life. But now? Now every semblance of hope and normalcy I'd had has been swept from beneath my feet.

"I… I've been better, Mom, but we're doing all right. W-what about you and Dad?"

"Oh, we're doing just fine over here. Just… going over our finances." Her voice breaks on the last word, telling me everything I need to know about how they really are.

"So, um, here's the plan," Oscar intervenes. "I talked to Maggie, and she's decided to come home for the time being. She's decided to take a temporary leave from school so she can find a full-time job to help contribute towards your… treatment costs until we can afford them. You'll probably be notified of the hold on her tuition payments, so I figured you should know why."

Mom's sigh is relieved but thick with emotion. "Oh, Maggie. Your father and I are *so* proud of the two of you. Thank you. I'd try convincing you against it, but it sounds like you've already made up your mind.."

I sniffle, wiping my nose pathetically with a tissue. "Of course, Mom. It is you we're talking about here. Ossy and I would do anything for you. You know that."

"And I would do anything for the two of you." Oscar and I share the same sad smile. "However, I must say, I'm so glad to hear you'll both be coming back home."

"Me too, Mom. Me too."

She releases a shuddery sigh before sniffling. "Well, I'll let you kids go. After your father and I finish up, we'll be starting supper."

Oscar swallows. "Sounds good, Mom. I'll see you tonight."

"We're looking forward to it! One of us could give you a ride if you'd like?"

Oscar glances over at me, and I shoot him a thumbs up. "It's okay. Maggie's gonna drive me."

"Oh, wonderful! I love you both."

"Love you," We chorus. Mom ends the call and Oscar shifts on the mattress. Leaning back against the wall, he sighs and crosses his legs.

"Well, I guess you should drop me off soon."

I nod along. "Sure. When do you wanna head over? You don't have to leave right away."

"It'd be better to leave now so I can get situated. Maybe you could stay for supper?"

As if on cue, my stomach rumbles. I sheepishly look up at Oscar. "I haven't had a homemade meal in a while…"

He grins and claps his hands together. "It's settled then!"

I grab my wallet, keys, and phone as I lead Oscar out of the dormitory. He follows close behind as I approach the parking lot and head toward the charging stations; as always, the only car parked in one is mine. I remove the pump before settling into the driver's seat while Oscar giddily climbs into the passenger seat. I turn on the car and slowly peel out of the parking lot.

It takes just under fifteen minutes to drive to Mom and Dad's. As soon as we turn onto Althorne Drive, the sight of the house fills me with bittersweet nostalgia. I take it in with a small smile, admiring the yellow-bricked building surrounded by dull, red-bricked houses. I can remember the day Mom decided to paint the house like it was yesterday; she'd wanted to paint it since she first moved in but couldn't decide on what colour until eight-year-old me suggested yellow to attract happiness. She told me that as soon as I said yellow, she knew that was the colour we'd use.

She took me with her to buy the paint and even let me help her paint the bricks I could reach. When it was all finished, I remember how proud I'd been to have helped paint our house after choosing the colour myself.

As I pull into the driveway, I take in the familiarity of the wide window sill overlooking Mom's garden to the right of the front door. Despite the thin sheet of slush covering the ground, I can still make out the paved set of slabs leading up to the front door.

Parking the car, I sit still for a moment, taking a deep, readying breath with my knuckles clenched tightly around the steering wheel. Even though I've come home more often than going to my dorm, it feels different all of a sudden. Knowing Mom is sick casts a vignette over the sunny bricks, tinting the happiness it's supposed to allure.

"You ready?" Oscar asks, placing a tentative hand on my shoulder.

I take a deep breath and nod as solemnly as I can manage, meekly meeting my brother's gaze. "I think so. Let's… let's go in."

I brace myself as I step out of the car, my childhood home foreboding as it looms over me for the first time in my life. Oscar catches my gaze and offers a small smile and a quick nod, to which I reciprocate. I follow as he approaches the front door, knocking resolutely. We stand in silence for a few seconds before the door swings open.

-FIVE-

Poignant Family Reunion

MAGDA

elcome home," Dad greets with a smile.

I sidestep past Oscar to envelop Dad in a tight hug. After snaking my arms around his torso and pressing my face against his shoulder like I used to do when I was little, I feel his shoulders begin to tremble, wracked by uncontrollable shaking. As he clutches me tightly against his chest, I allow myself to believe that rectification isn't as unlikely as I'd thought it to be. With Dad here with me, and I with him, I know everything will be okay.

The outside air on my back is what prompts me to reluctantly pull away from Dad, quickly wiping the tears beginning to stream down my cheeks. I hook my arm through Dad's as he leads me inside and closes the door behind us. Glancing between Dad and Oscar, I can't help admiring their resemblance; the same kind eyes and strong jawline, their identical mischievous grin, and broad statures. The only significant difference is Dad's pale skin tone versus Oscar's and my bronze complexion, Dad's short salt and pepper hair, and the light stubble caressing his jaw and upper lip.

"Are you staying for supper?" Dad asks.

"There's no universe where I'd ever say no to that," I answer.

"Plus, if coming home for food gives me a reason to see you guys, count me in."

He chuckles. "Good to know your priorities are sorted." He squeezes my hand before heading into the living room. "Alawa! The kids are here!"

A rasping cough is the only answer we receive from the living room. I cringe at the violent nature of it, thankful it subsides just as fast as it erupted. "Maggie too? How wonderful!"

I slip my shoes off and set them atop the shoe rack before tentatively approaching the living room, each beat of my heart sending shafts of icy trepidation through my already tense muscles.

I take a deep breath before turning the corner to enter the living room. The first thing I see is Mom curled up on the couch, so small and fragile it feels as though I'm looking at a newborn child.

For as long as I can remember, Mom has hidden her illnesses so well I never knew she was sick in the first place. But now, the realization that there are powers out there far greater than Mom's dawns on me all of a sudden, something I'd never bothered to consider until now.

Dark bruises blemish the skin beneath her bloodshot eyes, worry lines etched into her forehead. She's curled around herself in the corner of the couch like a wounded animal, wrinkled clothes baggy on her slim figure.

"Mom..." I croak. My knees buckle beneath me as I trip over my feet to get to her. I fall into her lap, clinging to her meekly as though if I put too much of my weight on her, she'll break. Any composure I had left shatters when Mom begins gently stroking my hair with a quivering hand.

That gesture takes me back to grade seven all of a sudden,

crying against Mom's chest in the parking lot of my school after being sent home for igniting a Bunsen burner without my partner and almost setting fire to myself.

Mom had been called from work to pick me up, and when she got to the school, it was impossible to gauge how she was feeling. Her expression was solemn and unreadable as my science teacher told her what had happened and openly chastised me for my recklessness and irresponsibility.

Still unsettlingly silent, Mom offered me her hand and led me out to the car without a word. The walk would have been no more than twenty seconds, but the tension made it feel like twenty minutes. When I finally reached the car, I slumped into the passenger seat. I braced myself for a scolding, only for Mom to say, "I never liked that teacher. She doesn't understand mistakes. But they happen, and I'm sure you didn't mean it."

She leaned towards me for a hug, one hand stroking my cheek while the other stroked my hair. Up until that moment, I'd kept the anxiety and depression I'd been dealing with bottled up inside—I didn't understand what it was, and I'd thought it was all in my head. But when Mom embraced me so lovingly that day, I couldn't keep it in any longer. I clung to her, sobbing openly for upwards of ten minutes. She didn't know how much I needed it that day, nor this one.

Just like that, I'm twelve again.

We remain wrapped in each other's arms for a few minutes before Mom weakly pushes against my chest. I let go of her and lace our fingers together, rubbing circles against her hand with my thumb. I smile at her through teary eyes, and she smiles back at me before turning away, a guttural cough scraping against her throat.

"It's not as bad as it looks," She manages when the hacking subsides. "I just have this cough, and I lose my breath more than before, and… and I've lost my appetite, but that's all. I'm okay. Right, George?"

I turn to Dad, expectant, and notice the way he holds Mom's gaze for a few seconds. He, too, looks unconvinced but turns to me with a tight-lipped smile. "Yes, she's doing okay. I wouldn't worry too much about her, honey. She's a fighter."

There's similar concern and skepticism beneath Dad's smile. As much as I wish Mom would just be honest with me about her condition, at the same time, I don't know if I'd be able to handle the truth.

"So, what's on the menu for tonight?" Oscar interjects, rubbing his hands together. "I'd be happy to help cook."

"That's my boy," Dad says with a laugh, clapping Oscar on the back. "Your mother was hoping we'd have pemmican, and I'd sure appreciate your help making it."

"Hell yeah!"

I smile and look down as Oscar and Dad disappear into the kitchen, leaving Mom and me alone in the living room. I wouldn't be too surprised if that's why Oscar asked to help Dad in the kitchen—to give me some time with Mom—although his genuine interest in cooking is explanative enough.

Mom's sudden lurch startles me as another bout of raucous coughs rattles her, and I instinctively begin rubbing her back, feeling the way her body convulses with each raspy bark.

"Mom, you're not fine."

"Are you sure it's the best idea for you to take a leave? As happy as I am that you'll be moving back in temporarily, I don't want you to put your future on the line for me. Especially when it's your last year."

"Mom, I'd rather work some shitty ten-bucks-an-hour job with you healthy than some billionaire doctor without you. No question."

She smiles feebly. "I forgot how stubborn you are."

My lip quirks upwards in a smile. "Where do you think I got it from?"

"Fair point." She takes a deep breath and squeezes my hand. "I love you, honey. So… so very much."

"Mom, please don't."

"Don't what?"

"Don't say your goodbyes."

"I'm not."

"Yes, you are. You're trying to say your goodbyes now, so there won't come a time where the opportunity is missed. Mom, you can't try to convince me everything's fine and then go and say goodbye. That's not how this works."

Mom bows her head. Her hands start trembling, and she looks up at me, embarrassed, and nods. "I know. You're right. I'm sorry. I shouldn't… I shouldn't contradict myself like that. I just… I don't want you to worry about me. But I'm… I'm scared."

Her admission catches me off guard. For the first time in my life, she's confessing to her malaise, and I struggle to comprehend it. "I am too."

I lean against her like I did when I was little, and we'd cuddle on the couch until I'd drift to sleep against her. And every single time without fail, I'd wake up the next day tucked into my bed, missing her comforting presence beside me.

Oscar's voice stirs me from the memory. "Hey, Mags? Could you get our drinks ready? I'm almost finished with the beef."

"Yeah, sure." I struggle to pull away from Mom and turn to her as I stand up. "What would you like to drink?"

"Oh, nonsense," She argues, pushing herself to her feet. "I

can get my drink."

"You *can*, but you won't," I insist, gently pushing her back down. "It's fine, Mom. Just let me do this for you."

A few moments go by before she acquiesces with an indignant 'hmph.' "All right. I'll have a glass of water, please."

"Sure thing," I head into the kitchen to pour two glasses of water for Mom and Dad, a glass of chocolate milk for Oscar and a glass of lemonade for myself (after confirming everyone's orders, of course).

Once Oscar finishes preparing our meal, I bring the drinks out and set the table with napkins, placemats, utensils, and plates, finishing just as he places a platter of pemmican in the center of the table. Not that I'd ever admit it, but if there's one thing Oscar's better at than making me laugh, it's cooking good food.

We all take our seats all the dinner table. Mom and Dad link their hands while gesturing for Oscar and me to do the same until we're all holding hands around the table.

"Our Creator," We chorus. "Help us and protect us; today, all. We are your children, all boys and men, all girls and women, and all others of all Nations. All people here, all over the world, we are thankful. Thank you."

As we talk and eat, Oscar perpetually elbows me to get my attention, only to flash me the chewed-up food in his mouth or pull a stupid face. It's only when he jabs me in the arm, and I turn to see his cheeks stuffed with beef that I spit out my lemonade, some of which shoots out of my nose, but the second I admit that is the very second I lose any credibility I have left to my brother. I settle for kicking him underneath the table while he just snickers, obnoxiously chewing up his food with an open mouth. I retch dramatically and turn away, stubbornly ignoring him for the rest of the meal.

"That was *so* good, Ossy," I say once I've finished my plate. I sag back in my chair and rest my hands over my stomach, smiling contentedly. "I forgot how good you are at cooking."

"Excuse me? How dare you?"

"It's not fair you can cook so well, but I'm left struggling to make myself peanut butter sandwiches."

"It must just be *so* hard to be the incapable sibling."

I kick Oscar under the table with a little more force than usual, and he gapes like a fish, grabbing his shin. "Ow!" He whines. "Abuse!"

I laugh and instinctively turn to Mom, catching her just as she slowly rises from the table. A morose feeling knots itself in my stomach, and I swallow it down.

"Mom? Where are you going?"

She stops her in her tracks as though she didn't expect me to notice her and pauses before answering. "Just… getting some fresh air."

Oh. She's going outside to smoke.

"You're… you're still smoking? I… I thought you quit."

"I did," She slowly begins. "But… well, after your father was laid off and the bills started coming in… the stress got to me, and… I started smoking again."

I've never struggled with addiction as Mom has, but I've done my fair share of research, and I understand better than most its physical effects on the human psyche. Despite that, I still feel a sense of disappointment that she's succumbed to the temptation once again.

"I'm sorry, honey," She whispers, hurriedly shuffling to the back porch. I open my mouth to say something but the sound of the door shutting has me closing my mouth.

I sigh and stand from my chair, grabbing my plate and glass

to deposit them in the sink before grabbing my shoes from the front door.

"Where are you going?" Oscar asks, following me to the front door.

"Outside," I answer, shoving my shoes back on. "To talk to Mom."

He doesn't say anything. I head back into the dining room and stop in front of the back door, taking a deep breath to steel myself. I put on a brave face and slide the door open to reveal Mom with a cigarette resting at her lips. Before noticing me, she takes a long puff of it and exhales contentedly, eyes closed. Her hands are trembling, and I can see the glint of tears rolling down her cheeks from where I stand.

I let go of the door, and it audibly shuts behind me, causing both of us to jump. Mom opens her eyes, and they widen when she notices me, her cheeks burning red. She almost drops the cigarette, scrambling to put it out in the ashtray next to her, and I can't deny the satisfaction it brings to see her put it out.

"M-Maggie," She stutters nervously.

"It's okay," I say, sinking into the chair beside her. "I mean, none of this is okay, but I'm not mad or disappointed in you. I know what addictions are. I've had to do countless assignments on them to know what it does to a person. I understand, I just hate to see what it does to you, and I hate being powerless to stop it. But please don't feel the need to hide it from me."

Tears stream down Mom's face, this time not out of shame but in relief. The red burn of her cheeks has died down into a rosy testament to the cold. She grabs my hand and squeezes it before pulling me into a hug, her fingers digging into the skin of my back as she presses her chin into my shoulder, trembling and wracked with sobs. "I'm sorry," she whispers into me. "I'm so sorry, Magda."

"Don't," I say, hugging her tight. "You don't have anything to be sorry about. Don't beat yourself up for being human."

I disregard the icy bite of the cold on my ears and face and the soggy, wet snow leaving a damp patch on my pants. I ignore the way I've started shivering from the cold and the way Mom's chin digs into my shoulder. I can't find it within me to care about any of it when I'm cradling my mom like she's always held me, allowing herself to express raw vulnerability like never before.

"You… you are *everything* I wanted when I knew I wanted kids," she whispers in my ear. "More than everything I wanted; everything I *needed*, then and now."

My heart stutters, and I'm rendered speechless. Smiling into Mom's shoulder, I relax, her words reverberating in my head: *"You are* everything *I wanted when I knew I wanted kids. More than everything I wanted; everything I* needed, *then and now."*

She pulls away to wipe her cheeks and smiles up at me like she's never been so proud of anything in her life.

Glancing at the clock in the dining room, I give Mom's hand one final squeeze before making a move to leave. "I should head back to my dorm now, but I'll make sure to call you guys later. Once I get my leave, I'll come straight home, okay?"

She beams back at me. "Okay. I love you."

"I love you too," I wrinkle my nose at the stench of smoke, but still, I lean forward and kiss her on the cheek. "I'll see you soon."

I head back inside just as Oscar finishes loading the dishwasher. "Mom's okay. I'm heading back to the dorm now, though."

He nods and grins as he closes the dishwasher with a click. "Okay. I'll come and visit soon, help you with things."

"That'd be great. I'll see you later, Os."

"Bye, Mags."

Hesitantly leaving the house, I approach my car with an easy smile and begin the drive back to my dorm in comfortable, satisfied silence.

–SIX–

To Make A Deal With The Devil

LARAMIE

y level of respect for humans has intensified more than I'd known possible since following and observing Magda and her family. Their ability to control and cope with their intense emotions is beyond me. Even more, their ability to discuss and understand them the way they do.

After debating whether or not to, finally, I stagger to my feet and over to the mirror in the tiny bathroom of Magda's dormitory that hangs precariously at an angle. The surface is foggy and slightly dirty, but I can still make out my reflection, and when I do, I stifle a gasp.

Despite having a moderate understanding of what I look like, I haven't seen my face in centuries, let alone given my newfound banishment. My face is deathly pale, and my halo is ashen, greying with only the slightest hint of gold lingering. My right horn is shorter than my left, the wide crevice curving the tips rigid and sharp. Already they're starting to pull away from one another as if being mutually repelled.

My hair is matted with my blood, and my skin no longer

glows; it's become a mix between my former fleshy tone and a solid grey, my face aged and tired, with dark bags beneath my eyes.

Something black glows through the fabric of my robe from the center of my chest. Frowning, I peel the material from my torso to behold the deep maroon silhouette of my heart, beating steadily against my chest. Trying to disregard my afflictions, I simply readjust my robe and ignore the reminder of my nominal status.

It's especially unsettling that I can see my eyes no longer concealed behind the blinding light my halo would produce. For the first time in my existence, I realize they're monolid with dark black irises, a startlingly hollow emptiness consuming them. It's perturbing to see something meant to be permanently hidden; seeing my own eyes makes me feel more vulnerable and exposed than my overall banishment.

I force myself to look away and pull my sticky, blood-soaked robe from my back, turning around to examine my wounds. Carefully gripping the fabric in one hand, I rip it from my back in one swift motion, pain erupting across my skin. I immediately stiffen, taking deep breaths as I wait for the ache to recede eventually.

The amount of blood coating my skin astounds me. I tenderly touch the lacerations between my shoulder blades, two thick pieces of skin protruding from my back surrounded by purple contusions. A deep bruise is forming in the dent of my back where the Powers' foot was planted, and the bones are visibly hacked off, which does little to help the churning in my stomach.

Allowing my robe to fall back around me, I carefully sit back down against the wall to try and think. Over the screaming in my head and pounding in my chest, I can barely process a single thought that swarms me. My eyes are sore and itchy from crying, and a headache throbs in my temples.

The fear of being alone—completely and utterly alone—suddenly hits me. My eyes shift beneath closed lids, and my mind soars, a plume of dread catching me off guard. I've never feared anything so much as the thought of being truly alone; it's so consuming, so lamentable, so... *lonely*.

Clenching my eyes shut, I settle against the wall somewhat peacefully until morning. I allow myself to imagine an alternate Heaven, one where I was never banished and am Razael's dutiful subordinate again. While I may yearn for that, I still maintain how unfulfilling it was to be an angel, especially when I have now experienced emotions. To go from being forced to serve another to granted the choice of deciding whom I devote myself to allows me such intense liberty in my actions for the first time in my existence.

Maybe, just maybe, being banished was the best thing to happen to me.

Anger burns bright within me when I remember the injustice of my banishment. I was sabotaged from the very beginning; Razael *knew* I would fail. He *knew* I would disobey him and still was the one to choose my punishment. *He* did this to me, consumed by the power imbalance in his favour.

I turn towards the window, relishing in the bright colours that bleed across the Stillfall sky. I smile softly at the thought of my choiren watching over me from Heaven during The Switch; looking up at the sky and knowing the Angels are inadvertently watching over me somehow makes me feel protected. Like I'm not as lost as I may feel.

My gaze drifts to the campus ground, and I take a few moments to appreciate the quiet atmosphere. I'm given less than a second to enjoy the serenity when a cold trickle of trepidation rolls down my back, an intuitive alarm.

Whirling around, I scan the dim dormitory, tense when the distinct stench of burnt flesh wafts through the air. I wrinkle my nose at its putrid scent and turn back to the window only to be met with a face on the other side of the glass, mere inches away from my own.

I fall backwards, frantically scrambling away from the figure staring directly at me. He's staring right at me. He can see me...

His complexion is pallid, his features exacerbated by the sharp bones jutting beneath his skin. His hair is unkempt and light, and it obscures his forehead, casting a shadow across his face. His eyes are dark and devoid of any emotion besides a wicked glint, his lips upturned in a macabre smirk. Long wings protrude from his back, allowing him to hover in the air.

My mind goes completely blank, and I can honestly say my heart has never beat as fast as it does seeing *him*—the figure I saw before.

Lucifer.

Before classifying the Angelic Choirs, the angels God created in The Dawn had emotions that intensified as more angels were amassed. Lucifer, the first angel, became consumed with greed and plotted to overthrow God with a rebellion. Because of this, God created Hell to be a penitentiary for those who wrong them as, initially, to contain Lucifer and his fleet.

Because they were created before the Angelic Choirs divided angels' celestial abilities, Lucifer and his demons have the combined powers of all choiren.

The demon's presence debilitates me; I can't bring myself to say anything to him. Intimidation weighs me down as I grapple with the reality that his powers emulate God's while mine has been stripped from me. I would stand no chance against him if the occasion arose where I'd be forced to fight for my existence.

He seems to sense my ambivalence and is the first to break the silence. 'As much as you would like to fight it, we are a great deal alike,' His voice is deep yet melodic, almost entrancing. He points to my chest, where the faint outline of my heart is barely visible. I suppress the urge to cover myself from him. 'As much as you have been taught to fear me, just know I was once an angel like yourself. I was cast away just as you in an attempt to voice my beliefs.

'Worry not, for I will not hurt you. I have an offer you may see fit to accept. All I ask of you is your unbiased attention. After that, you are free to make your decision.'

Wary of his true intentions, I know better than to believe Lucifer's lies. However, I also know that downright denying him will evoke his wrath upon myself and all of Heaven.

In the act of self-preservation, I acquiesce. "I will listen."

His smile widens, a sickly sight overtaking his expression. It's chilling, and I'm suddenly apprehensive of whatever is to come. *What have I agreed to?*

'Follow me,' Lucifer beckons before disappearing from the window. I race to follow, rushing through the University, thankful it's abandoned at this hour. I'm able to pursue Lucifer as he hovers towards a tree in the middle of the campus, landing swiftly on his feet. He comfortably seats himself at the base, curling his wings behind him. Jealousy blazes in my chest at the sight of his wings, still intact. Who is he to deserve such a gift while I'm left to suffer without?

I'm vaguely aware of the grass burning beneath his feet, his form poisoning the air with the promise of death. I force away my hesitancy, turning away from the smouldering terrain beneath him as I cautiously sit in front of him. Maintaining a conservative distance between us amuses him, however, I care only for my safety.

'God has been lying to all of you. They are not whom you think they are, nor are their abilities as exceptional as they express. Their real name is Az, and they are not the all-powerful "God" they feign to be. There exists another who holds a higher rank than them, the rightful creator of Humans and Earth, Ona.

'Unable to stand being seen as the lesser, Az evoked a war against Ona for ownership of the cosmos. Ona's ascendancy cursed angels with petrification when contact ensues between the two species. There was no nonsensical act of betrayal by a misled angel fuelled with "love." I predicted Az's defeat and offered Ona patronage alongside those who agreed with my ideology. Ona's compensation was to divide control of the cosmos to facilitate Az's downfall.

'Az feigned surrender after watching their angels succumb to Ona's curse and took advantage of our momentary susceptibility. They banished my allies and me to Hell and imprisoned Ona on Earth. Not only that, but they removed any encompassing recollection of Ona from existence.

'What Az did is unforgivable.' Lucifer's voice rises angrily. 'They incarcerated us, the only beings who still knew of Ona's existence, for all of eternity and confiscated any means of reminding Ona's children of their imprisonment. The cruelty of your precious *God* runs deeper than you could ever fully fathom.'

All the inconsistencies of Az's narrative amend in empyrean hues of revelation. That must be why Lucifer and his fleet still brandish their wings; Az exiled them before they had a chance to banish them properly.

No matter how hard I fight to disbelieve him, a part of me knows Lucifer's not lying. Perhaps altering certain circumstances of the tale to his advantage, yes, but the underlying facts are not fabricated.

Silence overtakes me for a few long seconds. All I can hear is the erratic beating in my chest as I process the sudden onslaught of information that will forever alter my perception of reality. For the alleged evil entity to expose God's—no, *Az's*—dishonesty is abhorrent; it's unheard of.

Our choiren was created to execute whatever task we're assigned, to accredit Az doubtlessly when they've kept such a pivotal truth from us. We were told the loyalties of our choiren require unwavering attention and fidelity to them when all they've done is blinded us with false rectitude and marred our recollection.

I force myself to meet Lucifer's gaze despite how intimidating it is. "Why is it that you've told me this?"

The mischievous glint in his eyes intensifies as he straightens his posture and raises his chin. 'I'd like you to join my revolution against Az. I can prevent your deterioration until we release Ona, who can forever halt your decay.'

His proposition makes my heart skip a beat. If I accept, I can exist longer than intended; just the thought of exceeding my foreordained expiration and refusing Razael's adjudication is satisfactory enough. Nevertheless, I consider my dilemma logically.

No matter what Lucifer has professed to me—the truth and answers I never knew I needed—I still cannot blindly trust him. He chose power, triumph and acclamation over his creator, and the only reason he's disclosed any of this is to benefit himself.

"As tempting as your proposal may be," I begin, deliberate with my word choice. "I have no incentive to join you, nor do I see fit to be a faithful follower to Az."

Lucifer's face immediately flares with anger and indignation, his eyes fogging over with ire. He rises on his feet, glowering above me as his wings fan out around him threateningly. I immediately jump back and find my footing, backing away from the irate demon. 'I offer you the fortuity to serve an honest god, and you dare refuse me? Is my honesty not incentive enough to pledge yourself to my superiority?'

"Wait, I—"

'You have fallen in love with a human,' He muses with a smirk. 'Magda Mercy, yes?'

Dread drains away any bit of confidence left in me. "P-please Lucifer, sh-she's not—"

His wings give a curt flap forward, and I flinch. 'You will regret your senseless decision. You say you have no incentive to join me? I will give you an incentive. I see now your weakness, the human girl who cost you your wings. You will eat your words, godspittle.'

With that, Lucifer rises menacingly in the air, maintaining his scowl. He doesn't drop my gaze as he soars out of sight, and I don't drop his until he finally disappears.

-SEVEN-

Adversary Arrival

LARAMIE

agda spends the weekend discussing a leave of absence with her counsellor. Once determining she needs to write a letter to the dean asking for permission, Magda spends her days sitting in front of her computer to draft the request.

Upon settling on a version she's satisfied with after many rewrites, Magda scrutinizes the acquisition, eyes scanning over it three, four, five times before eventually sighing and closing the laptop.

Late Monday evening, I follow Magda as she leaves her room, prints the letter, and after signing in, she promptly drops it off at the counselling office, passing the receptionist the envelope.

An unfamiliar man stands in the hallway facing Magda's door when she returns. There's recognition in her expression alongside surprise and unease. She subtly checks the time on her phone with furrowed brows, stopping a couple of feet away from her dorm; 6:43 pm—late Postmede early Lightlapse.

Magda takes a step to back away unnoticed, but as soon as she turns around to leave, the man notices her. A sinister smile plays on his lips, something about his expression unsettling in a way I can't describe.

She smiles nervously—fearfully—as the man approaches her and grabs her by the waist. His fingers dig into her skin as he spins her around in what could be perceived as a playful manner; however, it is decidedly not based on her startled expression.

Magda almost drops her computer and struggles from his grasp. I clench my hands into fists as I watch her attempt to push him away. Anger consumes me, so hot and fiery, its intensity frightening.

I freeze when I realize there's a thick accumulation of navy mist enveloping the man's head. Something glints in my periphery and I force myself to turn towards the end of the hallway, catching a blur of movement as a dark form slips from view; two large peach wings duck around the corner with him. I distinguish the thin trail of blue energy cast down the hallway where the figure just disappeared, and the familiar scent of burning flesh sends my heart plummeting in my chest. *No, no, it can't be...*

Lucifer is controlling the man.

"Don't!" I cry with a desperation I've never known. My mind screams at me to confront Lucifer, to intervene somehow, but I can't bring myself to leave the scene unravelling in front of me. And even if I could force myself to, I'm powerless to stop the demon. It's too risky; what if my interference only escalates things?

The man slides his right hand from where it's clasped around Magda's waist up to her face, her expression encapsulating the horror I feel forced to watch. She thrashes when his grip loosens, but his other hand only tightens around her waist while he cups her cheek.

All of a sudden, he leans in and kisses her. Magda's cheeks burn a harsh red in stark contrast to her ashen complexion, and I feel my heart sink in my chest. An inferno rages in my eyes.

"What's the matter with you?" The man's voice is deep and demanding, complaining upon pulling away to regard Magda intensely. She cringes at its sound as he brings his hand back down to her waist and tightly clamps down.

"Excuse me? What the *hell* are you doing?" She spits, her face now red with anger as she thrashes against his hold. "What are you doing here? Only students are allowed in the dorms."

"Why are you so bitchy today? Is it that time of the month again?"

"What the fuck is *wrong* with you?"

"Um, nothing," He states matter-of-factly. "I'm just here to say hi to my girlfriend."

Anger, resentment, and jealousy stew in my gut. She's with someone romantically? Why does she look so uneasy to see him, then? Does she sense something's wrong with him, too?

Whatever hope I still harboured that I may find a way to be with Magda depletes, engulfing me in heavy loss. How am I to watch her intimacy with another—with a partner—such as this?

"'Your girlfriend?' We've been broken up for, like, four months. I know you were pissed about it but don't try and act like it didn't happen. If this is your attempt to win me back, calling me 'bitchy' and asking if I'm on my period is not the way to go. Now answer my question: how are you here?" As much as her explanation eases my jealousy, a heavy cloud of disparity still weighs down on my chest.

"My dad got a job here, so I can drop by whenever I want," The man's grip on Magda lessens enough to reach into his pocket and produce a card. Upon closer inspection, it's a key card with an older man's face on it. He smirks, and Magda's eyes widen.

"Let go of me," She seethes, desperately trying to peel his

arms off her. "I don't care if you're my boyfriend or not or if you can drop by whenever you please. Let go of me *right now*."

"What's going on?"

MAGDA

When I twist in Nolan's arms to see Oscar turn the corner, I can already feel my heart settling down in my chest. It's beyond relieving to see Oscar eyeing Nolan suspiciously while he approaches us, clearly picking up on the fact that something is wrong.

"None of your business," Nolan growls quickly, tightening his grip on my waist. He barely acknowledges Oscar's presence, focused on me with a predatory glint in his eyes I can't shake off.

I turn to Oscar with the most distraught expression I can muster, terrified tears springing in my eyes; the second we make eye contact, he barrels towards us and shoves Nolan away from me with excessive force while one hand clutches a takeout bag from Quesada.

Nolan's grip falters, and he hits the hallway wall with an audible *thump*. As soon as I'm released, Oscar protectively steps in front of me with one hand keeping me behind him. My knees feel they're about to buckle at any given moment. I nervously peer over Oscar's shoulder to gauge Nolan's reaction.

Red, hot anger flashes in his eyes, a steady trembling settling over him. He clenches his fists at his sides, the veins in his forehead and neck bulging comically as he takes a threatening step towards us.

"Who the *fuck* do you think you are?" Nolan growls, taking slow, stalking steps.

"Listen, buddy, I don't care who you are, how you know her, or why you're here, but if my sister asks you to let go, you *let. Her.*

Go."

Nolan's expression and composure soften immediately. It's so abrupt that I flinch, wincing at the horrifyingly convincing easy smile that spreads across his face. The veins that were about to burst from his neck settle beneath his skin like a cat retracting its claws.

"You must be Maggie's little brother! Nice to meet you. I'm her boyfriend, Nolan." He casually offers his hand to Oscar.

I bite back a plethora of colourful curse words I wish I could scream, instead deciding on something less vulgar but just as scathing. "Like hell. We're not together anymore, dickhead."

Confusedly, Oscar glances back at me with no intention of accepting Nolan's handshake. He flexes his jaw, the tendons popping angrily as he straightens his brooding posture. "All right, *Nolan,* you're gonna calmly leave this building, and you're going to avoid Maggie like the goddamn plague if you have any semblance of self-preservation."

Nolan dares to look confounded. Without seeing Oscar's expression, I can tell we're both facing him with the same stoic sneer.

"I was just—"

"Don't make me repeat myself," Oscar interjects.

Nolan's mouth snaps shut as he turns to me for redemption. I flip him off over Oscar's shoulder, and his expression sours. He raises his hands in surrender and wordlessly seethes past us.

As I watch Nolan retreat down the hallway, I notice a couple of students staring at Oscar and me, bewildered, as they reach for their respective doorknobs. When they see Oscar and I look back at them, they immediately avert eye contact and start fumbling around with their keycards. I can even see their cheeks burning as their eyes dart back to Oscar and me—or, more specifically, to Oscar.

I whistle flirtatiously at Oscar, his cheeks going redder than the girls' when he registers my implication. He just waves shyly at them before turning away and hurriedly opening my door to usher me inside.

"Someone's popular," I tease with a small smile. "You've been here like, two days and are already more popular than I am after almost four years."

He clears his throat, the tips of his ears dipped in vermillion. He faces me, his eyes oozing worry as they flit across my body, assessing any damage. "Are you okay? Did he hurt you?"

My smile falters, and I feel my legs weaken beneath me. I collapse on my bed, my heart still racing as though I'd just run a marathon. "I'm… I'm okay."

"Why'd he say he's your boyfriend if you guys are broken up?"

I sigh, rubbing my eyes. "We dated briefly, but I didn't feel that… spark-thingy, so I broke up with him about four months ago, and kind of broke his heart. He, um, admitted to being in love with me, so he was pretty devastated by it. But I hadn't heard from him since, until now, and honestly, I have no idea why he's even here in the first place."

Oscar slumps beside me, carefully placing the Quesada bag on the floor to hold my hand with both of his. "Does he go here too?"

I shake my head. "Nope. His dad got a job here, so I guess that means he has no qualms about stealing his keycard to harass me or whatever it is he wants."

"If you want him out of your life, I can deliver the message for you."

As flattering as Oscar's offer is, I shake my head. "It's nothing.

Please don't make a big deal of it. I'll deal with it. But thank you, I really appreciate it."

Oscar nods, a soft smile playing on his lips. "All right. If you don't want my help, I'll stay out of it. But the minute he does anything, and I mean *anything*, call me, okay? And I'll make sure he doesn't bother you ever again."

I giggle, smiling into Oscar's shoulder. "I will." I wrap an arm around his torso, and he reciprocates with an arm around my shoulder. I smile up at him, the thought of Nolan being unable to find me once I move back home alleviating beyond belief.

LARAMIE

I could kill Lucifer if I had the means.

I can see the pain and struggle behind Magda's eyes, even in the way she sits, slouched and trembling, and the dart of her eyes whenever she hears a sound. Seeing her so afraid stimulates an agonizing ache that won't subside.

As Lightlapse falls, I admire the sunset.

The sun's yellow disc drifts toward the horizon, the sky melting into shades of pink and orange and purple and blue. A small smile tugs at my lips as the sun bleeds red before my very eyes, and I watch, fascinated, as the bright stars shine their light upon me through the veil of the ebony, inky sky. The moon is milky and full, and though very far away, the silver glow not only calms but reassures me with a fulfilling sense of virtuosity.

Knowing Lucifer can leave Hell whenever he pleases and the fact that he's using whatever means around him he has to besiege Magda's life is sickening. Unjustifiable pain and abuse inflicted upon her all to make me regret declining his offer. The barrage of guilt that Magda's newfound suffrage is my fault embeds itself into my chest like a knife lodged through my heart.

I can find at least momentary respite in knowing I chose to do the right thing now that Lucifer's shown his true colours. And yet how can I justify Magda's suffering? Maybe I should have agreed to let Magda's life go uncorrupted, the way it was meant to. Then perhaps she would've found peace.

It's too late to go back now, I bitterly remind myself. *What's done is done.*

MAGDA

Sighing, I idly tap my pen against my laptop, chewing on my lip as I continue to search for jobs. I shift against the wall, staring at my computer screen through squinting eyes, the light that emits from it bright and slightly dizzying in the dark room. While it's extremely bad for me to be staring at an almost blinding computer screen in a pitch-black room, that's honestly the least of my problems right now.

A muffled buzz beside me makes me jump. I rummage through my blankets before sweeping up my phone, my hands shaking as I unlock it. My heart immediately drops when I see who the text is from. *Nolan.*

Stopping by tomorrow at ur dorm for dinner. be ready at 530 & wear something sexy, k babe? ;)

I send a blunt 'not happening asshole' before turning off my phone and throwing it on the bed with a scoff. I glare at it until tears build in my eyes that I can't see behind, and I push the computer off my lap to wipe them from my eyes. They're dry and sore from crying so much lately that I don't know if I can handle any more.

Sniffling, I sit up and grab my phone again, dialling Mom's

number through the tears obscuring my sight. I have to dial it three times before getting it right, and I hurry to click call when I finally do. It rings for a few long seconds, giving me plenty of time to chastise myself for waking Mom up in the middle of the night for such a stupid reason. I'm about to hang up when Mom answers.

"Hello?" Her voice is raspy with fatigue.

"M-mom?" It feels like all worry ceases as soon as I hear her voice. *"Mom."*

"Maggie, sweetie? What's the matter, dear?"

"I need to talk to you," I admit bashfully. "Sorry for waking you up. Maybe I shouldn't've called…"

"Nonsense. I told you to always come to me first when you were a little girl. I'm pleased to know you're still following through with that." I smile into the phone, my eyes growing misty again. "Now, what's the matter, sweetheart?"

Sighing, I explain everything that's been going on with Nolan. I recount what happened earlier today with Nolan, despite how humiliating it is to tell her about a guy who's borderline harassing me, but, like always, there's no judgement in her tone when she speaks.

"I'm so sorry, baby," She says when I finish. "A lot's going on in your life right now. It doesn't help that on top of everything else, you're dealing with a boy who won't take the hint, hm? Dealing with this kind of thing is tricky. The best way to handle things is to give him an ultimatum; give him consequences if he chooses to seek you out again. Tell him if he keeps trying to contact you and visit you, you'll call his parents or even the police. You have to show him what he's doing is not okay."

Already I feel so much better. My body relaxes, even if only marginally, and I allow myself to fall back against the bed with a happy sigh. “Thanks, Mom.”

“Anytime. Now, is there anything else you’d like to talk about?”

“No, I don’t think so. I should let you get back to sleep since I’m pretty tired myself.”

“Okay, dear. I love you with all of my heart. Sleep well, angel.”

“I love you too, Mom. Thanks for always being here.”

–EIGHT–

You've Got Company

MAGDA

"Guess what?" Oscar exclaims, bursting into my dorm without warning. I startle, tense as I whip my head in the direction of the door from where I'm sitting cross-legged on my bed with my laptop precariously situated on my lap.

I relax when I realize it's Oscar at the door, but my heart continues to race, blood rushing to my ears. I try for a cool smile, closing the lid of my computer as I relax as best as I can. "You always know how to make a bang. Holy shit, Os. Warn me next time, wouldja?"

He flushes slightly, sheepishly muttering a small "sorry" before closing the door and actually vibrating over to me. Dude looks like a jackhammer with the way he's shaking in what I can only assume is excitement. "Guess what?"

"Hm, let me guess; they finally got the drop on that one dentist who doesn't recommend Colgate?"

Oscar snorts. "Honestly, they should probably get a hitman involved at this point. That last dentist is really ruining their rep."

"Honestly true."

"My *actual* news is that I landed an interview at that coffee shop! You know, the one we went to the other day? I dropped off my resume and got an interview this Thursday!"

"Oh my God, Os, congrats!" I grab Oscar's shoulders and give them a solid shake, beaming with pride. "Wait. Don't tell me this is all an elaborate plan of yours to get mega discounts on their muffins?"

Oscar snaps his fingers, feigning incredulity. "How'd you guess?"

"Because I'm awesome."

He rolls his eyes. "Seriously though, can you believe it? I could be serving coffee in like a week from now, fulfilling my small-town barista fantasies. Oh my God, what if I find my soulmate? I'm behind the counter, and when our eyes meet, this spark flies."

"You've been reading way too much fan fiction," I tease. "Though that's not too unrealistic. Personally, I think you'll make the cutest waitress, prancing around wearing your little apron with your little notepad and a pencil tucked behind your ear. You'd be irresistible."

He puffs his chest out. "I *am* adorable, aren't I?"

I reply by leaning over and squeezing Oscar's cheeks. He bats my hands away as soon as I pinch his skin. "And here I'd come to offer you a grilled cheese from my future employment." He holds up a small takeout bag I hadn't noticed he'd been carrying until now and shakes his head. "Shaking my head."

"I never asked you to get me anything."

"I did it out of the kindness of my heart."

"Still didn't ask."

He just thrusts the bag at me and throws his arms up. "Kids these days… so ungrateful."

I mimic him as I push my laptop down to grope at the food. While, yes, it was very kind of Oscar to bring me food, and as grateful as I am to have an excuse to get away from job hunting, the last thing I want to do right now is eat.

"Eat," he orders.

"Demanding much?"

"It's not like I'm pressuring you into doing drugs, Mags."

"Yeah, 'cause that's my job."

He laughs. "Are you gonna eat it or not?"

I feel a sense of loss, staring down at the few pathetic nibbles I've taken, and I shrug. "I'm just not that hungry."

"You still need to eat. When was the last time you had a meal?" My silence says more than I could with words. "Magda Celia Mercy—"

I cringe at his use of my full name. "Only Mom gets to use our full names to guilt-trip us, *Oscar Steven Mercy.*"

"Don't vomit or anything, but I'm gonna try to have a serious conversation with you," He cautions, his expression too stern for my liking. "This isn't the first time you've neglected to eat, even if it's unintentional. And you remember how that went last time, right?"

I was twelve when I'd started reducing my food intake for the first time. It wasn't deliberate, but it also didn't help that I already had a poor self-image. I forgot to eat more often than was healthy and began drastically losing weight, hiding it under sweaters and baggy clothes. Nobody suspected a thing until one day Oscar and I were playing outside, and I'd been hit with sudden overwhelming vertigo and passed out. When I briefly regained consciousness next, it was in an ambulance, the screeching sirens and blaring lights enough to put me back under.

The next time I woke up, I was in a hospital bed with Mom, Dad and Oscar sitting around me. The doctors told them how malnourished I was and diagnosed me with anorexia. The recovery was brutal, and I don't think I'll ever forget the fear in Oscar's eyes when he'd looked over at me, grimacing at my bony collarbones and sunken face. He was barely ten.

"Yeah, I remember," I mutter. Shame burns beneath my skin, and I fold in on myself.

"I'm not trying to embarrass you. I'm just worried about you. And... I remember it. Vividly. I don't think I've ever been so scared as I was when I saw you laying in that hospital bed looking like a corpse, boney and pale and sickly. Seeing The Shining at seven years old was relaxing in comparison."

I don't say anything. I can't argue with him when he's right. I *hate* it when he's right; it's so unsettling, like seeing a baby swear.

"I'm not your responsibility," My voice falters, and I take a shaky breath. *"I'm* the older sibling. I should be the one taking care of you. Not... not the other way around." All I feel is an unshakable humiliation when I realize I'm the immature one; I'm the one who's acting like a child when I'm older and should be wiser and shit. "Don't... don't do that to yourself. You don't have to worry about me."

"Have you met me? I'm not just gonna let you starve yourself, Mags."

"I'm not starving myself—" He cuts off my indignant grumbling when he thrusts his finger to my lips. *"Shh.* Obviously, I'm not just gonna sit here and watch you put yourself last, okay? So, come on. Eat your damn sandwich before I stuff it down your throat." He begins to roll up his sleeves. "You think I'm kidding?"

I don't doubt his sincerity for a second. Accepting the fact that I can't win this argument, I begrudgingly pick my sandwich up and lift it to my lips, wrinkling my nose when my stomach fills with nausea at the smell. I'm fifty shades of fucked up if a grilled cheese makes me want to throw up.

Not wanting to let Oscar down, I eat the stupid sandwich. It feels like a battle between my stomach and me as I fight to keep it from coming back up. Thankfully, it doesn't, and when I take my final bite, Oscar is infuriatingly smug as he claps his hands together to shake off invisible dust. I make a face at him, flashing the chewed-up food in my mouth before continuing to chew, emphasizing the smack of my lips.

"Ew," He complains as I giggle, trying not to choke on my last bite. "That's gross. You're gross."

Too much strength goes into forcing down my final bite. I burp, sucking air into my cheeks until I finally feel the food settle in my stomach. "You know you *looove* me."

"Unfortunately."

My idiot brother cackles maniacally at his own joke as I clean the remnants of my meal before reluctantly returning to my job search. I'm too focused on applying to a few part-time positions to pay much attention when Oscar leaves for the night. I absent-mindedly wave as the door clicks shut behind him, fingers flying across my keyboard as I submit my resume for a part-time information technology support advisor at a nearby IT company.

I receive an email from the dean of students accepting my leave request almost immediately after submitting my final resume for the night, and I instantly leap to my feet and call Oscar. He legitimately screeches when I read the email over the phone to him, and I can't help myself from laughing hysterically when I hear Mom and Dad scolding him in the background for startling them.

As soon as the call abruptly ends—the last thing I hear is Dad saying, "You can't just scream bloody murder when," before Oscar hastily ends the call, no doubt in for the reprimanding of a lifetime—there's a knock at the door. Expecting it to be the dorm manager, I open it without a second thought and can physically feel the colour drain from my face as I stare, dumbfounded, at Nolan in the doorway.

A burning stench hits me when I swing the door open, and I don't have any time to consider what it is or where it's coming from when Nolan greets me with a "Hey, babe" before leaning in to kiss me.

I turn my head before he can kiss me on the lips, forcing him instead to peck me on the cheek. I still shove him away from me, but he doesn't budge, looming over me with a disgustingly satisfied smile. I fight the almost irresistible urge to punch it off his face.

He looks me up and down, an eyebrow arched and nose wrinkled at what I can only assume is my lack of quote-unquote "sexy attire" like he so gentlemanly requested.

"I told you to wear something sexy!" Yep, there it is. "Ugh, whatever. Maybe after." He wiggles his eyebrows at me, and I consider slamming the door hard enough to break his nose. I don't, unfortunately, not wanting to damage the door.

"We're gonna catch up at the coffee shop on the corner. I think it's called 'Topped Off' or something. I didn't want to go anywhere too fancy since we haven't seen each other in so long, so how does coffee sound?"

"I'm not going out with you," My voice is surprisingly firm, but my heart is lodged so deep in my throat I worry I'll choke on it.

"Why do you always have to make things so difficult? I try to plan something nice for us, and you *always* have something negative to say about it." He sighs and rubs his face. "I'll let it slide this time, only because it's been so long since we've last hung out. I suppose we can hang out here instead." He pushes past me, sending me stumbling against the wall while he makes himself comfortable on my bed. "Maybe we could… get straight to dessert?"

"That's not what I meant," I spit vehemently, my fists curled tightly around the door. "Get out."

"What? Why?"

"Why? *Why?* We're broken up. You're not welcome here."

"What the hell are you going on about? Definitely that time of the month." He bristles. "We're fine, babe. What's gotten into you? Wait, is this because of your brother?"

I have the distinct urge to roll my eyes so far back in my head I pass out on the spot. The only reason I don't is that I get the feeling that my passing out won't stop Nolan from arguing, and I'd rather not be unconscious around him. "This isn't about Oscar. He has *nothing* to do with this. This is because of *you*. I broke up with you like four months ago."

"Did you hit your head or something?" He almost sounds concerned. "What the hell are you talking about? You never broke up with me; you just told me you needed to focus on your studies for a while. That's why we haven't seen each other in forever."

Exasperated, I scrub a hand over my face. "Look, Nolan, we're not together. I broke up with you. You cried, told me it wasn't fair because you still loved me, and then left. Gone from my life for four months. Don't try acting like that never happened."

"This is so not fair. I'm not letting you do this to me. If you think I'm dumb enough to let some jackass take you from me, you're dumber than I thought."

"I'm not yours for someone to take from you! Just swallow your pride and leave, or I'll call your dad."

He seems to consider my threat, dropping his head. He runs a hand through his hair before looking back up, features hardened and cold.

"I'm not leaving," he decides. "I'm not leaving you."

"Get out!" I shout, my heart racing. "I'll do it! I'll call your dad!"

"Do it! See if I care." He taunts, lunging forward to grab my arm. I yelp and thrash against his hold, choking on my own breath as he rips my hands off the door and slams it shut. "You're not getting away from me so easily."

"Let go of me." I manage calmly; how I have no idea. Nolan backs me into the room, and I flinch when my back hits the wall. He leans into me so close our faces are mere inches apart and snarls, "You are MINE. MINE AND MINE ALONE," through clenched teeth.

I scan the room wildly, lips parted preemptively to scream. I inhale sharply, but Nolan clamps a hand down on my mouth before I have the chance to cry out. Startled, I use my freed arm to try pushing him off me as he slides his hand down my neck and tilts my head up, completely disregarding my resistance. I stand there in mute horror as he leans down and starts kissing my neck, his teeth puncturing my skin. I scream, violated and horrified, but all my struggling seems to do is motivate him. His hand roughly grasps my neck where his face isn't pressed against it, and he savagely bites down.

When he finally pulls away, his lips are smeared red with my blood. The sight alone makes me want to projectile vomit all over his smug expression.

He effortlessly pushes me off the wall until the back of my knees hits the bed frame. I pound on his chest as adrenaline courses through me, but I'm no match for him. All it takes is one solid shove to send me onto the bed, crowding me until I'm splayed across the mattress. Ceaseless tears stream from my eyes as I beg Nolan to stop, but his hand remains firm against my mouth, my words incoherent babbles as I sob.

LARAMIE

I scream at Nolan, my stomach blistering with rage as I see Magda's neck beginning to bruise, tiny beads of blood bubbling from the shallow lacerations.

Lightning and thunder reverberate synchronously with my cries. I sob helplessly as Magda's terrified expression only intensifies from the thunder I created.

Nolan shifts his hand to Magda's body and gropes at her, pressing himself down in erratic bursts. He hungrily licks his lips, and breathy sobs escape Magda's as she claws at his hand still clamped around her face, to no avail. She uses her other hand to try and push him away from her chest, but his grip won't budge, his strength almost inhuman.

I briefly turn away to find Lucifer, following the trail of Grace that leads to the window, behind which I see Lucifer's face. His despicable grin douses me in pure dread, his eyes murderous yet soft with enjoyment.

He finds pleasure in Magda's suffering.

"STOP THIS!" I scream at him. Although I'm terrified to be mere inches away from Lucifer, I approach the window and glare at him nonetheless. "STOP THIS!"

'You should have accepted my offer,' He spits.

"STOP! *PLEASE!*" I turn back to Magda. Nolan has begun straddling her hips, grinning as he uses one hand to force her arms beneath his knees. Magda thrashes and struggles, but he pins her down effortlessly.

"STOP!" My voice is hoarse as anger writhes low in my stomach—tears streak my cheeks, my shouts echoed by the thunder and lightning striking outside. I feel like I can't breathe with my chest so tight. "DON'T DO THIS TO HER! PLEASE, STOP IT!"

'Such a shame you have no miracles left…' Lucifer coos, tone extenuating his delight as his eyes sparkle while watching the scene unfold. When I look back to see Nolan tugging at Magda's sweatpants and undergarments, my vision burns red. I feel something taking over me, a burst of energy clawing its way from deep within. I don't let myself question what it is as I unleash a bloodcurdling wail and focus on grasping the power with as much desperation as I can muster.

I'm glowering in pure rage as I raise my arm and curl my hand into a fist. I focus on the feeling of Nolan's being in the palm of my hand and swiftly thrust my arm across the air. Nolan is wrenched off of Magda and skids across the room before slamming against the door with enough force to leave him momentarily stunned, Lucifer's control over him wavering.

A look of confusion and disorientation flashes across the human's face as he glances around the room, dazed. Satisfaction sweeps through me in a kaleidoscope of dull lights and a burst of adrenaline that consolidates my pride.

Shock sweeps across Lucifer's face when his concentration is broken. He quickly regains his composure, shifting Nolan's expression from bewilderment to hardened rage in less than a second.

A rush of lightheadedness debilitates me. I find Magda cowering against the wall, blankly staring forward, her expression suspended in shock. The vacancy and resignation in her eyes purge any satisfaction I'd had upon intervening like a punch in the gut.

"You're lucky I've got a curfew," Nolan snarls, his swiftness sinister as he stalks towards Magda again. She scrambles back against the wall, but his hand shoots out to grab her arm and tugs her onto her back, seizing her throat yet again in another violating kiss.

When he finally pulls away, the man smirks at Magda, licks his lips, and shoves her one final time before climbing off the bed without looking back. He flings the door open and leaves, slamming it hard enough that it hits the doorframe with a heavy *thump* before swinging back open.

Lucifer glares at me with confusion and anger. 'Opposing my power will lead to nothing but forfeiture, worse than I intended,' He hisses, and any trace of his presence or power disappears from the window.

Magda straightens herself against the wall, lifting a trembling hand to her neck. She cringes against the touch and peers down indifferently at the droplets of blood smeared across her fingers upon pulling her hand away.

Overcome with fatigue, I allow the tides of repentance to crash into me. I slump to my knees, breathing deeply as my mind races to make sense of everything that's just unfolded. Something overcame me, and I used a portion of Grace that I thought I no longer had to intervene. But how?

I raise my hand, concentrating on the familiar tingling that usurped my fingers but feel only emptiness within.

How did I do that?

MAGDA

I feel drunk and high at the same time, minus the momentary alleviation alcohol and drugs provide—not that I'd know what either is like, of course.

My mind is foggy, and I can barely process everything that

just unfolded. The last thing I want to do is even *think* about what almost happened—I'd do whatever it takes to forget about it altogether.

I sag forward, weakly grabbing a fistful of my blankets in a blind struggle to find my phone. When it falls into my lap, I dial Oscar's number without hesitation, and after the second ring, he answers. "Hey, Mags, what's up?"

"Ossy…"

"Maggie? What's wrong? I'm here. Do you need me to come over?"

I bob my head up and down, too delirious to realize Oscar can't see me; I know if I open my mouth, I'll start sobbing, and I don't have the energy to deal with crying any more than I already have.

My head lulls onto the floor defeatedly as I focus on taking deep breaths to prevent myself from passing out.

"Okay, okay," Oscar must sense something's wrong based on the urgency in his voice. "I'm on my way now, all right? Hold on, Mags, I'll be right there."

NINE

Expeditious Salvation

LARAMIE

scar bursts through the open doorway, his dread and alarm palpable upon finding the door left ajar. He's panting erratically as he scans the room for his sister, a panicked plea alight in his dark eyes. His expression immediately softens when he notices Magda curled up in the corner, wracked by an intense trembling.

"Maggie…" Alawa and George appear behind him in the doorway when he barrels into the room, similar concern and horror painted across their faces.

Magda's head snaps up when she hears Oscar call her name, eyes filled with pure fear. She scrambles back as he approaches, arm held out weakly to keep him at bay.

"No!" Her voice wavers, and her lip quivers. "S-stay back. *Don't touch me.*"

Oscar freezes mid-stride. His eyes widen in horror and confusion, and I can almost hear his heart skip a beat, his shoulders shaking imperceptibly. "Okay. I-I'll stay right here. It's okay. I was just going to hug you. I'm not gonna hurt you." His voice breaks on the last sentence as Alawa and George take hesitant steps towards the bed. The only reaction Magda has to it is the tension in her muscles slowly beginning to recede as they grow closer to her. Carefully sitting on the edge of the bed, Alawa beckons Magda towards her with an outstretched hand. Magda's eyes brim with tears as she reaches out and grasps it, one hand still clasped around her neck.

"I'm here, honey. Nothing's going to hurt you now. It's okay. You're okay," Alawa soothes. I blink the tears I didn't realize had gathered in my own eyes and turn, a sudden chill sweeping over me. I rub my arms, taking a shaky breath only to stiffen when something catches on my hands. Confused, I lift my palm to find a long strip of skin caught between two of my fingers.

I look down at the wide aperture exposing a starry-night void of deepest blue with flecks of starlight underneath. My mind malfunctions as I drop my hand and, out of curiosity, poke the gap. Only then does the realization occur that my form is beginning to fade away.

Magda's quiet sobbing is what regains my attention. With swiftness yet reluctance, I peel off the strip, wincing as it withers away in the very palm of my hand. I look down at my arm, almost in a trance, as the long line of midnight sky begins to dissolve.

I try to ignore my impending doom as I turn back to Magda. She's still trembling minutely, now slumped against her mother's chest, who whispers comforting reassurances in her ear.

"Are you okay?" George broaches tentatively, his voice timid yet curious. He looks like he's been considering asking for the past few minutes, conflicted and slightly fearful.

When he reaches out to rub Magda's back, she cringes away from his touch. He whips his hand away as if burned but refrains from saying anything. "What happened?"

"I just…" Magda's voice is rough and broken, contrary to its typically soothing, velvety timbre. "It was sudden and… and… he was just…"

"Who?"

Realization dawns on Oscar. He sets his jaw and clenches his fists so tight his knuckles turn snow-white. "Nolan… he was here, wasn't he?"

Magda nods, silent tears spilling down her face. Alawa closes her eyes and gently tightens their embrace, beginning to sway slowly and assiduously in a soothing motion.

"That son of a bitch…" George seethes.

"I'm sorry we left you with that…" Oscar takes a deep breath, bowing his head. "What did he do? Did he-did he hurt you?"

Magda takes a shaky inhale and closes her eyes. After a few seconds, she pulls away from Alawa enough to remove the hand clasped around her neck, revealing the purple contusion and shallow cuts. Alawa inhales sharply, immediately averting her eyes. She buries her face in Magda's shoulder, squeezing tighter than before while Oscar and George imperturbably examine the injury. Magda winces when her father gently angles her head back to inspect the extent of the bruising.

"I-it's not much b-but…"

"Don't you dare underplay it," Oscar wavers, wiping the tears in his eyes before scrubbing a hand over his face. "What-what happened?"

A tear rolls down Magda's chin and onto her shirt, leaving a dampening blot that goes unnoticed. She sniffles and squeezes Alawa's hand for reassurance. "He-he backed me against the bed a-and… did this—" she motions weakly to her neck, "—I managed to shove him off me, then he said something about his curfew and left."

Shame burns bright against Magda's cheeks. She wasn't completely honest with them. Why? Is she embarrassed? Afraid of telling them? In denial, or still in shock?

"I-I can't believe he…" Oscar's voice trails off. He turns back to Magda. "He forced you down and gave you… a hickey?"

Magda nods, cringing.

"This-this is *unacceptable*. He can't just force his way into your dorm without permission, assault you and get away with it!" George bellows, his face a bright red. "We need to talk to someone about this. I-I can—"

"Don't…" Magda says softly. "I just… I need to think, and… he's…" she takes a shallow breath, "Give me a night. I'll figure it out." Alawa lets go of Magda's waist with one hand to stroke her hair.

"Honey, sweetie, look at you. You've got a blackening bruise on your neck, you sound like hell, and, no offence, but you look like a wreck. I-I can't just let that monster go after doing this to you." George firmly shakes his head. "I won't let him."

"Please…" She clasps her father's hand in a silent plea, tears cascading freely down her cheeks. "I can figure this all out, I swear. Just—please don't do anything. Not yet, at least. I…I don't want to be alone."

George's expression softens. When he pulls Magda towards him, this time she collapses against his chest and blinks back tears, all the tension siphoned from her body.

"Okay. We aren't going anywhere. I just… I just love you *so much*, and I can't stand seeing someone hurt you."

Magda's breaths start to even, her sobs lessening until she falls fast asleep. I can't imagine how exhausted she must be from what transpired—all because of me.

After a few long seconds, George looks down at Magda to see she's fallen asleep in his arms. He'd been about to say something but closes his mouth instead and delicately deposits her onto her bed while Oscar furiously wipes his eyes.

"We should take her home with us," Alawa whispers. Despite the wheeze in her breathing, she's clearly trying to be quiet so as not to disturb Magda, absentmindedly carding a hand through the girl's hair again. "We can't just leave her here."

"I'll grab her phone," agrees Oscar. "And anything else she'll need."

George gently lifts Magda back into his arms as Oscar gathers a few of her belongings before leading them back to the main entrance, where Alawa and George's car is parked just outside.

Oscar hops in the backseat as George gently lays Magda across the seats. Once he closes the door, Oscar cradles Magda's head for a few moments before warily rearranging it to rest on his thigh, careful not to strain her neck. Alawa settles in the passenger seat and holds Magda's hand across the console as George drives them home.

Oscar is the one who carries Magda inside upon their arrival. He takes her straight to what I assume is her bedroom and tucks her into the neatly made bed with tender movements. Alawa and George kiss the children goodnight before hesitantly retreating to the living room, whispering in hushed tones. Oscar is the last to leave Magda's bedroom, only to return after half a minute with a pillow and blanket to settle on the floor beside her bed.

MAGDA

I jolt awake with a gasp, drenched in sweat. My chest heaves as I struggle to catch my breath, pushing myself upright. I'm struck with an overwhelming surge of panic when I realize I'm not in my dorm room, and it only intensifies when I remember what happened with Nolan. I start hyperventilating, and my heart pounds ruthlessly against my chest when I entertain the possibility that Nolan kidnapped me. I can't breathe for a few seconds while I adjust to the darkness enough to recognize where I am; home.

My chest deflates, and I fall back against the bed, blinking back tears as I stare blankly at the ceiling, slowly coming to terms with what happened. I pull the covers up to my chin and squeeze my eyes shut, finally allowing the tears to fall.

As much as I hate Nolan, I hate myself more for allowing it to happen. I fought with all the strength left in me, but if I'd just been stronger or less pathetic, I could've stopped him. But I'm not, and I didn't. I let him hurt me because I'm not strong enough to stop him; because I'm me.

The urge to cut comes back with a vengeance, just as Nolan has all of a sudden. The temptation is almost too strong to resist, but I do, only because I'm too tired and lethargic to manage to make my way to the kitchen; had I not been, I probably would have relapsed for the first time in four or five years because of him.

No, because of me.

I sluggishly sit up and blink away the darkness enveloping me. I flinch violently when I see a silhouette on the floor next to my bed, thankfully realizing it's just Oscar before having another panic attack. There's a pillow wedged beneath his head and a thin blanket draped across him; it doesn't look remotely comfortable, however, his expression is nonetheless peaceful and relaxed.

My eyes linger on his form for a few more seconds before I turn away. The glint of something across the room catches in my periphery, so I turn back in its direction, where it's peeking from an unopened cardboard box next to my desk.

Mustering some semblance of energy, I slide off the bed and

carefully step over Oscar, quiet as not to wake him, and approach the box. I let out a soft laugh, a sly smile tugging at my lips when I push back the lids of the box to reveal a familiar teddy bear. I smile fondly, my heart aching with nostalgia as I gently grasp Bearley and inhale the familiar scent of Mom's perfume that clings to him. The long red ribbon tied around his neck in a bow tickles my chin with its frayed ends as I squeeze him to my chest, his cherished white fur splattered with hardened chips of green, blue, and purple paint.

I can almost hear the phantom laugh of six-year-old me running around the backyard holding him by his paw. It impacts me so suddenly, a memory I forgot I even had.

How could I forget about you? I wonder absently. My hand moves with a mind of its own to squeeze his left paw. I startle at the sound of Mom's slightly stifled voice emitting from the plush, *"I love you, Maggie. You're my little angel."*

Somehow, that's all I needed to fall back asleep. I slip back into bed and gently lay my head down on the pillow, still cautious of my tender neck, and wrap myself in the blankets with Bearley tucked protectively beneath my chin.

TEN

Home Sweet Home

MAGDA

he darkness is smothering.

Despite being unable to see my surroundings, I somehow know I'm kneeling on the floor of my dorm room. My head is hung, but I can't move when I try to look up, not even the slightest flick of a finger or a quick glance.

I'm paralyzed in place.

Cold disembodied hands pinch my chin and tilt my head, so I'm finally able to look up. A silhouette stands over me, and I can do nothing but watch as the shadow recedes until I recognize the figure towering over me, and of-fucking-course, it's Nolan. I'm unable to show any outward indication of my unease; my expression remains solemnly neutral, and my body stays firmly planted in place despite the pure horror overwhelming me.

"My sweet Maggie," He hisses, a ribbon-like forked tongue flicking from his mouth as he speaks. An ominous shadow is still cast across his face, so I can just barely discern his eyes; they're glowing a brassy-yellow with pupils slit like a snake. He grins at me with razor-sharp teeth as his grip tightens on my chin. "You *belong* to me. You have always belonged to me."

My surroundings suddenly materialize into my childhood bedroom; I realize I'm kneeling at the foot of my bed with Nolan standing over me.

When he drops my chin, it falls to my chest, and only then am I able to look down at myself to see my hands tied on my lap and ankles bound beneath me. I suddenly feel the thick strip of fabric tied around my mouth, preventing me from speaking.

I look up as Nolan turns his attention to something on the floor, and I follow his gaze to find Oscar fast asleep on the floor beside my bed. Nolan turns to me, grinning maliciously before advancing towards my brother.

My movements are stiff as I shake my head, the only means I have to protest Nolan's actions. I watch uselessly as he curls his hands around Oscar's neck, and the next thing I know, he has Oscar pinned to the wall by his neck. Oscar jerks awake, eyes comically wide as he starts gasping for breath with these awful croaky wheezing noises. Nolan throws his head back in a laugh and slides Oscar further up the wall until his toes can't even brush against the ground. His face goes beet red, his neck slowly turning purple from the asphyxiation.

I want to scream out to Oscar, writhing in my restraints to beat the ever-loving *shit* out of Nolan, but the only control I have over myself is moving my head back and forth. I'm left entirely helpless, forced to sit back and watch while my brother is strangled brutally in front of me.

"You will *never* take her from me," Nolan snarls, his face a mere few inches from Oscar's. "I won't let you take her from me. I won't let anyone *ever* take her from me."

He casually flicks his wrist, the nauseating crack of Oscar's neck reverberating in the empty air. The snap plays over and over again in my head, a deafening echo as all I can do is stare in horror as Oscar's body falls limp and his arms swing bonelessly at his sides. I can physically see the life drain from his eyes as they cloud over, empty and inanimate.

Nolan stalks forward until he's kneeling in front of me, waving Oscar's corpse in my face with a psychotic smile. "I saved you." He grabs Oscar by the hair to shake him for emphasis, shoving my brother's face so close to my own that I can almost feel the blood pouring from his nose, mouth, and eyes; I can't tear my gaze away from his vacant, bloodshot eyes that bleed profusely.

"I saved you," Nolan repeats. "Look at what I did for you—look at what I'm willing to do for you. I love you, Maggie. And I won't *ever* let anyone get between you and me. You are *MINE.*"

Oscar hits the floor hard, his head falling into my lap as Nolan disappears. Oscar's lifeless eyes bore through mine, and I would almost believe he's just asleep if not for the blood still sluggishly streaming from his face and his disconcerting blank stare.

"Maggie."

I squeeze my eyes shut and refuse to open them, feeling Nolan's presence in front of me.

"Maggie."

He starts vigorously shaking my shoulders, but I don't budge.

"Maggie!"

The whole world is thrust from beneath me, and I fall. When I hit the ground, I wake up.

I bolt upright in bed, sweating profusely as my heart jack-rabbits against my chest. I blink back the sleep in my eyes to find Oscar concernedly kneeling over me, his hands gently resting on my shoulders, grounding me. The mental image of his sallow, purple face with blood oozing from his eyes suddenly flashes in my head, and I immediately throw my arms around him in a hug.

He leans back for a moment before hesitantly reciprocating. I grip his shoulders and squeeze with all the might my still half-asleep body can muster, too tired to cry. Every time I close my eyes, his lifeless face is right there in front of me, so I keep my eyes open as I bury my face into his neck and cling to him. Eventually, he pulls away. "You okay?"

I nod shakily and gently slide my hand beneath his, using the other to rub the sleep from my eyes. "I'm fine. Just… just a nightmare."

He nods, his lips pulled into a tight line. "Ah. Do you want to tell me about it?"

I hesitate, flashes of the dream playing through my head; Nolan's snake-like appearance and deranged expression as he stands over Oscar's sleeping body, Oscar thrashing and wheezing as he's choked to death, his lifeless eyes perforating my very soul, sluggishly oozing red-hot blood.

I shudder and shake my head. "I can't. I'm sorry."

"Hey, no worries. That's okay. No pressure."

Neither of us says anything for a few seconds before I clear my throat and break the silence. "Wh-what happened?"

"Well, uhm, after… after you called me last night, Mom, Dad, and I didn't want to leave you alone at your dorm, so we brought you home. We didn't mean to spook you. We just wanted you to be home in case you needed us." I honestly can't imagine how panicked I would've been had I awoken in the middle of the night, alone at my dorm, hallucinating Nolan standing over me with those cold, evil eyes. "Thanks, Os."

"We're about to eat breakfast in the living room if you wanna join us," He suggests. "No pressure, just whenever you feel ready."

"Yeah, okay."

He shoots me a small smile and squeezes my hand before leaving, gently closing the door behind him. I sigh and shiver, hugging my waist protectively as the urge to wrap myself in my blanket like a burrito and stay there until I'm forced to shower entices me. I'm about to give in when my stomach rumbles loudly, motivating me to get up and get something to eat, so I don't pass out again from malnutrition.

I stumble to the bathroom and take a nice warm shower, hoping to cleanse myself of Nolan's violation, however, the phantom ghost of his hands possesses my own. My own hands and touch become Nolan's; my soft, slender fingers become thick and calloused and rough. I stop mid-shower, my arms falling to my sides as I let the water rinse whatever shampoo and soap still linger before frantically hurrying to get out and wrap myself in a towel.

I can still feel his hands on my body as I brush my teeth at the sink, unable to meet my own gaze. Instinctively, I go to push the hands off of me before realizing they aren't there; it's all in my head. I want to scream and cry and rip the skin off my very bones, but I don't have the energy or willpower to do any.

Returning to my bedroom with my towel tightly secured around me, I find my backpack leaning against the wall that Oscar must have brought for me. I probably break the world record for the fastest time getting dressed as I practically beam myself into my clothes. I rifle through the bag for my phone to shove it in my back pocket before heading to the living room, where I find Mom and Dad sitting on the couch and Oscar sprawled across the loveseat.

Mom is the first to notice me with a warm smile. "Good morning, Maggie. Help yourself to some breakfast. There should be plenty left for you on the stove."

I smile and nod, grabbing a small plate from the cabinet before scooping an egg from the pan on the stove and two pieces of bacon onto my plate. I don't bother to get any toast, just a knife and fork before settling on the armchair across from Oscar. At first, I stare blankly at my plate, too lost in thought to start eating. I can feel everybody staring at me, but I don't quite register it.

"Maggie? Are you okay, honey?" I snort at Dad's question, and he immediately looks down. "Sorry, that was a dumb question. Are you... willing to talk about it, yet?"

I don't even want to admit to myself what happened, let alone my family, but still, I feel like I owe them some answers. Besides, I don't have to tell them everything, just enough to satiate their concern.

I swallow nervously, pushing my cold plate onto the coffee table as I pull my knees up to my chest. "Yeah, okay. I don't know how much I can talk about yet, but I'll try to answer any questions you have. So, um, what exactly did I already tell you?"

Dad blanches. "Oh, um. You told us the general gist of what happened; how he... forced himself on you."

I cringe at Dad's word choice, despite knowing it's probably the lightest way to describe what happened. "Well, yeah, um, that's-that's pretty much what happened."

"It's tricky dealing with people like Nolan," Mom begins, reaching out to hold my hand in hers. "People who believe they have power over others and use it to make themselves stronger and feel more powerful. Please know that despite his efforts to make you feel inferior, there is no one out there who has the power to take your strength away from you unless you let them."

Abruptly, Oscar stands, and we all turn to look at him when he begins down the hallway. His expression is unreadable, but when I notice his slight trembling, I immediately know something is extremely wrong. "Where are you going, Os?"

"Bathroom." I expect him to duck into the bathroom beside

the kitchen, but instead, he ascends to the second floor.

I almost completely forget about Nolan as I watch Oscar disappear upstairs, concerned and confused. I turn back to Mom and Dad, a little girl again desperate for answers."Is everything okay with Oscar?"

"He's… he's taking this pretty hard," Dad confesses, leaning forward and lowering his voice. His eyes flick back up the stairs as he continues. "He feels like he abandoned you, and he blames himself for not being there to protect you."

"It's not Oscar's fault!" I exclaim incredulously. "Why on Earth would he think it's his fault?"

"The same reason you think it's yours."

I stiffen, squirming slightly, unable to meet Mom's gaze. I'm unable to find the words to say as my mouth suddenly goes bone-dry. I turn back to my untouched plate with contempt and ignore my hunger, too sick to my stomach to consider eating anything.

LARAMIE

After Magda's parents got her settled and moved back home the following day, they sat down for a hearty dinner of Oscar's preparation, who appears more satisfied by his family's raving than the taste of the food itself as they eat.

Afterwards, Oscar suggests they participate in a board game before segregating for the night. Magda eagerly agrees, tripping over herself to get to the bookcase, plucking a thick wooden box from the lowest shelf before returning to the couch with a smile. "Clue, anyone?"

"But you always cheat," Oscar whines.

"I have literally never cheated. You're just scared that I'll beat you for the, what, five hundred and twenty-eighth time?"

"You've kept count?" Alawa asks.

"No," Oscar argues. "It'd only be the five hundred and twenty-seventh time."

Magda raises her hands. "My mistake. You in or not?"

Oscar sighs and checks his bare wrist, feigning contemplation. "I suppose I can spare a few minutes to destroy you."

Magda laughs. "Good one."

He scowls but sits opposite his sister, facing her with narrowed eyes as she opens the box and assembles its contents. It takes seconds until they begin the game.

Magda periodically glances at her mother, a playful smirk dancing across her face, while Oscar's expression remains guarded and neutral, constantly fixated on her as if to catch her cheating. Magda casually glances indifferently between her family until the very end, where she enthusiastically proclaims her victory, much to Oscar's dismay. He defeatedly chucks his cards onto the table and throws his head back in frustration. "Bullshit. How do you always win?"

Magda grins triumphantly and crosses her arms. "Guess I'm just that good."

"Just so you know, I was *this* close to winning," He pinches his fingers together, nearly touching. "I had Colonel Mustard and the wrench but just not the room."

"This is payback. While my gift of absolutely annihilating you in Clue pales in comparison to yours for cooking, I *do* love how wound up you get when you lose," coos Magda.

"You're evil."

Magda explodes in a fit of maniacal laughter, and Oscar smirks but rolls his eyes. "You're so stupid."

"Can't spell stupid without 'u.'"

"Or 'I.' *Dammit.*"

Magda's exaggerated cackling becomes genuine laughter as Oscar shakes his head and storms to his room, muttering, "Stupid game. Whose idea even was it to play? So dumb," under his breath.

Giggling, Magda wipes the tears that'd sprung in her eyes, smiling softly as she bids her parents goodnight and all but floats to her bedroom. She hesitates outside Oscar's bedroom door upon seeing it left slightly ajar and gently nudges it open. Peering through the slit, she sees Oscar asleep in his bed, sprawled on his stomach with a blanket draped haphazardly over his torso. He snores softly with each rise and fall of his chest.

"Night, Os," Magda whispers with a fond smile. She quietly closes the door before grabbing a handful of clothes from her bedroom to change in the bathroom. I wait just outside while she changes, uses the washroom, brushes her teeth, and then finishes up by washing her face. Magda slips into her bedroom, throws her soiled clothes in a basket, and closes the door behind her.

She slumps on the edge of the bed with her bear wedged beneath her arm as she tucks herself into bed. As soon as she closes her eyes, her breathing deepens considerably, and, finally, her eyelids relax as she melts into the bed beneath her.

I glance back down at my arm to see the contusion from before fading exponentially more as countless other strips all over my body peel away in starry night skies.

I hesitantly pat my arm and watch as the skin snags between my fingers when I brush over it. I give it an experimental tug, watching in fascination as a galaxy explodes beneath the surface.

With nothing better to do and to try and clear my mind, I wander outside, unintentionally drifting to a nearby park. The sun is nowhere to be seen, and the half-moon glistens far away in the Stillfall sky as I slump against a nearby bench, allowing myself comfort in a moment of tranquil solitude. After a few moments spent focusing on my breathing, I open my eyes to find a crying child hunched on the bench, mere inches away from my being.

-ELEVEN-

Newfound Freedom of Choice

LARAMIE

anic overwhelms me.

I instinctively stiffen and hold my breath as I carefully shift as far away as I can from the boy beside me. My heart steadily hammers against my chest, my gaze unwavering from the child as I make slow, deliberate movements. Surviving (if you could even call it that) this far, only to seal my fate by accidentally brushing against a crying child, would be infinitely more humiliating than being banished in the first place.

Footsteps quickly approach. Despite my sluggishness, I whirl around to see a teenage boy advancing carefully towards us. The child turns upon hearing the footsteps, and when their eyes meet, his reaction isn't what I had expected.

There's recognition alongside an intense fear burning in his deep brown eyes. He hastily leaps from the bench, only to run into the teen's chest, who grabs his forearm and stops him mid-escape.

"Ghalen, please!" The child begs, his voice broken with fear. "D-don't, please. Don't make me go back there, please, I can't go back there. I can't. *Please.*"

"It's okay, shhh, it's all right," Ghalen reassures, pulling the boy into a reluctant hug. He gingerly touches the back of the boy's head but jerks his hand away to see blood smeared across his fingers. His eyes darken, and he grimaces, conflicted and contrite. "I'm not gonna force you to go back there, Kahlil. Honest. Shhhh, it's okay. I'm here."

"You-you'd never… hurt me, would you Ghale?"

Ghalen pulls away to make eye contact with the boy. "Hey, K, look at me," uncertain eyes meet Ghalen's. "I'd never hurt you. *Never.*" Kahlil nods slowly, clinging to Ghalen like his life depends on it. Ghalen hugs back, a transparent smile on his face.

"You okay?" The boy squeaks, his voice muffled.

"Am *I*—you were—how can you—*oh my God*. Yeah, I'm fine, bud. Why'd you ask?"

"I just…" Kahlil sniffles. "I just don't wanna lose you. Did he-did he hurt you too?"

Ghalen hesitates. "No, not really. I'm fine. But, what about you, are you okay?"

Kahlil shrugs in response, squeezing his eyes shut. "Not really. It hurts, Ghale. It hurts."

"Where? Where's it hurt?"

"My head," He mumbles. "I've got a headache. I-I miss Dad. Can we visit him?"

Ghalen sighs. "I dunno, bud…"

"Please," Kahlil whines, sobbing as he tightens his hold on his brother's middle. "Owen scares me, but Dad doesn't, and I miss him. We haven't seen him in *so* long… please?"

Ghalen pauses briefly before smiling at his brother. "Yeah, okay. Sure. Why not?"

Kahlil pulls away with a wide grin. "Really?"

"Really," His brother confirms with a chuckle. "You remember the way, right?"

The boy nods enthusiastically, his body vibrating with barely-contained excitement. He hugs Ghalen again, whispering into his stomach a soft, "Thank you."

Ghalen smiles and pulls away from the hug, only to lift Kahlil onto the bench. I stumble to my feet, avoiding contact as best I can while observing the boys from afar.

Ghalen reaches into his pocket, producing a fidget toy as an offering to the boy, who eagerly accepts it. The teen turns around and holds his arms out for his brother, who jumps onto his back, held in a sturdy grip.

"Ready?" Ghalen asks.

Kahlil nods as his brother takes him in the direction opposite where they came from. I don't even realize I've stood up and am about to follow them when a voice snaps me from my momentary trance. 'Ghalen and Kahlil Young. I have been following and observing them since I, myself, was banished.'

I spin on my heels to see Scribe Batair (or former Scribe, now) standing behind me. Her robe is tattered and bloody, and her skin is visibly faded in disproportionate patches. My eyes widen when I see her, and I can't help the gasp I release, relief and dread blending uncomfortably in my stomach.

Before I can say anything, she approaches the bench and calmly sits down. Overwhelmed with shock, I settle next to her and stare, unable to form words.

'I must admit, it is fortunate I found you, as I knew not of your location,' She says, her voice still powerful. 'Lonely as it may be, I assume for you the same.'

"What happened to you?" I finally manage, my voice trembling. "Why have you been banished?"

Batair turns away and lowers her head. 'Razael saw fit that I face the same consequences as you for encouraging your disloyalty.'

She was banished… because of *me.*

As bitter as I still may be about my own banishment, I've grown to accept it, however, to be responsible for the harrowing fate of another—and not just anyone, but Batair…

"Batair…" my voice falters, and I shake my head. "I had no idea you, too, would be punished. I… I'm so sorry."

She shrugs impassively. 'What is done is done.'

Overwhelmed by a sudden longing to embrace the angel, I hesitantly reach out to her but stop as I would had I been reaching out to Magda. She must notice my reluctance as she gently takes my hand in hers, a small smile gracing her lips. Tears build in my eyes at the sensation; her skin is warm, and she feels *alive*—well, as alive as we can be when we're not.

I reciprocate by squeezing her hand, unable to resist tackling her in a hug. She's initially hesitant and stiffens in my arms, however, eventually, she embraces me back. She must crave contact just as much as I do as she relaxes against me and takes a deep breath through her nose, sighing contentedly.

Tears form in my eyes. If I close them and focus hard enough, I can imagine myself embracing Magda; the very idea infuses me with intense fulfillment. I cling to it, to the feeling—to *her.*

After a few long minutes, Batair is the one to pull away. I let go and wipe my tears as we fall into a tense silence. I try not to stare but being with someone who can see and interact with me (and isn't Lucifer) is impossible to disregard. Even better is the ability to relate to her deteriorating state; it's somehow reassuring and makes me feel less alone.

'Tell me,' Batair begins. 'Tell me more about… feeling. Your emotions.'

Her plea catches me off guard. "My… emotions?"

'I want to know more,' She says, a glint in her eyes. 'Please, tell me everything.'

So that's what I do.

I go into vivid detail to explain what emotions feel like as someone who now has firsthand experience. Batair's attention is unwavering throughout my exposition; she seldom interrupts, only to seek further clarification or to ask me to elaborate. Not only am I helping her, as she clearly wants to know more about feeling, but she's helping me just as much by allowing me someone to confide in.

'I would like to feel, too,' she says when I finish.

"It would suit you," I agree with a smile. "Feeling everything all at once transcends feeling nothing at all." A silence settles over us again.

'If I may ask, what has become of the human you fell in love with?' She asks. 'And of you.'

"Well, Lucifer pursued me in hopes of enlisting myself as one of his demons. My refusal has driven him to torment Magda, the human I fell in love with."

Batair nods and stays silent for a few moments, regarding me with an unreadable expression.

'Strange.' Is all she says.

"What of the two boys you've been watching? Ghalen and Kahlil?"

'Their mother's partner is racist and abusive. Unfortunately, their mother remains unaware of the beatings they endure, particularly Kahlil, because he is autistic. It's unfortunate to see. Humans and needless conflict intertwine more than I had realized.'

She faces the direction Ghalen and Kahlil disappeared, scrutinizing the neighbourhood for a few seconds. 'Do you ever wonder why our existence remains so bleak in comparison to humans'?' I remain silent, beckoning Batair to proceed. 'Typically, humans are born into a world of vast possibilities and choice and freedom. A place they are allowed and entitled to make their own decisions and decide for themselves what they will do.

'Meanwhile, we are given life second to a pre-determined purpose, governed from our inception on what to do, how to do it, and when. We are deficient in freedom to do or say anything unless given permission by authority. We are just…'

"Servants," I finish. Batair turns to me and nods. 'Exactly. I've found myself wondering lately what choices I would make for myself if I were human. If I was allotted life on this mortal earth and given such a large spectrum of choice, what would I choose?'

Batair's words impact me in a way I hadn't expected. Beyond envying humans' range of emotions, I hadn't considered how lucky they are to have life for themselves and not just as a servant for another, born as individuals with the power to make their own decisions. I'm hit with another wave of calamity at the prospect of my entire existential function being my willingness to obey another.

'Do you?' Batair asks.

I turn to her, cocking my head to the side. "What?"

'Do you ever wonder why we were made as an extension of another while humans are made for themselves?'

I shake my head. "Honestly, I hadn't considered that before you mentioned it. But now… now I do. And I, myself, wonder what I would choose if I were a human."

'From what knowledge I possess, I surmise I would enjoy baking.'

I smile, the image of Batair in a bakery wearing an apron splattered with flour forming easily in my mind. I can even picture her stirring some sort of batter in a silver mixing bowl, smiling contentedly to herself while a sweet aroma wafts through the air. “I can see you enjoying that.”

Batair grins. ‘I think I would too.’ She goes quiet for a moment. ‘Before I return to Ghalen and Kahlil, I’d like to thank you.’

“Thank me? For what?”

‘This may sound odd, but… for my banishment. I never realized how much I was missing out on in Heaven. All I knew about mortal life was from words on a piece of paper, and I never got to experience this.’ She gestures to the world around us. ‘Nothing I could have read about the world would even come close to being able to see and experience it all. For that, I thank you.’

Taken aback by her sincerity, I struggle to come up with what to respond with for a few moments. “I’m… not sure what to say. You’re… welcome?”

Batair smiles and stands, offering me her hand. ‘It’s time for me to return to my humans, as I’m sure is the same with you.’

I pull myself to my feet beside her and nod. I consider asking for another hug when she pulls me into one, this time startling me with the embrace.

‘Thank you.’ She whispers.

“I’m glad this was all for the best.” I hold onto her for a few seconds, cherishing our brief contact while it lasts. When I pull away, I give her a soft smile.

She nods. ‘Me too.’

-TWELVE-

Uneasy Living

MAGDA

hursday morning, I'm awoken from a broken sleep cycle (less than three hours, if I had to guess) to a knock on my door.

Immediately, my heart leaps into my throat before I remember I'm safe at home; I almost pass back out from the rush of alleviation, but a second knock is what fully wakes me.

"Come in," I mumble into my pillow. Oscar opens the door timidly with a small smile, and I greet him with a listless wave before falling back against the bed, still half-asleep. "Hhh."

"Morning, Mags. Sorry for waking you. I was just wondering if you could, um, help me get ready for my interview, maybe?"

My eyes snap open. Immediately, I surge out of bed, almost toppling over from an intense rush of vertigo, but I stabilize myself by pinwheeling my arms.

Instinctively, Oscar moves to catch me. "Woah, you okay?"

I give a curt nod before wordlessly grabbing his arm to drag him to his bedroom. He doesn't say anything, but I catch a slight smirk tugging his lips up as I pull him along.

I help him pick out an outfit; a dark grey cardigan and black khakis rolled up slightly, and when he's agreed with my choice, I all but throw him into the bathroom with a towel for a shower, slamming the door behind him. I go full mom-mode on him by ironing his clothes (even though he specifically told me not to because he said he'd do it himself and blah, blah, blah,) and I pick out a pair of casual black running shoes, making sure they're not too scuffed.

When Oscar comes out of the bathroom with a towel around his waist, he sees his freshly-ironed clothes folded neatly on the bed and looks at me with a mix of irritation and appreciation. I flash him the most obnoxiously sweet smile I can muster before he trudges into his bedroom and slams the door behind him, but there's no real animosity behind it.

Upon dressing, Oscar goes back to the bathroom to adjust his outfit, and I follow him with a smile as he fiddles with the sleeves of his sweater and rolls his shoulders.

"Want me to braid your hair?" I offer, stifling a yawn.

"Please?" He implores, bashfully glancing at me through the mirror.

I pull a stool in from my bedroom and sit Oscar down on it, grabbing a hairbrush and two elastics as I hover behind him. I start by brushing his still-damp hair before sectioning his hair into two. He hums as I begin braiding, my fingers moving swiftly as I thread tuft over tuft.

"How long do you think the interview's gonna be?" I ask, tying off the first braid and placing it over Oscar's shoulder.

"I honestly have no idea. How long do they usually last?"

"Depends on the place and if they like you, I guess."

"You probably won't see me 'till tomorrow, then. Nobody meets me without falling head-over-heels in love."

I snort, almost messing up his second braid. "You should add modesty to your resume if you don't have it listed already."

Oscar giggles, and I shake my head at him. When I finish braiding his hair, he stands up and regards himself in the mirror, brushing the wrinkles from his sweater and readjusting his pants.

"Do I look okay?" He asks, checking his teeth.

"You look great, Os. Lighten your hair a bit, and you could pass as a young Leo DiCaprio."

Oscar turns to me, dramatically slapping a hand to his chest. "That's the nicest thing anyone has ever said to me."

I playfully punch his arm. "You'll do great, Os. You're very charismatic. I wouldn't worry too much about them not liking you."

He nods and takes a deep breath. "Yeah. Right. Cool. Okay."

LARAMIE

Magda bids Oscar well before he leaves, visibly consolidating his doubt with a hug. He clings to her for a few long seconds and gives each of his parents a hug before nervously stumbling out the door. Magda watches from the window until he turns the corner and disappears from sight.

She mutters something about continuing her job search as she stumbles to her bedroom to retrieve her laptop and sprawl across the couch. George gives her an encouraging pat on the back before he and Alawa leave to go grocery shopping. Magda waves distractedly as they go, begrudgingly pulling her laptop onto her lap to begin browsing job listings.

The light that emits from the computer screen casts a shadow across her features, illuminating the sunken bags beneath her eyes, the way her lips are curled downwards into an unintentional scowl, her too-pale skin and the small medley of bruises still staining her neck. I grimace at the sight of the tender-looking purple contusions, confident that if I could do anything in this very moment, I want nothing more than to be able to kiss the bruises away and replace her pain with my love.

Three job applications and an hour later, Magda's head lulls back, and her eyelids droop. Her eyebrows unfurrow, and the worry lines creasing her face relax and smoothen. Her grip loosens on her laptop, and her lips part as her chest rhythmically rises and deflates; she's fallen asleep.

I admire the peacefulness that cleanses the human's face of any previous irritability, watching as her eyelashes twitch and her body naturally melts into the couch cushions. There's a piece of hair falling over her face that I'm tempted to brush from her eyes. I almost do, reaching out instinctively, but I freeze when I hear the sound of keys clicking against one another coming from the front door.

Magda and I turn to the door in unison as it's unlocked and pushed open. She shifts her chin to rest atop the armrest of the couch, tiredly watching as Oscar's smiling face greets her at the door.

"Heyyy. You're home," She slurs, grinning up at her brother. It appears to take a great deal of effort to lift her arms, however, she does, making a childlike grabbing gesture with her hands. Oscar gives her an inquisitive look as he approaches to hug her, leaning over the couch to do so.

"You okay?" He asks, letting go of their embrace to sit beside her, gently nudging her feet from the cushions. She gives him room, and he stares at her sleepy expression with furrowed brows. "Did you get any sleep last night?"

She hesitates. "Sure. Plenty."

"How much equates to plenty for you? Seven? Eight hours?"

"Erm, not quite."

"Mags," Oscar's tone deepens, his expression concerned and accusatory like a parents'. "How many hours did you get?"

Magda sighs, seemingly too tired to argue. "Three, maybe."

His eyes widen. "Oh my God, Maggie. Why didn't you say anything before I left?"

"'Cause you were so excited for your interview and… and I didn't wanna ruin your mood. S'not your fault I couldn't get to sleep till, like, six am, cause I had n—um, my brain was just too wired for me to sleep, I guess." Oscar catches the way Magda stops herself from admitting the cause had been nightmares, but he doesn't pry. "'Nuff about me. How—" yawn, "—was it?"

Oscar looks conflicted but inevitably answers. "Good, I think. I was pretty nervous, but the general manager who interviewed me—I think their name was Kamari?—was super nice and even had a few laughs with me. I don't want to jinx myself or anything, but I'm honestly pretty confident I got the job."

Magda beams like the sun incarnate. "I'm so glad it went so well." She looks like she wants to say something else but stops herself. Oscar can predict what she was going to say, as he smiles and says, "I missed you, too."

A burst of colour erupts in Magda's cheeks as she repositions herself upright against the couch. Her stomach growls loudly; she doesn't seem to notice (or chooses to ignore it), but Oscar hears it all too clearly.

"Have you eaten yet today?"

She pauses before answering. "Not yet, no."

"So, hypothetically, if I were to go back to the coffee shop and buy myself something to eat—this is all theoretical, of course—and accidentally ordered another meal, what is your preference?"

Magda sits up slightly straighter. "Aren't you tired? Y'know, from the interview and everything?"

Oscar sputters indignantly, dismissively waving his hand. "Just answer the theoretical question."

Understanding Oscar's stubbornness far outweighs her energy to argue, Magda concedes. "I guess… I guess if you got me a chipotle chicken wrap, I wouldn't throw it back in your face. Hypothetically."

Oscar grins triumphantly. "I'll be back in fifteen. If I accidentally buy anything, I expect you'll be a good sister and take it off my hands for me, okay?"

Magda nods, smiling tiredly. "Love you, Os."

"Love you, too."

MAGDA

I don't realize I've fallen back asleep on the couch until I'm awoken by the sound of my phone ringing incessantly in my ear. Tired and sluggish and feeling arguably worse than I did before, I struggle to grab my phone, not bothering to check the caller before answering.

"Hello?" I cringe at my sleep-heavy tone, clearing my throat to try again. "Hello?" Somehow, it comes out worse that time.

"Hi, it's Teresa Brown. Is this Magda Mercy?"

I instantly bold upright, suddenly wide awake, my heart already pounding. "Um, yes. Yes, it is."

"On behalf of the Web Basics team, I'd like to invite you to interview for the position of part-time Information Technology Support Advisor at our offices."

A grin breaks out across my face, and for the first time in forever, I find myself shaking with excitement. I'd applied shortly after I submitted my leave request, and it's the only job I've applied for that I don't think I'll completely loathe, and I have an interview for it.

"The time and date we have set for you is Tuesday, October 12th at 10 am. Does that work?"

I nod eagerly. "It does."

"Perfect! I will follow up with an email to you shortly detailing the interview process and any items we would like for you to bring. We're looking forward to it, and hopefully, this will prove to be a great match for us both."

I somehow manage to calm down enough to reply coherently with, "Likewise. I'll see you then," before promptly ending the call and squealing in excitement.

My exhaustion upon just waking up from an admittedly gross nap after less than three hours of sleep is long forgotten with the relief and fervour that I have an interview. Maybe Oscar was right. Maybe we *can* do this.

As if on cue, I hear voices just outside the front door and turn in time to see Mom and Dad struggling to carry bags of groceries inside while Oscar holds a takeout bag while bickering with them about taking some of their bags.

I compose myself enough as humanly possible before triumphantly exclaiming, "I got an interview!"

THIRTEEN

In God We Trust(ed)

MAGDA

My alarm seizes me from a fitful sleep when Tuesday finally rolls around.

I barely crack open my eyelids before I lazily throw my arm towards my bedside table, feeling for my phone. When I finally find it, I pull myself against my headboard and squint past the brightness of the screen as I fumble to turn off the alarm.

Falling back on my bed, I close my eyes for a few seconds and contemplate whether or not getting a job is important enough to warrant leaving my bed. After spending far too long weighing my options, I finally get up, nausea suppressing any hunger I feel just thinking about the interview. I do my best to ignore the churning in my gut as I get out of bed and approach the bathroom.

I take a quick shower and braid my hair in two sections, carefully pulling a blue turtleneck over my head to hide the bruise still visible on the side of my neck. I slip into a pair of black jeans and shrug on a black blazer, carefully fastening a low-hanging necklace around my neck with a feather at the end that Mom made me when I was thirteen.

After resentfully scrutinizing myself in the bathroom mirror for a few seconds, I nervously wander downstairs to the kitchen just as Oscar finishes frying some french toast on the stovetop. The dining room table has been set, so I sit down and oblige myself to have a quick bite to eat before I leave. My stomach gurgles dangerously as I force the food down, but I ignore it as best as I can, knowing it's in my best interest not to go to my interview on an empty stomach.

"Best of luck, sweetie," Mom says as I pull on my coat and moccasins to leave. "Not that I think you'll need it."

"You'll do great today. I know it," Dad adds with a warm hug. "I love you lots, kiddo. See you soon."

"I love you too, Dad."

"Don't forget about little old me!" Oscar pipes up, sweeping me off my feet. He swings me around a few times like they do in all those cheesy rom-coms, but the moment is neither cute nor movie-like with the threatening swish of my stomach's contents. Not only that, but it inadvertently reminds me of Nolan's repeated despotism over me, a bitter reminder of the ease with which he could push me around. Fighting my inner revulsion, I nervously demand to be put down, willing my voice not to falter or crack. Oscar complies after swinging me around once more, setting me on my feet in time for my stomach to settle, my limbs still trembling.

"Make your little brother proud, you hear me?"

I beam with a tight smile. "'Course."

Mom approaches and envelopes me in a gentle hug. I relax into her arms, the scent of her perfume a sedative for my nerves.

"I believe in you, Maggie. I'm right here with you."

As soon as I return from my interview, I throw the front door open like I'm in a movie and emphatically announce, "I'm home from my interview!"

I stand there for a few seconds, awaiting the enthusiastic replies welcoming me home. Instead, I'm met with a disconcerting silence.

At first, I don't move. A part of me still anticipates their response, even if it's a little delayed. Ten seconds go by, and a pit settles in my stomach as I tentatively close the door behind me. I remove my coat and shoes before nervously wandering the house, half-expecting Oscar to jump out of every dark corner and scare me.

"Hello? Anyone home?" My anxiety exacerbates tenfold with every vacant room until the whole house has been established empty.

A gnawing panic replaces my enthusiasm. Of course, the only theories I consider are negative, a barrage of pessimistic improbabilities that threatens my composure.

Everything's fine. I try convincing myself. *They probably just went out to get groceries they forgot to get last week or something. There's no reason to be jumping to conclusions. Everything's okay.*

I shake off my worry in favour of changing into a t-shirt and sweatpants, my neck itching from the chafe of the turtleneck. I scratch the irritated skin as soon as the shirt is wrenched over my head, momentarily forgetting about my bruise until my nail grazes the clotting scab and opens it, the sharp pain an unwelcome reminder of its origin.

Cradling my tender neck as I stagger into the bathroom, I run a washcloth under the tap to dab at the beads of blood beginning to ooze from the shallow cut. I press the cloth to my neck before returning to the living room, trying to ignore the images that plague me with each throb in my neck.

Pulling my phone from my pocket as a distraction, I consider calling Oscar to ask where he went and get my mind off of Nolan. My finger hovers over the call button when his contact flashes as an incoming call. I answer quickly, turning it on speakerphone before flipping it onto the couch.

"Oscar, hi. I was literally *just* about to call you! I—"

"Maggie," His voice is broken and shaky; a myriad of dissonant sounds nearly deafen it. "Mom's being taken to the hospital." As if on cue, the piercing blare of a siren wails, knocking the wind out of me. I genuinely stop breathing for a second as my heart rate skyrockets, the world ripped beneath my very feet when I realize my worst assumptions were true this time.

"What?" I barely register Oscar's voice as I sink back against the couch, dazed and dumbfounded. Blinking past the tears beginning to obscure my vision, I notice the disarray our living room is in; the contents of the coffee table are strewn carelessly across its surface—some are even overturned on the floor—the couch cushions are somewhat upturned (how the *fuck* did I not notice that until now?), and the rug on the floor is slightly pulled out from underneath with its corners folded down. The realization that a struggle took place anchors my heart to the pit of my chest as a sickly heat encases my throat.

"They said that Mom might be suffering from something called malignant pleural effusion," Oscar's voice draws me from my thoughts. "Basically, the fluid containing cancer cells is building up in the place surrounding her lungs. Dad and I are following the ambulance in his car. You need to come and meet us at the hospital. The paramedics think things may…" His voice falters, and he takes a deep, shaky breath. "…be getting worse. Please come."

LARAMIE

A deep laugh reverberates in the crestfallen atmosphere. I immediately tense, turning slowly to find Lucifer sitting atop the staircase, a grim shadow cast across him in the dull light. He grins and waves to me, his eyes sparkling with a twinge of manic satisfaction. I cringe at the intensity of his expression, unable to even try to hide my fear.

He did this.

"I…" Magda's expression is unsettlingly unreadable as she struggles to form words. She slides limply to the floor, clutching her phone tightly in trembling hands. "I-I don't…"

"Maggie? Maggie?" She opens her mouth to respond but can't seem to find the words. Resigned, she just hangs her head.

"Maggie? Can-can you hear me? You need to come now; this may be the last time we see—" Oscar cuts himself off and takes a shaky breath. "It's just… Mom, she-she's in a lot of pain and n-needs you to be here for her. We all do. Please, just… come as soon as you can. It's the hospital downtown, the one we usually go to. Please."

Magda nods slowly. A loud sigh and incessant sirens are the last we hear before Oscar ends the call.

I turn back to Lucifer, who stands motionless at the top of the stairs. "Please, Lucifer, don't do this."

'Can't you intervene?' He bites with a smirk. 'Can't you stop this? Go ahead. We're waiting.'

The energy to argue depletes before I have the chance to open my mouth. I look back at Magda curled around herself on the floor and whisper, "Stop this, now. *Please.*"

Lucifer hums contentedly. 'As much as I just *love* hearing you beg, I'm afraid I can't do that.' He lifts his hands and laughs, boisterous and garbled. 'Well, I *can*, but where's the fun in that?' With that, he vanishes.

Magda starts screaming again, or maybe she never stopped judging by how hoarse her voice has become. It's shrill with startling anguish and misery, borderline nightmarish with a lilt of unbridled grief.

Dropping to her hands and knees, Magda throws her head back in an almost deafening scream. When it dies down, she bows her head and begins slamming her fists against the floor in rapid succession with each sob that wracks her body.

I can't look away, but the sight of her devastation has me freely weeping, provoking rainfall and the distant rumbling of thunder.

This is all my fault.

Fists clenched at her sides, Magda slowly climbs to her feet despite the furious shaking of her legs that threatens her mobility. She doesn't even bother to grab a jacket—or even slip shoes onto her bare feet for that matter—as she grabs her keys and phone and marches outside, unbothered by the snowy cement beneath her feet.

She unlocks her car with considerable difficulty until she can finally collapse in the driver's seat. Slamming the door shut behind her, she wipes the tears and rainwater off her face before gripping the steering wheel with white knuckles. It's only now that I realize how raw her knuckles are rubbed, bleeding from being slammed violently against the ground. She unknowingly smears blood across the steering wheel and car handle, carmine streams running down her arms to drip into her lap.

I reach out to gently clasp her bruised hands in mine but stop when I'm a fraction of an inch from touching her. My body erupts in an overwhelming surge of frustration. I scream into the sky for no one to hear, sobs bubbling up my throat in an intense flood of emotion.

I don't notice the skin that splits across my neck and cheek from screaming or feel the heavy beating of my heart against my chest. At this point, I've lost the motivation to care about anything that isn't Magda.

"WHY?" She screams, her hair plastered against her face from a combination of rain and tears. She drops her forehead against the steering wheel, her shoulders trembling sporadically. "Why?" She mewls. *"Why?"*

She calms down marginally before lifting her head back up and turning on the car. It soundlessly roars to life, and an unfamiliar melody fills the air as she stomps down on the gas, swerving the car out of the driveway.

Time slows when I see a car speeding towards Magda's, too fast to stop in time not to hit her. Amidst the rain and darkened sky, I discern a familiar hue of blue light encasing the car. Following it, I find Lucifer hovering nearby, grinning as the vehicle accelerates.

Unable to ignore the hatred concentrating within me, I cling to any strength I still possess, grasping the rear of Magda's car. My eyes burn with tears as my chipped nails dig into the brittle metal of the trunk, denting the vehicle with a shrill grinding noise.

Once I feel like I have a good grip on the car, I push with strength I didn't even know I had. Waves upon waves of Grace-like energy surges through me, enough that I manage to shove Magda from the car's trajectory with a fierce thrust. The car Lucifer controls collides with the backseat of Magda's instead of the driver's side door, sparing her from the brunt of the impact. The force sends Magda's car drifting in a full circle before coming to an abrupt stop on the side of the road, with a deafening screech of tires. The other vehicle immediately skids to a halt behind Magda, Lucifer's control over it extinguished like a candle alongside his immediate presence. It provides momentary relief to know the worst of Lucifer's intervention has elapsed.

Magda's breathing is laboured, and her body shakes furiously as she processes the accident, visibly going into shock. She leans back in her seat, her face swelling from a blistering cut across her right temple, eyes wide. She's trembling so intensely she almost looks still as she pushes open the car door and collapses on her hands and knees. The rain washes the dripping blood from her knuckles onto the damp concrete as she takes a deep breath before promptly vomiting onto the ground.

"Magda, I…" My voice comes out just above a whisper as I kneel next to the human, my arm hovering around her back. I know she can't hear anything I say, but I feel the need to apologize to ease the guilt burdening me. "I-I wish you could know just how sorry I am. This—everything—it's all my fault and… and your mother… I'm so sorry."

She slowly stands on weak legs that barely support her weight with her arms limp at her sides. She seems unbothered by the hair that obscures the majority of her otherwise doleful expression as she stares forward blankly, swaying on her feet.

"Oh my God, miss, I am so sorry," A man stumbles out of his car and approaches Magda, something about him familiar in a way I can't quite identify. "I-I didn't even realize I was going that fast. I'm so sorry." He turns to her car and runs a hand through his hair. "I'll pay for all the damages, I swear. Again, I'm so, so sorry. You aren't hurt, are you, miss? Miss?"

Magda's eyes flutter closed, and without warning, she falls. The man lunges, and surprisingly enough, catches her just before she hits the ground.

The distant rumbling of thunder and lightning claps synchronously with my scream of, *"LUCIFER!"* I glance down at Magda's motionless form and can do little besides watch as the wet strands of hair covering her lips fluctuate rhythmically with her breathing. My pulse pounds in my ears, and my head swims with nausea and vertigo. I can no longer hear my own screaming; voices keep hissing taunts in my head, so I shriek as loud as I can to drown them out, ignoring the searing pain it engulfs my throat in.

The distant wail of sirens quickly approaches courtesy of a woman who had driven up on the scene and called for help almost seconds after the collision took place. An ambulance careens down the street and parks as close as it can to Magda and the man, whose face is flushed with relief when he notices their arrival. The paramedics unload a stretcher and hurry to load Magda onto it while the man frantically explains what happened.

-FOURTEEN-

Chaos Aftermath

LARAMIE

very second after unfolds in slow motion for me. I watch as the ambulance pulls into the Emergency Department at the hospital and the paramedic's wheel Magda inside, unable to hear the man's explanation of what happened over the pounding in my head. A wave of dizziness overtakes me, and I fall to the floor in a heap, awaiting any indication of Magda's condition. Defeatedly, I allow myself to slump against the wall in the corner of the lobby, somewhere I won't have to worry about my proximity to any humans.

While a part of me knows with complete certainty that Magda will recover, another part keeps screaming, *what if she won't? What if she dies?*

I refuse to consider what would happen if Magda does die. Instead, I allow myself to fixate on the incomparable hate I feel towards Lucifer, something that has never been so intense.

He could have killed Magda… he *would* have had I been unable to intercept and still may make another attempt on her life. Meanwhile, I'm left as the only one who has any—albeit diminutive—chance of preventing it. And who knows, there may come a time I can no longer stop Lucifer, or maybe when I finally fade away, I will unintentionally leave Magda to his mercy.

Despite recollecting being an angel vividly, I can't seem to remember what it was like before I had Magda in my life. She's everything to me now, and losing her would be the greatest loss I could experience; it would be the worst Hell to deprive me of her presence. Ironically, there's nothing I wouldn't do for her, yet there's very little I can.

A small part of me wishes I'd never met Magda, solely to preserve her from the pain that permeates my being. It hurts more than I knew possible to realize my very presence is what causes the one I love most the worst pain, to realize my absence may be the only penance I'm capable of providing.

Not only have I imperilled my choiren, but I've inadvertently endangered the human I risked Heaven for in the first place.

I'm incapable of anything beyond failure and calamity.

It takes an agonizingly long time for the doctors to return with confirmation that Magda is okay. When her doctor approaches Nick—the man who'd hit her introduces himself as—he immediately springs from his seat. "H-how is she? Is-is she okay?"

"She'll be just fine," The doctor answers. "She has a bruise on her head from the impact but no concussion or cerebral injury. Unrelated to the accident, she's dehydrated and slightly malnourished, so we started an I.V. with fluids. Her hands are bruised quite heavily, and from your description, we're still unsure how that happened. We're in the process of determining the cause of the cuts and scrapes on the bottom of her feet as she was barefoot upon admittance. Can you confirm whether she was wearing shoes at the scene of the accident?"

Nick shakes his head. "No, not that I can recall. She wasn't wearing any when she stepped out of the car."

The doctor nods and jots down a note on his clipboard. "Thank you for the information. All in all, she'll be just fine. From your description, she must have some guardian angel watching over her."

"Can I see her?"

"I'm afraid not. Unless you are immediate family to the patient, you aren't permitted to visit for liability reasons."

Nick scrubs his face. "Is there any way I can see her? Can you ask her? Bring a doctor while I visit? Anything?"

The doctor glances down at his clipboard and hesitates. "It's typically prohibited, but…" He sighs. "I'll have someone see you up if you're so concerned. Ishaan—" A nurse walks over at the mention of his name, and the doctor lowers his voice to address him. "Please see Mr. Williams up to Magda Mercy's room. I've permitted him to visit the patient just to see that she's okay. Please keep an eye on him."

The nurse, Ishaan, nods, and Nick smiles gratefully at the doctor. "Thank you so much, Doctor—" He squints to read the name clip pinned to the doctor's right breast pocket. "—Young."

"No problem," The man responds with a smile, disappearing somewhere within the hospital. I'm struck with the realization that the doctor is Ghalen and Kahlil's father and instinctively turn to tell Batair. I deflate, however, when I realize she's not with me; the sudden emptiness of her presence finds me longing for another hug. I can almost feel her pressed against me in a warm embrace, and I cling to the sensation, willing the tears not to fall from my eyes.

I follow the nurse as he guides Nick to the elevator, where it stops on the second floor for a woman. Upon noticing a gift shop when the doors open, Nick says he'd like to get a gift, with Ishaan following from an appropriate distance. He buys a bouquet of orange orchids and purple lilies alongside a 'Get Well Soon' plush before hurrying back to the elevator, where the two ascend to the fifth floor alone this time.

Ishaan leads Nick to a door labelled 504 and gestures him in, standing by the entrance to supervise their interaction. Magda is just awakening when they enter her room, and recognition ignites on both hers and Nick's faces.

MAGDA

"M-Mr. Williams," I croak, sitting up stiffly. What… what is Nolan's dad doing here? And… am I in a hospital bed? What's going on? "W-where am I?"

"Maggie?" Mr. Williams asks, his voice faltering as he sets a bouquet down onto the table next to me. Wait, flowers? Did he bring me flowers? For what? "You're at the uh, the hospital. I… I hit you with my car earlier tonight. I-uh, I didn't realize I was going so fast, and I wasn't paying attention. I didn't mean to hit you. I could've sworn the stop sign was farther away." He nervously clears his throat. "I'll pay for all the damages to your car and all the, uh, hospital bills."

Last night's events hit me like the world's worst hangover. The rapid beeping of the heart monitor next to me only worsens the painful pounding in my chest that induces it in the first place. "Oh, um, thank you. That's… very kind."

"It's the least I can do considering—" he gestures at me, and I instinctively curl in on myself. He briefly turns to the nurse hovering at the door before looking back over at me. "I think I should be going now. You, uh, have my number, so just let me know when you go to have the car repaired or if you need anything else."

"I will. Thank you. Really—thank you."

"You should get some rest; you're still pretty banged up. Again, I'm so sorry," When he takes a tentative step forward to offer me a Get Well Soon teddy bear, I manage to repress recoiling from his approach, and instead, I gingerly accept the plush. He gives me one last small smile before turning and leaving, and the nurse that'd lingered behind closes the door behind them.

As soon as the door clicks closed, I sag against my pillow, my skull throbbing with a headache as last night's events bombard me like the gunfire on a battlefield. I squeeze my eyes shut, the sickly sensation of bile rising in my throat the only warning I get to hurl myself over the edge of my bed before emptying the measly contents of my stomach onto the hospital floor.

I'm only distantly aware of the door to my room opening behind me before a teal basin is held up to my chin, and hands pull my hair back as I heave, vomit dripping from my lips. Once I stop retching, the same nurse from before asks me a few questions about how I feel. My face burns in embarrassment as he helps me sit back down on the bed, and I thank him feebly, averting eye contact as he leaves and calls down the hallway for 'clean up' in my room. If it was ever at all possible to die of embarrassment, I would have at that moment.

A thin sheen of sweat clings uncomfortably to my forehead. I notice a plastic bag on the table beside my bed, catching a glimpse of my phone through the transparent material. Immediately, I reach for it, barely able to hold my phone steadily in my hands, let alone dial a number. Despite that, I still furiously attempt to call Mom.

The first time it goes to voicemail, my heart drops. With shaking hands, I call again, waiting with bated breath for an answer.

Again, it goes to voicemail.

I continue to call until my phone slips from my sweaty hands, clinging to any denial I still maintain, feeling as though I slipped past reality into a world of hysteria. When the final fragment of disbelief becomes a heavy realization, I allow myself to scream and thrash freely. The room around me spins in a hazy white blur, slightly obscured by the tears that don't stop flooding from my eyes.

I don't hear the door opening or the nurse running in. I don't feel her touch as she tries to calm me down, something I don't even think is possible at this point. I don't feel the sedative she injects into my I.V. line; I only feel its effects as I begin to drift to sleep. It's only then that my head clears enough to feel the bed beneath me and the sheets pulled up to my waist. I feel as though I melt into it, tears drying in my eyes as I welcome the familiar darkness.

Waking up, I feel groggier than I ever have. My body is excruciatingly hot and numb, and my mouth feels like it's stuffed full of sand. My eyes ache as I slowly come to, the glaring lights above me only tempting me back to sleep. It's only when I notice Oscar sitting beside me that I force myself to stay awake.

He tenderly holds my bandaged hand, his head bowed against the bed as he takes deep breaths. Blearily glancing around the room, I shift in my spot and blurt out a cough that garners his attention; he lifts his head, slightly disoriented, and turns to face me with eyes red and puffy from crying. The colour immediately returns to his face, and he smiles when he sees I'm awake.

"I was so worried," He mutters, unable to meet my gaze. "Your doctor told me you'll be fine, but I was still pretty scared.

He said you'd be free to leave once you wake up but still… I hate seeing you like this…" he takes a shaky breath. "What-what happened?"

I sigh, dreading however anticipating the question. I muster up the strength to rest my back against the backboard, licking my chapped lips as I blink back the sedative. "After you told me about Mom—wait, *Mom*. How is she? Is she okay?"

Oscar looks down, trying to hide the thick tears beginning to roll down his cheeks as he takes a deep breath, shoulders trembling as sobs wrack his body.

"She's… she's gone."

–FIFTEEN–

Tribulation

MAGDA

"No... no, she can't be... she's not..." I can't bring myself to say it, vigorously shaking my head. Oscar's confession overwhelms my indignation. "She-she was fine this morning... b-before I left and... and she was good! She was fine. She was okay. She's not... she can't be..."

Oscar shakes his head and wanders over to the door. He faces away from me in what I can only assume is an attempt to hide his tears, but the way his shoulder shake gives it out immediately.

"Ossy... Ossy, please... tell me it's not true."

He answers by sliding to the floor, sobbing hysterically while corroborating my worst fear.

No, no, no, this can't be happening. Mom's fine... she has *to be. She's not... she can't be...*

She's dead.

She's... she's *actually* dead.

A knot of emotion ruptures in my throat when I realize I never got to say goodbye, and I'll never get to tell her how much I love her and hear it back.

My heart feels as though it's doubled in weight, heavy and

aching with heartbreak. I pound my fists against my head, uncaring of the pain that ignites when I hit the sensitive bruise on my forehead.

I look up only when Oscar grabs my hands and forces me to stop. The position is horrifically familiar, especially when Oscar's face is replaced with Nolan's when I blink. His looming figure pins me to the bed, the weight of his grip digging into the skin of my wrists as he grins sadistically.

"NO!" I scream, delirious and desperate for freedom. "GET AWAY FROM ME! *PLEASE,* NOLAN, DON'T—"

As soon as the name passes my lips, horror dawns on his face, and when I blink, it's Oscar looking down at me again. The respite it provides lets me sag against the bed, taking deep breaths to calm down. I squeeze my eyes shut and bury my face in my hands, bringing my knees up to my chest. I've never felt more demoralized than I do now, plagued not only with the death of my mom but the horrors of my past.

"Mags," Albeit small, Oscar's voice rings in my ears. I face him through my tears; seeing him calms me more than I thought possible. I immediately relax and gaze into his bloodshot eyes, watching the tears silently streaming down his cheeks. My sudden burst of adrenaline evaporates, but I still can't stop crying.

He offers me his hand, and I take it, squeezing tightly as I sob and shake for the better part of five minutes while he rubs his thumb in comforting circles and reassures me that everything is okay.

Once I've calmed down, he lets go of my hand to slump against the bed beside me, so his head rests against my side. I shakily comb through his hair with my bandaged hand without realizing, still dazed in a trancelike state of grief.

After a few seconds of silence, I slow my movements before

resting my hand on Oscar's head. He takes a shuddery breath before saying, "Mom… she was admitted last night, and… passed a few hours later," without making any effort to move, his voice muffled through the sheets. "While she was sl-sleeping. I-I got a call a little while later. The doctor told me I was put down as your emergency contact and that you were involved in a, uh, an accident. I didn't expect to see you *and* Mom both admitted to the hospital, but…" the end of his sentence hangs in the air.

I look down, guilt-ridden. When Oscar finally lifts his head, his hair is stuck to his face in disproportionate patches from both tears and snot. Any other time I'd make fun of him and call him Snotscar, but I don't have it in me to joke. Instead, I brush the hair from his face for him to see. He smiles appreciatively before looking down, and when a grin breaks out on his face, I return it with confusion.

"Where'd you get that?" He points to the Get Well Soon bear tucked under my arm that, truthfully, I'd forgotten was even there.

"Oh, yeah. Um, the guy who hit me gave me this along with those flowers over there," I point in the direction of the table, and Oscar follows my finger. "And he also offered to pay for my hospital bills and the repairs to my car."

"That's… wow."

"Yeah," I answer with a snort. "Who knew Nolan's dad was such a good person."

Oscar's eyes immediately widen, and he scans the room as if expecting an attack. "The guy who hit you was *Nolan's dad?*"

"Oh, yeah, uh, Nick Williams."

"Was Nolan here?"

I shake my head. "No, just his dad. I mean, at first, I was scared to see him 'cause I thought he'd be with Nolan or something, but instead, he just… apologized."

Oscar falls back in his chair. He pauses for a few seconds before squeezing my bandaged hand—a gesture I can't feel but am just as comforted by—and beginning to stand. "I can go get Dad now if you want?"

I take a second to compose myself before nodding and pulling the blankets off me. "Yeah, that'd be good. I'll come with you."

He stops me with his hand. "Woah, woah, woah. Are you sure you're up for it? I mean… I still don't know what happened, for that matter."

I hesitate, and Oscar takes that as his cue to sit back down. "Well, u-um after you called me about Mom, I, uh, I was pretty… shaken up. I got in my car to drive to the hospital, but I was crying so much that I couldn't exactly see… clearly. Nick's car suddenly speeds through a stop sign and slams into the rear of mine. I hit my head on the steering wheel and my knuckles… I uh, I kinda… punched the ground until they started bleeding."

Oscar bows his head, swallowing thickly as he leans forward and reaches for my hand again. I hesitantly place my bandaged hand in his. "Mags, I'm so sorry."

"It's…" I pause. Well, no, it isn't okay, but it isn't Oscar's fault; he has nothing to apologize for. "I'm all right now. Don't be sorry."

LARAMIE

I thought it impossible to be any angrier with Lucifer, yet I'm proved wrong by the fresh ire burning like molten lava throughout my body.

Magda stumbles from the hospital bed with help from Oscar, who threads his arm under her despite her reassurances that she doesn't need his help. Upon standing, Magda tugs on her gown, shivering as goosebumps spread across her skin and a pink blush tints her cheeks. Oscar wordlessly removes his coat and drapes it over her shoulders, and she thanks him softly before they proceed towards the door, wheeling along a pole with a tube connected to Magda's arm.

They take the elevator down to the first floor, and Oscar leads them to the waiting room. When they round the corner, they see George sitting in one of the closest chairs. Immediately, the man turns to them, his expression bleeding from confusion to relief as he blinks back tears. He leaps to his feet and spreads his arms to hug Magda, who smiles weakly as she slumps into his arms.

Oscar takes George's seat. Magda cries steadily in her father's arms—with her face pressed into his shoulder, they're softened marginally, and after a few long minutes, George finally pulls away.

"Oh, Maggie," he cups her face and gently wipes away her tears with his thumb. "I was so worried. You—" he stops as if regarding her in a new light. "It sounds stupid since I saw you just yesterday, but… I forgot how much you look like your mother."

She smiles and looks down. "Dad, I…" She falters, her voice wavering.

George just nods, removing one hand from her to wipe the tears streaming down his face. "I know, honey. I know." He pauses, gently carding his fingers through her hair just as she had done to Oscar earlier. "A-are you okay?"

"Yeah, Dad, I-I'm fine. Seriously, it wasn't-it wasn't serious. Just a few bumps and bruises, that's all."

He nods, gently clasping her bandaged hand in his. "Do you need to stay longer, or are you okay to leave now?"

Magda turns to Oscar, who gives her a thumbs up. "I, uh, I

think I'm good to go now."

On their way back up to her room, they run into Dr. Young, who confirms Magda's free to go and briefly explains how to treat her injuries at home. She asks more questions while Oscar and George awkwardly watch, uninterested. Eventually, Oscar tells George which room to pack up while waiting for Magda to finish.

Dr. Young leaves only when called to another patient; Magda's visibly disappointed the conversation is cut short but nonetheless returns to her room with Oscar. He grabs the bouquet while the same nurse as before removes her I.V.

Oscar and George pack up Magda's modest assortment of belongings just as the nurse finishes with her and leaves. She thanked him for his time before heading into the bathroom to change into the pair of clothes Oscar had brought. Halfway through struggling to get into her pants, she feebly asks for help. Oscar doesn't hesitate to help her with her pants and even rolls a fresh pair of socks over her feet even though she hadn't asked.

"Where're your shoes?" He asks after putting her last sock on.

She rubs her neck. "I, um, wasn't wearing any."

"Wait, what?"

"I wasn't exactly thinking straight, and it was all so hectic that I kind of… forgot."

Oscar hands George the bouquet before pulling off his shoes to offer them to Magda. She stares at him for a few seconds before refusing to accept them, which turns into soft bickering that ends with the older sibling begrudgingly sliding the footwear onto her feet.

Lastly, she picks up her teddy bear and takes one last look around the room before following Oscar and George to the elevator. She ensures she says bye to her nurse and doctor when she bumps into them on her way out, to which they wish her a speedy recovery, and in return, she thanks them sincerely for their help.

Despite the slush and dampness, Oscar remains unbothered in just his socks walking out to the parking lot. When they approach George's car, he opens the trunk and has Oscar deposit the flowers beside a large cardboard box that had been haphazardly thrown inside.

Magda hesitates at the sight of the vehicle, fear sparkling plainly in her eyes. She slowly shuffles into the backseat while Oscar climbs into the driver's seat, leaving George in the passenger side as the car slowly pulls out of the parking lot.

–SIXTEEN–

A Stressful Night's Sleep

MAGDA

s soon as the car starts to move, flashbacks of the crash flicker through my mind. I can almost feel the impact again, the way the car spun, and the jarring weightlessness of my body before I came to a sudden halt. The phantom drip of blood runs down my face, and I find my hands suddenly sore.

Squeezing my eyes shut, I dig my bandaged fingers into the car seat and take short, shallow breaths as I attempt to distract myself with something else. I manage to stutter a weak, "Please be careful," to Oscar, who peers back at me in return and, upon seeing my expression (which I can only assume is unbridled fear), promises to be as careful as he can. Trusting Oscar, I allow myself to relax ever-so-slightly, my fingers still digging into the polyester seats and my eyes firmly clenched shut.

The second the car comes to a stop in our driveway, I throw my door open and tumble onto the snowy ground, my knees scraping against the hard concrete, but I don't feel it. When I stagger onto my feet and stumble towards the house, I notice my car in the driveway ahead and approach it, my breath hitching at its sight.

There's a wide dent across the back of the car, countless

scrapes chipping the paint away. Something catches in my periphery, and I stop, approaching to get a better look. Indented in the hood of the trunk are small, deep gashes that resemble fingernails, almost like claw marks. My mind goes completely blank when I examine them, unable even to begin speculating what caused it.

I reach out and brush my fingers along the cold metal, dumbfounded. When I touch the marks, something tingles in my fingertips, and I immediately retract my hand as if burned.

"What's that?" Oscar asks from behind me.

"Nothing," I dismiss with a shake of my head. "Must've been from the crash." I leave the conversation hanging in the air, and luckily Oscar doesn't get a good enough look at the scratches to question me.

I stand back as he approaches the front door and unlocks it, sighing into the familiar atmosphere. He dips his head before turning to meet my gaze, his cheeks and nose painted pink with dysphoria. I hesitantly join him and instinctively tense upon stepping into the house, eyes growing misty as I look around. The once comforting atmosphere of my childhood home feels suddenly so dark and harrowing without Mom; her absence casts a grey tint over what once was my sanctuary.

Leaning against the doorway, I'm hit with a sudden wave of memories; Mom cooking breakfast in the kitchen while I hum at the dining room table, Oscar and I arguing over who gets to stay with her while Dad goes off on a business trip, Mom kissing me on the forehead before tucking me into bed and singing me to sleep. The gentleness of her touch whenever I scraped a knee or fell off the monkey bars, the soothing tone of her voice as she'd console me, *"You're such a brave one, Magda. Such a warrior."*

As the memories fade to darkness, my knees buckle beneath me, and I crash to the ground.

Oscar's hand sparks warmth and feeling in my shoulder as he grabs me and pulls me onto my feet. He helps me to my bedroom, where I slump onto my bed in an emotionless heap of exhaustion, falling asleep almost instantly.

I'm in a dark room.

A single light ahead of me illuminates a casket with flowers propped against it and the altar of a church to its immediate right. The rest of the room is shrouded in complete darkness, the atmosphere cold and dangerous. The hairs on my arms stick up, and goosebumps ripple across my body.

There's nowhere else to go but forward, so I slowly approach the casket. Leaning over it, I flinch when I see Mom lying there, eyes closed and deathly pale, her hair greasy and thin. Her lips are chapped and cracked, and there's a bruise on her forehead and what looks like a dent in her jaw. It's gory and gruesome and shakes me to my core.

I go to take a step back when Mom's eyes snap open, and she turns her neck, a grisly crack emitting from the movement. Her hand shoots up and grabs my collar, yanking me close to her. I don't dare move, her face mere centimetres from mine. The whites of her eyes are yellow and bloodshot, while her irises are blood red.

"You," She hisses, her voice gravelly and unnaturally warped. "Look at what you did to me! You weren't there. You left me; you *abandoned* me. What reason could you possibly have to abandon your own *mother* after everything I've done for you? How could you?"

My vocal cords snap in my throat as Mom pulls me further down until my torso is tilted completely into the casket with her, and I brace my hands on the edge.

"What? Have you got nothing to say to me? You are the greatest disappointment in my life, Magda Celia Mercy. I just had to give birth to a little fuck-up who can't do anything right, huh? What is the *MATTER WITH YOU?*" Tears stream down my face, thick like blood. "Death is a relief to me now. At least now I don't have to put up with you anymore. That goddamn responsibility is off my shoulders; I'm finally at peace."

Every word she says shatters me, each in a different way. Suddenly, the ceiling starts to melt as a dark navy sludge fills the casket. Mom shrieks and yanks me down, submerging my head within the liquid. I immediately hold my breath, instinctively struggling against her grip to no avail. Her hands seem to solidify around my collar, securing me beneath the rising goo.

I scream beneath the surface as my whole body is engulfed in it. My eyes are squeezed shut, but I can still see Mom's face frowning angrily at me. Her eyes glow red as I slip into the black abyss.

LARAMIE

When Magda jerks awake in a cold sweat the next morning, she locks herself in her bedroom without food or drink and refuses to leave. Oscar grows concerned, so he prepares her some homemade jerky and bannock. Holding a tray of the food in one hand and a water bottle in the other, he approaches Magda's bedroom door with a satisfied smirk and knocks gently on the door. After a few seconds of silence, he raps again, and this time, Magda responds with a quiet, "Go away."

"Mags? It's me, Oscar. I have some food and water for you. Can you let me in?" Silence fills the hallway. Oscar leans his head against the door and closes his eyes with a sigh. He shifts in place, his feet planted firmly in the doorway. "Maggie, please… I'm worried about you. Please just… let me help you." His shoulders sag when more silence fills the air. "Mags, please, just let me in so I can see you."

"No. Just… leave me alone."

"Please, Maggie. Mom's gone and… and I can't lose you too. I need my sister." His voice wavers. "I just… I want to know you're okay. I… I miss you." He pauses. "Are you-are you doing anything to… hurt yourself…?"

A quick response on Magda's part. "No. No, I'm not."

Oscar exhales in relief, his chin and lip quivering steadily. His forehead brushes back against the door, and he slowly opens his eyes. "Please, just let me in," he sobs, his voice breaking as he looks down to the ground.

It feels as if an eternity goes by before Magda shuffles around the room and unlocks the door with a click. Oscar waits patiently for her to invite him in, and a reluctant response finally comes after an agonizing few seconds of silence. "Come in."

Per Magda's permission, Oscar practically bursts through the door, scanning the room for his sister. He sees her hair peeking out from the top of the bed on the other side of the room and approaches to find her leaning against the bed with her legs pulled up to her chest, hands wedged underneath her.

Oscar settles beside her and places the food on the floor to her right. He wordlessly offers her the water, to which she ignores him despite being able to see it in her periphery.

"Come on, Mags. Don't make this harder than it has to be. Please drink."

Her eyes glisten with tears as she hesitates. She slowly slides her hands from beneath her and turns to accept the water bottle from Oscar. Both of us stare in shock at the sight of her bare hands, her knuckles stained with angry splotches of red and yellow, minor cuts running up and down her fingers with dried blood crusted to her palm. Only then do Oscar, and I suddenly notice the unravelled gauze bandages strewn on the floor beside her.

As Magda holds her trembling hands out for the water, Oscar just sets the bottle down and gently envelopes her hands in his. Her eyes instinctively widen, and she tries to pull away.

"I-it's all my fault and," She stutters through her sniffling. "I shouldn't've… I just—"

"It's okay. You're so incredibly strong and—"

"Me? Strong?" She scoffs. "Barely. I'm anything *but* strong."

"Anything but strong?" Oscar echoes, looking up in thought for a second. "All right. You're… tough, tenacious, headstrong, um, staunch—"

That elicits a laugh from Magda, a small one but a laugh nonetheless. She quickly stops and hangs her head. "Idiot. You know what I mean. I'm not strong."

"Mags, listen to me. Just because you're struggling now doesn't mean you're a weak person. Hell, if you think so, you should've seen me when Mom and Dad told me about Mom's cancer. I was *livid.* Does that make me a weak person? Do you think I'm weak because of that?" Magda slowly shakes her head. "My point exactly. Stop being so hard on yourself. You're honestly not the asshole you seem to think you are—sometimes."

She giggles, smiling slightly. "I've never felt so flattered to be called an asshole before."

Oscar grins and wraps her in a hug. She reciprocates eagerly, cringing when she's face-to-face with her bruised hands. Her smile wavers, but she simply closes her eyes into the hug.

–SEVENTEEN–

Grave Circumstances

LARAMIE

he next few days go by like a blur to me.

Oscar and George take it upon themselves to prepare for Alawa's funeral as Magda oversees the final decisions. A traditional wake is planned alongside the burial that lasts Wednesday the 20th through to Friday the 22nd at a nearby church to commemorate her Indigenous heritage.

Magda visibly avoids the casket and remains across the room throughout the wake as various friends and relatives contribute memories they shared with Alawa. I see tears running down Magda's face as she listens intently to the numerous stories they choose to share; no matter what tone the story is told with, all are conveyed with the same fond sentiment.

Some sing and pray, but I keep a healthy distance, more than ever before feeling like an intruder on the intimacy of the wake.

When Alawa's funeral encroaches the following Monday, after a particularly dismal breakfast, Magda dresses in her bedroom while Oscar and George dress in theirs.

She weakly sifts through her closet until finding a black dress that fits surprisingly loose on her small frame. Although the garment practically drapes over her thin form, it emphasizes her body perfectly; the black, silky fabric flows elegantly against her skin, and the sleeves reach her low shoulders with ebony lace that cascades down her arms to her wrists. The heart-shaped neckline rests mid-chest, and the cinched waist allows the dress to fall to her knees slightly accentuated.

She opens the large wooden jewelry box sat atop her dresser, a myriad of colourful aboriginal depictions painted across its surface with a golden 'M' painted in the middle, and gently retrieves a necklace. The chain is a brown leather cord bearing a smooth piece of ochre wood carved into an angels' wing, painted in a cacophony of red, yellow, black, and white strokes. Magda surveys it softly and flips it over in her fingers, revealing a message on its back that reads: '*For my angel, happy sixteenth*' in red.

Securing the necklace around her neck, Magda pulls her hair back as she allows the accessory to fall onto her shoulders. She approaches the mirror and takes a deep breath before smiling at her reflection.

She returns to the living room to find Oscar and George waiting to go. They both look up when she enters the room, smiling shyly from their attention.

"I guess you look okay," Oscar bristles. "You're no me, though." Magda laughs and playfully punches his arm, to which he holds his hands up and chuckles. "All right, all right. You look great," he pulls her into a brief hug and gives her a quick kiss on the forehead. "Thanks."

Oscar himself is wearing a pair of black slacks, a white dress shirt, and a jet black overcoat buttoned-up mid-torso. A blue tie with purple, pink, and orange designs is fastened around his collar, and his hair is split, again, into two braids.

Meanwhile, George sports a head-to-toe black outfit, black slacks and a black dress shirt barely visible beneath his various layers. Directly overtop of his dress shirt is a black vest, one with a set of four buttons pulling the fabric together in the shape of the square. Finally, he wears a long black overcoat and a pair of what appears to be worn black leather dress shoes.

"Dad…" Magda says proudly. "You look… dare I say twenty-five years younger."

George smiles, his eyes crinkling in sadness. Oscar awkwardly interrupts to say they should probably get going now, and they vacate the house one by one.

Magda reluctantly hops into the car, visibly frightened, but this time, Oscar chooses to sit with her in the backseat, offering his hand to her during the drive. She clings to him, squeezing until the skin turns both white and red, but he doesn't say a word about it.

They arrive within ten minutes and shuffle nervously into the church. By the time the service is about to start, the church is almost at full capacity, and I can't help but feel proud that Alawa had so many friends and family; that she touched so many people during her lifetime.

When the priest opens his mouth to begin the service, the front door creaks open as if on cue, garnering the entire room's attention. Any semblance of imperturbability I'd had is ruined when I look over to see Nolan slipping into the church.

Lucifer brazenly sprawls on the large cross at the far end of the church, his fingers dancing with the navy mist that binds Nolan's person to his influence. An angry fire fans in my stomach, sending a powerful tremor through my body. As truly evil as I know Lucifer to be, I had at least expected him to allow the family to grieve uninterrupted. I realize now how foolish it was to expect Lucifer would allow them any peace or comfort after all he's done.

Nolan scans the church before meeting Magda's wide and horrified eyes. A smile spreads on his face as he eagerly strides inside. "Thank God I made it!"

"Whoa, whoa, whoa, hey, hey," Oscar intercepts, planting himself in front of Magda as the three Mercy's rise to their feet to face Nolan. "You shouldn't be here."

"Why not?"

"This is a private funeral. You have no reason to be here."

"This is Nolan?" George whispers to Magda, who just nods, the colour draining from her panic-stricken face.

Nolan makes a face and wrinkles his nose. "Maggie and I aren't broken up, so I can be here. We just had a disagreement the other day, but I'm pretty sure I showed her what we mean to each other."

Oscar's face burns with an ill-concealed fury. "Bullshit. You assaulted her." He spits vehemently, voice low enough that only the four of them can hear.

"Um, actually, I was just trying to explain myself when she got all crazy and flipped out on me. I was just trying to calm her down so we could have a conversation."

"That is so *not* what happened," Magda mutters in the arms of her father.

"You need to leave," Oscar snaps. "Make it easier on all of us and just go."

Anticipation churns in my stomach as Nolan frowns, his lips pressed into a straight line. He's practically glowering, his fists clenched by his sides as the veins begin to bulge from his neck. "Who the hell do you think you are telling *me* what to do?"

"Excuse me, sir," The pastor interrupts, turning to address Nolan. "It's apparent you're not welcome here. Please respect the wishes of Alawa's family and kindly remove yourself from our premises." Nolan doesn't say anything, his glare unmoving on Oscar. "Sir? Did you hear—"

Nolan advances swiftly, punching Oscar in the face. I flinch when I hear the crisp *smack* it emits but can do nothing besides stare in horror as Oscar staggers backwards from the unexpected blow. Magda screams as Oscar straightens and quickly ducks to avoid the next attack. George holds Magda firmly to his chest as his face flashes between anger and fear, contemplating whether or not to intervene.

Oscar manages to grab Nolan's arms from behind and kicks the crook of his knees, forcing him to crumple to the ground. He holds his attacker's arms tightly and straddles him once on the floor, pressing the man's wrists to the small of his back with one hand. Glancing between the pastor and his family, Oscar calmly says, "Call the police."

"Get the hell off me!" Nolan screams, wiggling fruitlessly beneath Oscar's firm grip. "What the hell is wrong with you? Let me go, you asshole!"

"Oscar…" Magda whispers breathlessly. She approaches her brother tentatively, her eyes flickering towards Nolan every few seconds. Oscar just looks up at her, inadvertently brandishing his reddening cheek. She cringes at the angry bruise beginning to form. "Are you okay?"

He just rolls his shoulders and nods. "Yeah, I'm fine. Just gotta keep him from making a break for it until the cops get here."

"They're on their way," The pastor announces, pocketing his cell phone.

Oscar nods and glances back at the remaining guests watching from afar at the furthest end of the chapel. He and Magda exchange guilty expressions, glancing down at Nolan with their respective distaste and rage.

Nolan continues cursing at Oscar, who collectedly ignores him until the police burst through the doors. When they approach the two, Nolan is finally exhausted enough to remain still, however, not silent.

"I'm gonna kill you!" He screams as Oscar releases him so that the police officers can pull him to his feet. Another officer pushes Oscar away from Nolan.

"You bastard, I'm gonna kill you!"

"Woah, woah, hey, calm down," An officer growls at Nolan, who immediately pales when he realizes there are police officers present. "There's a service going on. Let's take this outside."

Once led outside, Nolan and Oscar give their separate statements to the officers. All I hear when listening to Nolan's side of the story is how "none of you understand!" and "we love each other!" and "she's just confused, and I'm trying to help her!" His dispassionate explanation catches me off guard. How can Lucifer believe he's fooling anyone with a story like that? The fact that he does nothing to come up with a contradictory version of the altercation is worrying and leaves me feeling uneasy.

The officers determine Nolan as the perpetrator and stuff him in the back of their car, despite his crude threats and objections. I can't help the triumph I feel upon seeing him persecuted, however, something sinister negates my optimism.

"Ossy, are you okay?" Magda asks once Nolan and the police are out of sight.

"Yeah, I'm good," He answers, experimentally tapping his cheek. He unexpectedly flinches at the contact but tries to play it off. "'Tis but a flesh wound."

"It looks pretty painful."

"It's not *that* bad. I'm good, seriously."

Magda rolls her eyes, leery of his sincerity, as she approaches

George's car. "Yeah, you're the picture of health. Come on." She throws open the passenger door before grabbing a red bag from the compartment between the seats, placing and unfastening it on the trunk. She gestures Oscar over. "C'mere."

"Seriously, Mags, I'm fine—"

"Shut the fuck up and get your ass over here."

While I, myself, have known Magda a short time, her stubbornness is palpable for any onlooker. Oscar neglects to argue further, all too familiar with her adamancy and concedes with a dramatic sigh. He stands in front of Magda as she uses a small pad doused in disinfectant to sterilize the shallow cut before gently applying a bright pink bandage over the bruise.

Magda reorganizes the kit and stuffs it back into the car once satisfied with Oscar's condition. She closes the car door as the pastor approaches and asks, "Shall we continue the service?"

The family exchanges dismal expressions before nodding and returning to the church. They give a brief apology for the interruption before allowing the service to proceed, and the room flourishes from the singing and praying and the rhythmic beat of drums, alive with spirit. The fervour is maintained even as the service concludes and the burial is initiated, and mourners gather around Alawa's casket to take one final look at her. They take turns distributing tobacco within the coffin and sweetgrass in her right hand before following her casket as it is loaded into a funeral hearse and taken to the graveyard reservation.

The casket is secured to a contraption that lowers it into the ground. Magda crumples into her father's embrace, steadily sobbing as Oscar morosely drapes a blanket over it before it begins its descent. Magda's hands are clasped tightly around her father as the empty contraption is lifted from the grave.

A man who resembles Alawa a great deal taps George on the

shoulder to offer flowers and tobacco. George accepts, after thanking him, and turns to Magda and Oscar to hand them each a flower, leaving the tobacco to deposit himself.

They gently toss their offerings into the grave, the air thick with grief. Magda kneels at the edge of the grave, attempting to suppress her tears as George places a comforting hand on her back. Oscar looks away as dirt is shovelled over the coffin, his eyes glistening with tears that he wipes before they have a chance to fall. He turns away from it, taking shallow breaths as he calms himself down.

Movement draws my attention to a nearby tree, where an unusually angry-looking owl is perched atop a low branch, its eyes trained directly on me. My heart stutters when I find his eyes locked on mine, boring into my very being. His gaze paralyzes me, his wings raised threateningly above his head. I suck in an anticipatory breath as he tenses before leaping into the air to fly away. He twists his head around to glare at me as he soars in the opposite direction, his maroon eyes unsettling in a way I can't quite describe.

I try to relax, but the feeling of being watched remains even as I turn back to the burial. Oscar and Magda hold each other as they stagger towards the church, following the crowd. George lingers for a few seconds, visibly reluctant—perhaps to leave or just about the whole day—before joining the congregation, bloodshot eyes shedding ceaseless tears.

EIGHTEEN

Finality

MAGDA

'm gonna miss you, Ossy," I sniffle pathetically as I tidy some of his things, helping him pack his bags as his thirtieth day of leave looms, also the 30th day of October. "You've only been back for a month, but I can't picture you leaving again."

"Mhm."

He's been unusually quiet and uninterested since Mom's funeral, and to chalk it up to grief is understandable enough. Still, the iciness of his words and actions is something else altogether. Despite being unconvinced that it's unrelated to Mom's passing, I have a feeling that it is. And typically, when I have a weird intuition like this—especially with Oscar—it ends up being right.

Still, I don't want to press him when he's so upset. As hard as it is for me to ignore his distress, I understand that if he wants to talk about it, he will. The last thing he needs right now is more pressure than he must already be feeling.

"I can't believe you're leaving the day before Halloween of all days," It's a feeble attempt to provide at least a semblance of levity to the overwhelmingly uneasy atmosphere, but an attempt nonetheless. "We can't even go trick-or-treating together. I was gonna dress up as a piece of shrimp and buy you a sexy chef costume."

"Mhm."

I don't think I've ever known Oscar not to return my quips, especially regarding his appearance. I'd expected a response that wasn't an indifferent hum, something along the lines of, "as soon as I put on a regular chef costume, it automatically becomes sexy." Because even after breaking his leg when he was eight, Oscar still cracked a "that's what she said" joke between screaming in pain when I asked how bad it hurt.

The severity of whatever's bothering him is nothing I've ever seen, and it's so unnerving that I feel dread steeping in my very bones.

I slow my packing to a stop, glancing worriedly at Oscar as I bicker with myself over whether or not I should say something. Unable to keep pretending like I don't notice Oscar's obvious distress, I carefully consider how to broach the topic. "Ossy?"

"Mhm?"

"Are you o—"

"I'm fine," He snaps. "Don't worry about it."

I press my lips together. "You don't seem fine. Is there… is there anything you wanna talk about?"

"No."

"Are you sure?"

"Yes."

"Positive?"

"Yes!"

I take a deep breath before approaching my brother, gently sitting next to him. "Ossy, please talk to me—" When I place a hand on his knee, he immediately leaps from the bed and leaves the room without a word.

It's bittersweet when I realize I've been treating Oscar the same recently, refusing help and denying his presence. I've been given a taste of my own medicine, and I can't even be mad about it.

I know firsthand how important it is to be given space when you're in such a fragile place, and despite not knowing exactly how he feels and what he's going through, I sympathize with Oscar. I want to be there if he needs someone; I'm just worried about him.

This must be how he felt when I was the one being withdrawn and cold.

The need to apologize to Oscar accumulates in my stomach like a snowball rolling down an icy hill. I leap to my feet and scramble to the living room.

"Oscar?" I turn the corner to see him sitting silently on the couch, absently staring at the far wall. "I'm not here to badger you or anything. I just… I just wanted to say I'm sorry."

That piques his interest. He seems to snap out of whatever daze he's in, turning to me with an unreadable expression. "For what?"

I tentatively sit down on the loveseat opposite Oscar, my movements slow so as to not startle or scare him away. "For being such a bitch to you."

He cracks a smile at that. "That's… not exactly what I was expecting you to say."

"I'm taking a page out of your book on being blunt. You like it?"

A small smile eases its way across his lips. He mutters something under his breath that sounds suspiciously like, "they grow up so fast," but I pretend not to hear it.

"Seriously though, I've been a real bitch to you recently, and I wanted to say I'm sorry. I wasn't trying to be. I'm awful at handling shitty situations."

Oscar takes a deep breath, leaning forward on the couch. "I'm not mad at you if that's what this is about."

"I didn't think you were. I just had this epiphany and felt the need to apologize to you. Don't expect another one from me, though."

Oscar wheezes softly, shaking his head. "I hate how good you are at making me laugh."

"Now you know how I feel, constantly."

"Yeah…" He smiles at me. "Thanks. I forgive you, or whatever."

"Your sincerity never fails to flatter me."

"It's all a part of my charm."

"There's the Oscar I remember."

I stand back up and pat him on the shoulder, feeling a sudden wave of pride for alleviating whatever he'd been worrying about. *I* made him smile and laugh when he didn't want to, the very thing *he* always does to *me*. "Good talk, champ."

"Champ?"

"Would you prefer dickhead?"

"Yes, actually."

Now it's my turn to laugh. "Duly noted."

The next day is the dismal day Oscar returns from his leave. "Is this it?" I manage.

"I guess so." His voice is small and quiet, wildly unlike his usual boisterous tone.

I yank him into a hug, willing myself not to cry for the billionth time over the last month. Immediately, he hugs me back, his face buried against my shoulder while mine is planted almost in his armpit. "Jesus, Os, when was the last time you showered?"

He scoffs indignantly, a trace of a laugh in the sound. He pushes me away from him and crosses his arms. "I'll have you know I showered this morning."

"Hey, no need to get testy," I raise my arms in surrender, feigning ignorance. "I was just asking out of concern. You smell fine."

"I hate you."

"I love you, too."

A rivulet of sadness pelts me between the eyes when I remember this is a goodbye, but I try to shove past it, putting on a brave face for Oscar. "I'll miss you, Os."

His smile holds too many emotions to detect them all; sadness, disappointment, hesitancy, shame and pain, just to name a few. He squeezes my hand. "I'm gonna miss you, too, Mags."

"You take care of yourself out there," Dad's voice wavers as he says, "I love you, Os." Oscar and Dad embrace for a few seconds, the air thick with melancholy.

"I love you too, Dad." Suddenly, Oscar sounds like a five-year-old boy refusing to let go of his dad as he's being dropped off at school. A slight tremor ripples across his body, and my heart breaks when he whispers, "I don't want to go."

LARAMIE

Watching Oscar and Magda say goodbye hurts more than anything Lucifer could inflict upon me.

Watching them mournfully exchange farewells stings worse

than when my wings were removed from my back because I can physically *see* Magda's helplessness. I can *feel* the desperation in her heart as Oscar waves to them one last time before closing the door behind him.

She watches him leave as though she'll never see him again, as though this goodbye is their last.

There's something poetic about the way I deteriorate faster when Oscar leaves, the way the few pieces of my skin left dissolve with sudden urgency. My face—or lack thereof—and the faint outline of my body is all that remains; any panic or fear of what awaits me after I disappear returns as a bitter debilitating uncertainty.

I peer down at Magda as she curls against the couch, sniffling while blankly staring at pictures of her family spread across the coffee table. My inability to do anything besides watching her suffrage (and sometimes even exacerbating it with the storms I cause) is tiresome beyond comprehension—it's frustrating and aggravating and utterly *exhausting*.

I yearn to sit next to her without hesitation and cradle her in my arms, to stroke her hair and wipe her tears, to soothe her trembling and offer her comfort. I yearn to divulge consolations until she finally understands her significance not only to me but in this world. Until she finally understands her inner beauty and merit.

I long to be the one who ameliorates her pain, so every morsel of sadness dissolves from her heart and body. I yearn to be the cause of her smiles and the benefactor of her happiness and self-confidence, to be the first thing she thinks about in Lightlift and the last thought at Lightlapse. I want with every fibre of my being that she may meet and fall in love with me just as I have with her.

Something about her lures me in, and I find myself unable to resist any longer. Still, I falter when I realize I've reached out for her yet again, the transparency encapsulating my arm reminding me of the inevitable consequences.

What even is there left for me in this world? I've been exiled from my only home and thrust into an existence surrounded by nothing but loss and pain inflicted upon the one I've learned to love. Perhaps, before I fade away completely, I may make an impression on the human world, be it insignificant and reckless as it may.

What is there to lose when I've already lost everything?

I scream at the sky, I scream at Az for this damn rule, and I scream at Razael for doing this to me. I cannot bear being forced to watch as Magda tears herself apart anymore. My powerlessness is an itch just beneath my skin, one I can't quite relieve myself of, and I know there's nothing I can do to untangle the riproar of my heart.

Magda straightens on the couch, pushing the blankets away from her unhealthily slim waist. I cringe upon seeing her skeletal frame enveloped beneath the thin shirt. When I catch a glimpse of my face on the black television screen, I quickly look away. Any minute now, I'll be gone, reduced to nothing but a mere conjecture of Az's.

Never in a billion years did I think I would understand what heartbreak truly is. Now, however, with everything I've had to endure after becoming enamoured with a human, I can finally say I know what it feels like. And as much as I'd like to say none of it was worth this, I would be lying. Magda was worth every bit of pain I experienced and more.

I confidently approach my human in a last-ditch effort to assume control over at least one aspect of my existence. A burdensome weight I hadn't even realized I've carried ceases when I finally allow myself to succumb to my desires, and I settle on the couch beside Magda to gently embrace her.

The warmth she exudes is scorching compared to Batair's, but it's welcomed all the same. I thread my arms beneath hers and pull her tight, gently resting my forehead against hers. I worry she'll feel my heart beating against her chest as I melt into the embrace, still concerned over my physical impact on her.

The intimacy is everything I could have asked for.

Despite my heart screaming at me not to, eventually, I pull away. Magda instantly stiffens and confusedly glances around the room. A sense of peace I'd never thought possible alleviates any doubt I'd had, knowing there's a possibility Magda felt our embrace.

My heart slows as the thick propinquity of bliss settles in my system. Magda's face is the last thing I see as I begin to dissolve, a rush of energy coursing through my faded body. I welcome my demise like an old friend, like this was always destined to be my end.

Depleting my final remnant of energy, I thrust my arm out, my fingertips barely grazing her cheek before instantaneously solidifying. The stone travels fast across my body, and a frigid pain rushes across my back. I stare at Magda, her features the only image important enough to be ingrained in my mind, so important that the only thing that bothers me now is the thought of forgetting her.

My eyes remain open, my corneas and eyelashes each solidifying into marble one by one, an eternal smile on my face.

NINETEEN

You Again

MAGDA

n unfamiliar tingling sensation encompasses my forehead and torso like a phantom hug planting itself on me. It's faint yet palpable, and despite how unnerving and startling it is to feel the ghost of someone holding me, the feeling is comforting and *safe* somehow.

I don't know what it is, but it's a welcomed respite from constantly being plagued by the haunting sensation of Nolan's hands; times where I swear I can feel them clenched around my arms, my wrists, my neck. Every time the horrifying tangibility of his presence torments me, I feel violated and exposed like it's the first time all over again.

But this time… this time it's everything but that. It's a feeling of immunity and mitigation; it's not unwanted or inflicted upon me, but a warm, encompassing feeling of being surrounded by love and protected from harm.

Bringing a tentative finger up to my forehead, my fingertips graze against the soft flesh, and I stiffen when the tingling sensation begins to drain from my body.

What *was* that?

I stand and wordlessly shuffle upstairs, the cotton in my ears muffling Dad's voice as he calls after me. I almost slam the door behind me as soon as I burst through the doorway without meaning to. Collapsing on my bed, I glance back up at the calendar beside the mirror above my desk to stare at the only uncrossed date: October 31st.

I clench my fists and squeeze, the bite of sharp nails digging into my palms grounds me. I scoot back on the bed and curl onto my side to face my bookcase, narrowing my eyes at the sight of a picture stuffed between a few books. Curiously, I lean forward and tug it from its place, flattening the dishevelled surface before flipping it around. Instantly, my heart lodges in my throat.

Halloween 2012. It's a picture of my first girlfriend and me, age fourteen, celebrating our first Halloween as friends. Bianca wears a Princess Peach costume while I wear a Rosalina costume. The photo captures us holding each other close.

I gaze wistfully at her dark, spirally hair that flows just beneath her ears. She's grinning widely with eyes nearly squeezed shut in happiness. My hair is brushed over one eye, but I, too, am smiling, admiring the girl while I hug her tightly.

My eyes begin to water, and my lip quivers. My hands tremble profusely, gripping the photograph in an unforgiving grip.

I hang my head as tears begin to spill. One drop splatters on the film before sliding off its waterproof surface and into my lap. Soon, I'm full-on sobbing. I press the picture against my chest and fall backward on the bed, crying until my throat becomes too raw to continue.

Sobs turn to soft whimpers, and my tears slowly dry until I'm left staring at the ceiling. I close my eyes for a second. Everyone I love is gone. Everyone leaves me… God, why does *everyone* have to leave me? My first girlfriend, my brother, and my mom. I need someone, *anyone.*

I throw the picture across the room as my emotions bleed into an all-consuming emptiness. I feel so weak, and everything feels so forlorn; I don't have the energy to do anything except lay there, motionless and unfeeling. Hugging my pillow over my face, I scream into it until the fury burning in my chest goes out, and the anger inside me is finally released.

I compose myself before sulking back downstairs after taking a minute to calm my erratic heartbeat by breathing deeply. Dad leaves the kitchen just as I walk by, and we nearly collide, but I swerve in time to avoid it.

"Mags, hi. I didn't mean to startle you. How are you feeling?"

"I'm fine, thanks." I massage my temples as I stumble into the living room and fall onto the couch.

"I was just about to head up for a nap. Give me a shout if you need anything, all right?"

"Got it."

He glances over at me with one last sad smile before disappearing upstairs. Barely even a second goes by before there's a quiet knock at the front door.

My heart instinctively starts to race, but I ignore the almost painful panic as I hesitantly approach the door. My hand shakes violently as I reach for the doorknob, and a sudden overwhelming trepidation stuns me.

I peer through our peephole, but all that does is intensify the nauseating déjà vu of standing on one side of the door while *he* stands on the other.

Nolan.

My blood runs cold as memories flash before my very eyes, my body locking in place. An overwhelming heaviness sends my thoughts into complete disarray; I suddenly feel dizzy, nauseous, and terrified all at once.

My legs buckle underneath me, and I slump to the ground, kicking at the floor until I've backed myself against the couch. My chest heaves violently and painfully, and I can't speak, move, or breathe; I can't breathe, I can't breathe, *I can't breathe*—

I dig my nails into my arm with all the strength I can muster. The pain grounds me; slowly, I start to feel the floor beneath me and the couch behind me. My breathing evens, and my heart settles in my chest, my limbs still heavy and numb.

I let go of my arm and sag, exhausted and lightheaded, when another knock at the door has panic creeping back up.

"Shit," I whisper, desperate not to spiral again. I manage to make it onto my feet, stumbling towards and bracing myself against the door, panting. "Go away."

"Maggie?" His voice is soft. "I know I'm probably the last person you want to see right now, but I really need to talk to you."

I shake my head adamantly. If I say no, he'll probably break the door down, but if I say yes, I'll have to face him again. Not only that, but alone, and in my own home. What could he possibly want now? Control? Vengeance? Power? It's too risky to say no. The last time I rejected him, he forced his way in and… and…

Maybe if I let him, he'll finally fuck off for good. Plus, Dad is in the house, so if push comes to shove, I can scream bloody murder and have backup to beat Nolan's ass.

"Fine," I finally say, my voice trembling. I struggle to unlock the door, alarms blaring in my head as it clicks unlatched beneath my fingers. I weakly open the door, cowering behind it for as long as I can before Nolan steps inside.

I instinctively flinch when I see him, throwing the door shut, so I have more time to distance myself from him. I stagger into the opposing wall and brace myself against it, anticipating an attack.

When I finally look up at him, I almost don't recognize him; his expression is sombre and ashamed, and he makes no move to approach me, his actions slow and exaggerated so as not to scare me.

Looking at him, rage burns in my chest and drowns out any fear or embarrassment of being in his presence. Seeing him is a bitter reminder of everything he's done to me and what he did to Oscar. He *punched* Oscar, my little brother, in the face and tried to… and assaulted me.

He glances nervously around the house. "I'm not here to… hurt you, I just… I need answers, and you're the only one who can help me. Please, Maggie."

It's unsettling to see him so desperate and placid; the look in his eyes is so unnaturally kind. There's no hint of malice or anger in his gaze or body language.

"Five minutes."

He swallows thickly but nods.

Refusing to tear my gaze from him for a second, I maintain a reasonable distance between us, my hand protectively clasped around my phone in my pocket. I narrow my eyes at him, suspicious and wary, as he tentatively sits down on the couch.

"I know it's gonna sound like some lame-ass cop-out, but I swear I'm telling the truth. I-I think I'm going crazy. I can't remember things, small things, and it's kind of gone now, but I'm scared this won't be the end of it.

"It started when I showed up at your school. I don't even remember going there or visiting you. I swear that I don't. All I remember is looking around your dorm, and that's it. I don't remember leaving my house or coming home; it was like I was at home, then I was looking around your room, and then I was back at home. It's really fucking freaky, and I don't know what's going on with me. I don't remember going to your mom's funeral… I didn't even know she died! All I remember is being driven to the police station handcuffed in the back of a cop car. They thought I was just trying to get out of trouble by asking what happened, so all I know is I assaulted your brother and was charged with assault. My dad bailed me out, so I just have to report regularly to the police, but I'm extremely confused because I honestly don't know what happened. I was hoping you could help me."

The way his voice shakes and his hands nervously fiddle, and the guilt and fear in his expression, are, admittedly, sincere. He's always been a shit actor, anyways.

Seeing the desperation in his eyes is genuinely unsettling, especially when if I close my eyes, I can still picture him looming over me with a sinister smile and a demented gleam in his eyes.

"You don't remember… anything? Did you… did you go to the hospital? Maybe you could have amnesia."

"No one believes that I don't remember anything. I tried seeing a doctor, but they just told me I don't have any of its symptoms besides being unable to remember what happened. I'm especially losing credibility because I can't remember the specific instances I was accused of assault."

I take a deep breath and bite my lip. He's telling the truth, I know that much for sure, but what the hell does that even mean? He can't remember ever hurting me or attacking Oscar…

"Okay," I start. "Okay, um, how-how exactly do you want me to help you?"

"Well, uh, I just thought that if you could tell me what happened, maybe I'll remember," He suggests. "Maybe it'll jog my memory. Even if it doesn't, I need to know what happened. It's killing me."

My heart rate skyrockets at the prospect of telling him about... well, everything. There's no way I'd be able to tell him everything when I couldn't even tell Mom, Dad or Oscar about it.

"Also, um, is your brother here? I'd like to apologize for what happened."

My voice swells in my throat. "He-he's not here. He... he left earlier today."

His face falls, but he nods. "Oh. I'm sorry. If you could tell him I'm sorry when you get to see him next?" I nod. "So... what exactly happened at the church?"

I take a deep breath and repress the tears forming in my eyes as I prepare to reiterate everything. It's not easy to bring back those memories, especially after I've made an effort to forget about and move past them. And, as much as I want to tell him to forget it, I know he won't take that for an answer, and if he's telling the truth here, he deserves to know what he did.

His face grows paler with each word I utter. I find myself genuinely wondering if he has a deranged evil twin I don't know about. It fits the prerogative, and honestly, at this point, I wouldn't even be that surprised if he did.

By the time I'm done, he looks horrified.

"Oh my God, I can't believe I... I mean, I know we didn't have the best breakup, and I was kind of a dick, but... I swear, I never would have done that to you knowingly. I honestly don't know what possessed me to do that... I'm so, so sorry."

"I know." While his apology does nothing to erase what happened, knowing he regrets it makes me feel a bit better about the fact that it transpired in the first place.

He sighs. "You didn't deserve—"

"What the hell is he doing here?" Dad suddenly roars from atop the stairwell.

We both blanch when he storms down the staircase, anger blazing furiously in his eyes. I stand between him and Nolan, preventing him from advancing on Nolan. The latter timidly backs towards the door.

"Dad, no, it's okay," I plant my hand firmly on his chest. "He was just—"

"You get the hell out of my house!" Dad snaps, an accusatory finger pointed at Nolan. "Get the hell out of my house, and don't *ever* step foot on our property again."

"Dad, wait—"

"No, he's right," Nolan agrees, scrambling to the door. "It's okay, Mags. I'm sorry for everything," He opens the door and steps outside, closing it behind him after whispering, just loud enough for me to hear, "Thank you."

-TWENTY-

A Wolf in Sheep's Clothing

ad fumes after Nolan and hastily locks the door behind him. I scrub a hand over my face, suddenly weak in the knees. They're about to buckle when Dad gently places his hands on my shoulders, holding me upright, and meets my gaze with concern. "Are you okay? What was *he* doing here?"

"I'm fine, Dad. He just… he just wanted to talk."

"About what?"

I hesitate, contemplating whether or not I should tell Dad the truth. Would he believe me, or would he assume Nolan was lying and scold me for falling for his lies and for willingly letting him into our home?

As much as I'd like to tell Dad everything, the fact that I don't even know what's going on with Nolan means there's not much I can say without sounding insane.

"He was apologizing," I finally decide on. Which, again, is technically true. "He was sincere, too. I don't forgive him, but it makes me feel a bit better."

"That was it? Nothing else?"

I nod. "Said he was feeling guilty and wanted to apologize. I thought hearing him out might make me feel better, so I said yes. I know it was stupid and dangerous if that wasn't his intention, but… he looked genuine and… I wasn't afraid of him."

Dad pauses for a second. "Did it help?"

"Yeah, I think it did." An awkward silence settles over us for a few long seconds. "I'm, uh, I'm just gonna head up to my bedroom for a while. Wind down a bit. Feel free to go back to bed if you want."

Dad waves a hand at me. "I'm already up. I couldn't fall asleep anyways. Let me know if you need anything. I'm right here."

I smile appreciatively and nod before wordlessly sulking to my bedroom, struggling to close the door behind me. I sit on the edge of my bed and begin to scroll through my blocked numbers, hesitating on Nolan's. Maybe if I text him, we can find out what happened and why he can't remember anything. Maybe there's something we're missing.

But there's nothing I can do for him. I'm not a doctor (yet) or a psychologist; I don't know what would make someone lose such vital pieces of their memories, and select few at that. Talking to him would just make things worse for both of us; the constant reminder of him still present in my life might end up being detrimental to my already declining mental health, and our continued correspondence might make him grow to resent me considering he doesn't remember what happened and why it led to his arrest.

Sighing defeatedly, I lock my phone and toss it aimlessly on my bed, squeezing my eyes shut. Taking deep breaths, I try to alleviate the pounding of my heart in my ears and the ceaseless trembling that overtakes me, only to throw myself against the wall when I look up to see a figure standing at my closet door.

He's pale, like a ghost, and has wavy blond hair, horns growing from his temples and wings billowing from his back. His eyes are unsettlingly unhinged, masked behind an over-compensating friendly face. Excluding his wings, horns, and the off-putting armour he's wearing, he looks relatively normal, and that's what scares me most.

A pungent odour wafts through the room, and I wrinkle my nose at its scent—searing meat. I suppress a gag, the familiarity of it on the tip of my tongue but just out of reach. *Why is it so familiar?*

'You have no reason to fear me,' He says calmly. I back myself against my headboard, eyes blown wide in fear as I stare at the *Thing* standing in my room. 'I am not here to hurt you; you must understand.'

He pauses to give me a chance to say something, but my debilitating fear prevents me from doing so. I pinch my arm as hard as possible, and dread settles in my stomach when the sensation of my nails digging into my skin confirms what I'd feared;

This *isn't* a dream.

What the fuck?

I settle for a shaky nod. It seems to satisfy him. "W-why do you have horns?" I blurt without thinking. Immediately I slap a hand over my mouth and cower in fear.

He holds his hands out. 'It's okay; please, you don't have to be afraid of me. I know I look scary, but I can promise you I don't want to hurt you. Before I had these—' he gestures to his horns, '—they were connected into a halo and glowed with heavenly light. I was banished and therefore lost that power. My name is Laramie, and I was banished because I fell in love with a human.' He looks me in the eyes and smiles fondly. 'I fell in love with *you*.'

The air is punched from my lungs. He's… *it's*… an angel? An angel who fell in *love* with me? How? Why? What? What even is my life anymore?

"I-I don't understand."

'That's fair. There's a lot I have to explain.'

I shake my head, confused and paranoid. Something feels… off. Wrong in a way I can't determine, and it leaves me on edge. "Why? Why tell me anything?"

'You deserve to know the truth after everything you've been put through. You deserve clarity.' I'm beyond confused at this point, but it only gets worse. 'A month ago, I was sent to Earth to complete an assignment. I did not know at the time that—whom you would know as God—was trying to determine whether or not angels are ready to feel again, so they cursed me with emotions and sent me to Earth. I blindly followed a human I fell in love with—you—and thus directly disobeyed their orders and was banished upon returning to Heaven. Since then, I have been imprisoned on Earth, forced to experience and endure your pain.

'Nevertheless, I wouldn't trade my love to go back to Heaven. The "God" you know is not whom you may think. They are called Az and allow humans to suffer on Earth, uncaring while using angels as their pawns to build power for themselves. They chose to punish me by hurting you.'

I know the term "blew my mind" is just a metaphor, but I'm pretty sure his explanation ignites something explosive in my head. I'm still skeptical and paranoid, but a feeling in the pit of my stomach tells me he's not lying. Why am I suddenly so good at reading people?

"Wha—how? Um, what?"

'Az used people. They used Nolan to hurt you and killed your mother.'

Oh.

Oh.

God—Az—was controlling Nolan, and *that's* why he can't remember attacking Oscar or… or assaulting me; because he wasn't in control of himself. The same God who… who killed Mom because an angel fell in love with me? Because… because *he* fell in love with me.

I didn't ask for any of this. I'd finally found a semblance of stability in my life, only to have it revoked by a goddamn deity for something I have no control over.

"You…" My shoulders shake, no longer in fear but anger. "You did this to me? My mom is dead, and… and I was nearly… he almost…" I choke on my words—I still can't say it. "Because of *you?*"

Laramie hangs his head. 'Indirectly, but yes. I did whatever I could to intervene, but, unfortunately, I am as powerless as you to prevent what transpired.'

Hot tears form in my eyes, and I can't suppress the anger swelling in my chest. "Why would I want to see you? You… you *ruined my life!*" I'm seething in anger, but it doesn't hold much weight. It suddenly dies like a flame burning out as tears begin to stream down my cheeks in frustration; I can barely wrap my head around anything.

Even worse is that somehow, I know it's real. Maybe I've finally gone mad, but I believe him, and that just makes it harder to comprehend.

I take a deep breath, relaxing my shoulders. I meet his gaze with a solemn one. "Tell me everything."

He smiles softly before calmly relaying an extremely complex retelling of the Dawn of Creation; the more Laramie explains, the closer I come to experiencing an existential crisis that will ultimately launch me over the same edge I've intermittently dangled my legs from since learning the harsh reality of our fucked up world. It almost feels like every single time I've ever thought the world was out to get me has now been proven true.

'This is where you come in,' Laramie continues. 'I need your help in finding and liberating Ona from their captivity. That way, what has happened to you may never happen again, to anyone.' He takes a step towards me. I'm not sure why but it exudes a threatening aura, so I instinctively scoot back. 'Humans deserve to have their rightful Creator back. I can save Ona and regain your world so Az may no longer control them—or control you.'

A throbbing headache pierces me. I cradle my head in my hands, willing the pain to subside since a headache is quite literally the last thing I need right now. "If you don't know where Ona is, what makes you think I would have or know how to find the information you need?"

'Humans understand more than you may fathom.'

I shake my head. "Doubtful. And, besides, what exactly will come of this?"

'We can conquer Az, destroy their angels and reclaim yours and Ona's Earth. With Ona in control, you will feel peace like you never have before. I don't want this for me. I want it for *you* because… because I love you and know you are deserving of it more than most.'

My head starts spinning, and pain engulfs my skull. "I can't do this."

I look up in time to see Laramie's expression fall. 'What do you mean?'

"I can't start something like this. I can't be responsible for the fu–um, for the fate of humanity when I shouldn't even be responsible for my own. You… I'm not the right person for this.

I'm sorry."

'You *have* to. Your life depends on it. I'm trying to help you.'

"I'm sorry," I say. "I really am, but I just… I *can't.*"

Laramie looks down, exasperated and angry. His body starts practically convulsing in rage while he takes stuttering deep breaths. 'You don't want to listen to me? Fine. Just know I warned you. You've tempted fate, but not in your favour.'

—TWENTY-ONE—

Leverage is a Powerful Thing

ey, Mags," Dad knocks quietly on my door before pressing it open, smiling over at me. I attempt to smile back, but I can tell it's just as disingenuous as it feels. "It's Oscar's birthday today, and I was thinking you and I could give him a call and say happy birthday. What do you say?"

My heart drops when I realize I completely forgot. Glancing over at my calendar confirms that it is, in fact, November fourth, Oscar's birthday. Instead of being happy like I usually am on birthdays, this time, it makes me feel sad. It's Oscar's birthday, yet we don't get to celebrate with him in person; we won't even get to see him for another year.

I shake my head. "Sorry, Dad, but I don't feel up to that right now. Maybe later."

I don't even have to look up to see his disappointed expression. He just nods and gives me a tight-lipped smile. "That's fine. I understand. I love you."

"I love you too."

He closes the door behind him, and I look back down and

sigh, a constant feeling of unease settled over me. It's been three days since I last saw Laramie, and a part of me is too scared to call out to him. The last thing he said sounded almost like a threat, talking about warning me and that whatever happens is my fault.

My thoughts drift back to Oscar, and my phone suddenly weighs heavy in my pocket, a sense of obligation pressing down on my chest. As shitty as I feel, I should at least call and let Oscar know I'm thinking about him—at least acknowledge his birthday. It's the least I can do, and I'm sure it'll mean the world to him.

Forcing a smile on my face, I grab my phone from my pocket and call Oscar. I turn it on speakerphone before dropping it in my lap, my heart beating quickly against my chest as the phone rings.

And rings.

And rings.

And rings.

"You have reached the voicemail for Private Oscar Mercy."

That's weird. Oscar always answers his phone. It's like his super-power; he always knows when it's ringing and answers it after the third ring. I have to remind myself that it's his birthday, and he could be busy or left his phone somewhere, or the battery died or something.

Taking a deep breath, I clear my throat and decide to leave a voicemail. Whenever he gets the time to check his phone, he'll get my message, and I'm sure he'll appreciate it whenever that is.

My phone beeps and I start blurting out "happy birthday" over the receiver, no matter how depressing and un-enthusiastic I sound. I manage to laugh at myself when I'm done, so Oscar doesn't worry too much about me, whether or not it's warranted or justified.

"Happy birthday Oscar," I say when I finish singing. "Sorry I couldn't catch you when you weren't busy. I hope a voicemail is enough. Happy twenty-first! I love you and will celebrate hardcore when I see you again." I swallow thickly, trying to hold back the tears threatening to spill from my eyes. "Next time you're home, I'll take you out to a bar so you can have a drink and make a complete ass of yourself shitfaced in public. Until then, I hope you have a terrific day. I love you, Os. Happy birthday. Bye!" I probably end the call too soon, but I can't help it with the looming feeling that life keeps beating me down when I experience even the tiniest bit of reprieve.

I've barely been around Dad recently; I don't go downstairs unless it's for food, and, to be honest, I miss him. But I can't face him—not now that I know it's all my fault Mom died. And what happened with Nolan… it's my fault it happened in the first place *and* that he has to suffer the consequences, too.

It's all my fault.

There's a knock at my door, and I mumble a quiet, "Come in."

Dad slips into the room with me. "How are you holding up?" As much as I feel everything eating me up inside, the last thing I want to do is worry Dad, but if I tell him anything, that's exactly what'll happen. So, for his sake, I keep it bottled up.

"I'm okay. Same as before. You?"

He shakes his head. "Yeah, no, I'm doing fine." He clears his throat. "I, uh, I was just wondering if you would be okay here, alone, if I were to go grocery shopping for an hour or so."

I instinctively tense at the prospect of being home alone, but I relax after letting Dad's words sink in. It's just an hour of grocery shopping. Of course, I'll be fine. I have to be. I'm not *that* weak and incapable.

I think.

"'Course, Dad, I'll be fine."

"You know you can call me if anything happens, right? Even if you're just feeling lonely, I'm always just one call away."

"Yeah, I know. Thanks. Thank you."

He beams. "Now that we've got that all settled, I'll be back in about an hour. I'll let you know when I'm on my way home so you can help me bring the groceries in, okay? Maybe you should stay in the living room, so you're ready when I get back."

"Sounds good to me. See you in an hour."

He leans over and kisses me on the forehead. I hold him back for a few seconds, praying he doesn't notice my trembling as I relish in the much-needed embrace. The comfort Dad provides me is stripped too soon when he pulls away and smiles before leaving my room. I listen to his footsteps as he descends the stairs, and I follow him down after a few seconds.

I curl up on the couch with my phone and watch as he grabs his keys, wallet, and some reusable bags from the kitchen counter.

He begins to leave, calling out, "Bye, sweetie. See you in a few," before closing the door behind him.

I'm instantly cast into a cold, dark abyss of loneliness. The second I'm left alone in the one place that has always placated any doubt or worry I'd harbour, it suddenly feels like a volatile battlefield I've been left for all of eternity to suffer in. Abandoned and alone, susceptible and defenceless, weak and vulnerable.

Not even ten minutes after Dad left, there's a knock at the front door. I instinctively tense before tiptoeing over to look through the peephole, my breath caught in anticipation. My eyes widen when I recognize the two men standing there as armed forces members; one looks like a clergy member by his clerical collar, and they're both dressed in military uniforms.

My hands shake as I pull open the door with all my might, feebly hiding behind it as they look up at me. I can tell my smile comes across as uneasy and slightly fearful from the quivering of my lips alone, but still, I manage a nervous, "Um, m-may I help you?" As I glance between the men.

"Are you Magda Celia Mercy?" The man on the left asks, his arms politely clasped together in front of his waist.

Oh God, oh God, oh God, oh God, oh God. "Y-yes, I am."

"Miss Mercy, I am Commanding Officer Paul Seifert of the Canadian Armed Forces, and this is Private Chaplain Emmanuel Erlich. May we step inside?"

I hesitate before nodding, moving out of the way. "Y-yeah, of course. Come right in."

They nod politely upon stepping into the depressing living room. The fear of what could've happened to bring a Chaplain and Oscar's Commanding Officer home—and without Oscar—makes my heart pound painfully against my ribcage.

"We… regrettably are here to inform you of the passing of Private Oscar Mercy."

At first, I don't understand what he says; my mind just goes blank, and my whole body freezes. Time slows for a few seconds until their words hit me hard, and instead of acceptance, I cling to denial, as though it may have the power to alter reality.

"He's not dead," I refuse. "No. No. He can't be. There's no way. He's just not. I… I don't believe you. There… there must've been a mistake. You have the wrong guy."

An involuntary shaking overtakes me, despite the fact that I still don't believe them. I shake my head adamantly, feeling the strength drain from my body as my mind completely shuts down.

I cover my mouth with trembling hands, barely able to inhale a proper breath as my chest heaves with a panic attack. *This has to be a nightmare. There's no way all of this is happening to me right now. This can't be real. It can't. It isn't.*

"His passing continues to be under investigation. However, our preliminary investigation strongly suggests that Private Mercy died by… suicide."

I'm hit with a sudden wave of vertigo that makes my legs buckle beneath me. I manage to catch myself on the wall before falling, the world swimming around me with the familiar agony I felt when I'd been told Mom had died. My mind does nothing but scream a cacophony of, *'NO, NO, NO!'* repeatedly, as if that word alone has the power to revive my baby brother.

The realization that Oscar… that he took his own life on his birthday devastates me in such a profound way I never knew I could feel. Not only is my baby brother dead, but… he killed himself on his *own birthday*.

Something glints in the window behind the two officers. My eyes widen in both shock and fear when I see Laramie standing there, smiling wickedly as he waves to me.

At that moment, everything clicks.

He did this. He killed Oscar.

"On behalf of the Secretary of Defence and the Canadian Armed Forces, we extend our greatest sorrow and condolences. Private Mercy was a fine soldier." Paul finishes with a sad smile.

All I can seem to think about is the fact that I'll never again be forced to sit through Oscar's corny jokes even though I secretly love them, or get to see his lopsided smile again after being apart for too long, or get to annoy the crap out of him for no reason, or just simply have a younger brother.

He's gone.

He's really gone.

Anger and condemnation cloud my mind. I blame Laramie. I

don't even know how he did it if he can't touch humans, but he *killed* my brother. He said he loves me but… why would he kill Oscar if he's feeling anything but love?

Emmanuel and Paul duck their heads and silently approach the door. They give me one last nod before quietly leaving. Once left alone, my stomach folds, and I feel the grossly familiar sensation of bile rising in my throat. I barely make it to the kitchen in a dead sprint before vomiting into the sink, coughing, and heaving up every bit of food I had eaten earlier, which, admittedly, isn't much.

I hold my hair back, spitting out the remnants of my stomach acid and regurgitated food to feel a sudden presence looming over me. I whirl around and instinctively flinch away from it, only to see Laramie standing over me.

'I didn't want to have to do it,' He says. 'I was hoping you would agree and save us both the grief, but… regrettably, you didn't. And if you wouldn't listen to Laramie, there was no other way I could willingly convince you to do this. It *is* a shame it didn't work. I was hoping you wouldn't push me to do this.'

"What are you talking about?"

He sighs, annoyed, and looks down at me with disgust. 'I am not Laramie. I'm Lucifer.'

Oh.

Oh.

"You… you lied to me."

He smiles. 'Yes, well, I did what I had to do. It's a shame you weren't more compliant; you could have saved yourself the loss. I hoped it wouldn't have to come to this, but you forced my hand.'

"You… you said you wanted to help me. Humanity. But, to do so, you kill a human."

His eyes flash with anger, and he kneels in front of me. I back myself up against the kitchen counter as he leans forward, invading my personal space. 'Whether one human lives or dies is of no significance to me. Oscar is an unfortunate casualty of war; an innocent bystander caught in the crossfires meant for more, meant as an incentive in my endeavour to persuade you for my cause. I did what I had to do to convince you to save humanity.'

Every part of me wants to scream at him that it's all bullshit, and he *decided* to kill Oscar, but my common sense reminds me yelling at The Devil will just make things worse for me.

'You have some time to grieve. I am no monster,' The irony in what he says makes me want to laugh; here he is, literal *Satan*, telling me he isn't a monster. 'But I expect your compliance. And if you choose not to help me, there are other methods I can erect to convince you to give in. Tomorrow, we will begin.'

When the sickly feeling rises in my throat again, I spring to my feet and stumble into the bathroom, where I dry heave into the toilet before collapsing exhausted against the wall.

Fuck.

–TWENTY-TWO–

Less Than Alone

espite how trapped I so clearly am, I at least know I still have one final escape. If I'm no longer alive, Lucifer can't use me; if I'm dead, I'm useless. No one else needs to get hurt if I'm not here to instigate it.

Closing the bathroom door, I get to my feet and brace myself against the sink counter, immediately looking away when I see my reflection in the mirror. I'm far too disgusted with myself after killing my family to acknowledge my existence; I *deserve* this.

I open the medicine cabinet behind the mirror, grabbing the closest bottle—acetaminophen—and popping open the cap. Turning away from the mirror, my hand trembles as I take a few deep breaths to steel myself before bringing the bottle to my lips to down the pills.

When nothing happens after a few seconds, I open my eyes to find my hand empty, cupping nothing but empty air. I whirl around in confusion, my mind racing to keep up with everything that's happening. Did I drop the bottle? It isn't on the floor. It's just… gone.

The hairs on the back of my neck stand up when the feeling of being watched returns, and I turn to face the window. There stands Lucifer holding the bottle I just had, an infuriatingly smug smirk on his face. Still determined, I lunge for the medicine cabinet to grab another bottle only to find it empty.

'You really thought you could get away that easily?' Lucifer mocks, his laugh a bitter taunt. 'So are you ready, or should I make plans for dear-old-dad?'

As much as I hate to admit it, the only way I can stop all this is to give in. I glare at him before hanging my head in defeat. "I'll do it."

'I knew you would come around eventually.'

I squeeze my eyes shut, exhaling only when I feel he's finally gone. I open my eyes and collapse limply against the toilet lid. Not only have I lost my mom and brother, but my life is no longer mine. I've been renounced the power to end it.

I don't hear the front door open before the distinct sound of approaching footsteps echoes from the hallway. I don't have it in me to stop crying, too overwhelmed with grief to think about anything else. Who knows, once Lucifer gets what he wants, there's no telling whether he'll keep Dad alive. I have no reason to trust him, and that scares me like nothing else.

Dad knocks on the bathroom door, and I instinctively flinch at the sound. "Maggie? Sweetie, are you okay?"

I sob harder into my palms as Dad opens the door. He gently places his hands on my knees, and initially, I cringe away before relaxing into his grip.

He pulls me into a hug, cupping my head against his chest. "Shh, it's okay, honey," He whispers into my shoulder. "You're okay. It's okay. Everything's okay. Just breathe."

I spend the next few minutes focused on steadying my breathing, unable to muster the strength to push away from him (not that I even want to, for that matter). When I finally stop crying long enough to tell Dad about Oscar, I choke on the words, barely able to string together a cohesive sentence. Still, I eventually manage to admit Oscar's gone.

Dad wails as though I'd just stuck my hand in his chest and ripped his heart out—which, I guess, I did, in a way. We cling to one another for at least half an hour on the floor of the bathroom; neither of us has the energy to move. It feels like my life is genuinely ending, but I don't even get the privilege of deciding whether or not it is.

To say Oscar's death destroys me is an understatement. I should be the one to go first since I'm older; I've always felt responsible for him, whether as his guide on his first day of high school or when it came to him getting bullied. No matter the circumstance, I made peace with my duty as the older sister to take care of Oscar no matter what.

What am I to do now that I no longer have anyone to protect? Who am I now that I'm no longer his older sister? There's a word for a child who's lost their parents and a person who's lost their partner, but there's no word for someone who's lost their sibling. What am I now that he's gone?

Those are some of the countless questions that keep me awake that night—alongside the impending doom that pursues me with Lucifer himself.

If someone had told me a week and a half ago that my mental health could deteriorate even faster than it was, and my life would keep getting worse, I would have laughed. But now that I'm here experiencing it all, I can't help but wonder how my life could get any worse in anticipation it will.

As if the death of my mother wasn't enough, my little brother's just had to come next, and only barely two weeks later on his birthday. I can't help the guilt I feel knowing how disappointed he'd be to see the person I've become, if he knew I was the reason he died. And yet, it only magnifies my guilt to know it's my fault he isn't here to see whom I've become.

Just as promised, Lucifer returns at dawn the next day.

I barely got any sleep anyway, so at the very least, I wasn't awakened by him, however, tossing and turning in bed to see him standing in the corner of my room was nonetheless startling.

I sit up and rub my eyes, looking up at the demon expectantly. I don't even say anything; I just wait for his orders.

'Desk.' He commands. I pocket my phone without bothering to change or go to the bathroom and wordlessly sit at my desk. He scowls at me. 'Notebook. Pen.' It feels hugely degrading for his vocabulary to be reduced to single-word sentences as he orders me around, but I'm in no position to contradict him. I obediently grab a blank notebook from the first drawer and grab a pen. 'You are going to write down everything in the exact order as I say. Do not change a thing.'

I nod and proceed to record everything Lucifer explains he knows about 'Paradise,' the supposed place Ona is imprisoned. I write down everything he says, given no time to think or allow my mind to wander. I don't ask for a break, not even when my hand throbs, my wrist cramps and my bladder aches. I keep going in fear that merely asking for a second will invoke his wrath.

I don't even filter his words as I write them down. It's like everything he says goes in one ear and out the other. My hand and wrist throbs, my eyes strain, and my body aches from sitting in the same position all morning. My stomach grumbles, but I ignore it and instead eye my water lustfully, even when my bladder feels like it'll burst any second.

I stay like that until noon when Lucifer "generously" gives me a five-minute break. I immediately limp to the bathroom, pee, and fill up a water bottle, only to race back in time. I take a long gulp of my water and sit back down to resume my role as Satan's secretary.

He has me research Paradise's location this time, standing stiffly by my shoulder to regulate my notes. He gives me another break at six o'clock, and then we proceed again until midnight. He "allows" me to get some sleep (which, spoiler alert, I don't get) before waking me at six o'clock am the following day to keep going. He maintains that routine until noon, when Dad knocks at my door.

The sudden knock startles me. I flinch and look up at Lucifer in a panic. He just disappears, yet I can hardly relax when I'm still able to feel him lurking nearby.

My voice wavers, and I clear my throat before inviting Dad into my room. "C-come in."

He opens the door, sympathetically regarding me where I sit stiffly at my desk. "Hey, kiddo. I haven't seen you in a while. How are you?"

"Fine. You?"

He nods slowly. "I'm… all right. I, uh, I just wanted to let you know that Oscar's f… Oscar's funeral is being held a week from now, on the eleventh. It'll be the same as A-Alawa's."

I hold back a humourless laugh. Oh, the irony of Oscar's funeral intersecting with Remembrance Day. The world really *is* a cruel place. I can't help but wonder if that was the way Lucifer intended it to be; I wouldn't be surprised to learn that he did that intentionally.

I glance over Dad's shoulder to see Lucifer standing behind him, grasping a large carmine blade ending with three serrated points. Its metal is glistening, and the veins on his arm holding the pitchfork glow red. He angles it over Dad to kill, and I manage to mask my fear and shake my head, who just looks at me with an eyebrow raised, a silent demand.

"I'm not going," I declare, my leg bouncing uncontrollably underneath my desk. *'I'm no monster,'* my ass; Lucifer won't even allow me to say goodbye to my baby brother.

"What do you mean you're not going?" Dad admonishes.

"I mean, I'm not going."

"You can't just *not* go."

"I don't want to," I blurt without thinking. My eyes widen when I hear myself, and Dad looks at me with similar horror and disappointment.

"I know grief shows itself in different ways, but… how could you skip your own brother's funeral?" Dad begins. "I get you're still dealing with everything, and this is your way of coping, but you have to snap out of it. You're angry; at the world, at yourself, hell, I'm sure you're mad at me, too. But please, for my sake, try to get away from the anger. It just makes everything worse for everyone.

"In the meantime, if you *do* decide you want to come, you're very welcome to. But please, *please* come. I just know you'll regret it if you don't."

I remain silent, somehow still seeing the frustration and disappointment in Dad's expression even after turning away from him. I force myself not to dwell on it as I hear him close the door after leaving.

Lucifer returns to my side and smiles. 'I had the perfect opportunity to kill him, you know that? One puncture, clean through the heart, and it's done.'

I can tell he's waiting for me to say something, to burst or explode or start screaming at him, but I keep my mouth shut and cringe at the satisfaction it provides him.

I spend the next few days scouring the internet for everything I can find about Paradise and its location. Just as luck would have it, researchers can't agree on where it may be, and every time I get a lead, I find out it's been debunked. I have to be the unluckiest person alive.

In my mind, I'm just a dumb human who was unfortunate enough to be at the wrong place at the wrong time. Lucifer didn't pick me for this because I'm special; he chose me because Laramie was cursed to fall in love with me—something that makes banishment look like a luxury in comparison.

It's all just shitty luck. I don't deserve an award for surviving (I'd deserve one if I could successfully kill myself) because Lucifer's kept me alive. Maybe I deserve some form of compensation for the trouble, though.

As nice as it is to be unfeeling, I wish I was at least tired. At least then I'd know there's still a part of me unwilling. But the fact that I don't question Lucifer or fight back anymore (granted because I don't want to face the subsequent repercussions of my father dying) just means he's broken me.

I don't smile, I don't frown, I don't even cry. I feel like I've been purged of emotions, void of happiness and sadness, instead filled with an emotionless exterior prohibiting me from feeling anything anymore. I assume that's precisely what Lucifer wants, which makes sense. I've turned into his mindless, obedient slave forced to do whatever he orders. I'm not even tired anymore.

Just numb.

Because of Lucifer and the measly two five-minute breaks I'm permitted a day, I stop eating as much, basically anything for that matter, and am left sequestered in my bedroom. I'm only ever allowed to leave for food and water or the bathroom, and I practically live in the same pair of pyjamas, too depressed even to consider showering—not that I even have enough time for it, anyways.

To say I'm a wreck is so much more than an understatement, especially during Oscar's funeral and wake.

They're held at the same church as Mom's (the wake on the 8th to the 10th and the final burial on the 11th), as Dad said, but I don't go because I can't—because Lucifer won't let me. Instead, I wait until midnight on the 11th, when I can finally see Oscar's grave without Lucifer breathing down my neck.

Putting on a fresh pair of clothes, deodorant and dry shampoo for the first time in days, I quietly pull on my boots, jacket, mitts and hat before sneaking out of the house. Luckily, Dad's fast asleep, and the cemetery isn't far, so I'm able to walk since there's no way I'd be able to drive myself.

Oscar's grave is easy to find since the spot is freshly dug, and there's barely a thin sheet of snow covering the dirt in front of his tombstone.

It's dark, and I can't see that well, but I still feel sick to my stomach to see all but a tombstone commemorating my beloved brother. His full name is written across the stone slab, his identical birthday and death date underneath accompanied by his official army title and rank.

I can't hold back my tears as I take a step towards his granite remnants, my boot crunching softly in the layer of snow that blankets the wet grass beneath. My tongue feels dry and heavy in my mouth, and I can't seem to force anything past my lips. That's no surprise since I haven't spoken since I last talked to

Dad, which was a week ago, now.

It takes a few minutes of glaring at the headstone before I can even begin to think about what to say. What even is there to say? Oscar's gone. He's dead, and it's all my fault. What can I possibly say that would help me—or even begin to reduce my guilt? Nothing, because I deserve it. *I* killed Oscar. Why shouldn't I suffer for it until I inevitably join him?

"This-this isn't how I thought I'd see you again," I whisper, averting my gaze to the snow beneath me. "I, uh, this-this is really hard for me to do. Saying goodbye, I mean. In general, I'm a pretty awkward person already, but when it-when it comes to things like this..." I falter. "I know what you'd say if you were here: *'you did great at Mom's funeral, but now you're tongue-tied? What—I don't even get a 'see you later?'*

"With you, it's harder because I... I have to come to terms with the fact that I... that I killed you. I'm so sorry, Ossy. If I could take everything back, I would. You don't deserve this; *I do.* If anyone should be dying, it should be me. And yet, I'm the only one stuck living.

"I know now that you were struggling too; I can't even begin to imagine what it was like. I know you tried your best to keep up this strong front, but you didn't have to. Maybe you thought keeping the family together and keeping us from falling apart was your responsibility. But it wasn't. I wish I had a chance to tell you that before..." my voice falters. "But I didn't, and I'm sorry. I know what's done is done, and I can't go back in time and stop you, but... I don't know. I guess a part of me is trying to convince myself this," I take a deep breath, shifting on my feet. "I love you, Ossy. I love you *so* much. I promise I'll never forget you."

–TWENTY-THREE–

To Bleed or Not To Bleed

I start crying when I bury myself beneath my bedsheets that night and can't stop after visiting Oscar's grave, too overwhelmed with the unshakable guilt of missing his funeral—so intense that on my way home, I stopped by the nearest convenience store and bought a pack of razor blades (and a bag of Doritos so the employee wouldn't be too suspicious), and as soon as I got home, I cut myself until I couldn't feel the pain anymore. But cuts heal. Death isn't nearly as forgiving.

After that, I couldn't find it in me to do anything but sob into my pillow as my arm smeared blood all over my sheets. I don't care; I don't care about anything anymore except keeping Dad alive.

I struggle to lift my head when I hear what sounds like a knock at my door, but I don't say anything as the door creaks open. I lay my head back against my pillow and listen to the footsteps approaching my bed before the mattress dips under Dad's weight, and he asks, "Maggie, honey? What's the matter?"

I don't have the energy to speak, so I just stay quiet, casually burying my arm beneath my blankets so I won't hurt Dad more than I already have with my self-harm.

He sighs when I don't reply, and I feel bad for ignoring him, but I do so in favour of appeasing Lucifer. Who knows what would happen if he found out I told Dad about him? He'd kill him, point-blank, no questions asked, and then keep me alive just so I can suffer. And then, only then, will I finally have nothing left to live for.

"Maggie, please talk to me. It's been days since we've had a proper conversation. I need to know what's going on with you… how I can help." I don't reply. "I just scheduled an appointment with Dr. Soni for myself. I wanted to suggest you schedule one for yourself too. I'm sure it'd help."

A tear trickles down my cheek. He's trying to get me to see a psychiatrist at both the best and worst time. As much as I need it, I can't have it. Not when Lucifer will find out about it and punish me for trying to 'betray' him.

"Mags, I know things are tough right now, not just because of your mother and b-brother, but you can't just give up. You don't deserve to be in pain like this, Maggie. You don't." I hear the sound of him rubbing his face tiredly before sighing. "Please, honey. I need you to get back on your feet. It's not gonna be easy, and it certainly won't just happen overnight, but I need you to at least try. Try for Alawa, try for me… try for Oscar."

This, *this* is Hell, feeling like I'm betraying my values and my own father. I'm making him think I don't care about Oscar and that I don't care about him when the truth is I do, more than anything. More than I care about myself. He's the one I'm doing this for, the only life I'm trying to spare at this point.

"If… if Oscar were still here, you know he'd agree with everything I've said. You know it. He wouldn't want you to put your mental health last; he'd want you to get up and fight because he knows more than anyone how strong you are. You *can* do it, and you should, for Oscar.

"I can't do anything for you. I can't force you to make an appointment, and I can't force you to go to it. All I can do is encourage you to do this for yourself. I'm here if you need me, and I'd be happy to help you schedule it if you decide to. I won't judge you no matter what you choose. I just want you to do what's best for you."

I can feel Lucifer's presence lingering over me, and I know if I open my mouth, things will come out that will just worsen the whole situation. Maybe I'd let it slip about the razor blades, or maybe I'd say something about my increasing suicidal thoughts, the fact that I attempted and was only stopped by Lucifer himself, or the feeling of helplessness that won't leave ever since Oscar's death.

Either way, I know that as soon as I open my mouth, everything will be so much worse. So, to save Dad the worry and guilt, it's in his best interest if I just keep it all inside.

"And remember, I'm always here if you need me, all right, kiddo?" Silence. "I'm going back to bed now, but please don't hesitate to come to see me anytime if you need me. I'm always happy for the company. I love you."

He gets off the bed and leaves the room without even waiting for a response. It breaks my heart to know he wasn't expecting me to say I love you in return; that's what makes me finally break down.

I try to be quiet, but there's only so much I can do when I'm so far gone, when I'm a trembling, hiccuping and wailing mess. If there's ever a moment I had to identify when I truly felt the worst, it would be now.

The more I think about it, the more I realize how constantly afraid I am, most of the time without cause. Two weeks ago, I attempted suicide after my brother's death, and now I've relapsed back into self-harm from grief. I haven't felt this alone and in pain, since I last stopped cutting when I was what, sixteen? Seventeen?

Regardless of when it was, the familiar feeling makes me queasy no matter how little is in my stomach nowadays. And just knowing I fell back on those old coping methods feels like defeat. Like I've finally failed myself and everyone who loves me. Again.

As much as I'd like to listen to Dad and seek out professional help, once again, I'd be forced to go to a psychiatrist to fix my issues, issues I'm not strong enough to fix myself. Not only that, but I don't doubt that Lucifer physically wouldn't allow me to see anyone.

Speaking of, the demon arrives promptly at six o'clock that morning and watches as I continue with my research. I get my lunch break and resume until six, when he stops me.

'Get into your car and drive to the nearest library,' he says. 'We must exhaust all earthly means to locate Ona.'

My face loses all colour. "C-couldn't I ask Dad to drive me instead?"

His expression falls, and he fixes me with a predatory gaze. 'You said it yourself; you may not involve your father lest he admits you to a corrupt mental facilitation in disbelief.'

Hope drains out of me, and I begin feeling lightheaded—although that could just be from my lack of sleep and permeating unease considering I've barely eaten, barely slept, and barely moved for the past week and a half. It's no surprise I feel so terrible.

I open my suddenly dry mouth to say more, but Lucifer's expression shuts me down. There's no way I can convince him otherwise. He's expecting me to do this, so come what may, I'm doing it.

Bracing myself, I pull my boots, hat and coat on and slip out of the house unseen. My hands shake as I hold the keys to my car and approach the vehicle in the driveway. I haven't touched it since Dad took it in to fix it since my newfound phobia of driving is still so raw. I never thought I'd ever get back into it to drive. Well, before now, there's a lot of things I never thought would happen to me, but here I am despite it all.

My hands tightly clasp around my keys as I wrench open the door and take a deep breath. I plunge myself into the driver's seat, the lingering feeling that I'm succumbing to my demise no longer unsettling but relieving.

I turn the car on with trembling hands and fasten my seatbelt tightly to my chest before beginning to pull out of the driveway. I slowly climb towards twenty kilometres as I pull out of our neighbourhood and head into the main roads. Just seeing the other cars driving by does nothing to abate my already heightened anxiety. I clench my knuckles around the steering wheel until they're white and taught, but I can barely even feel them over the rush of blood roaring in my ears.

Come on, Maggie, you can do it. It's an eight-minute drive, stop stressing so much and just relax. You've driven miles and miles in this car, but one accident is what determines your luck on the roads? Just be safe, and everything's gonna be okay.

The fear of being in another accident constantly looms over me like a silent promise that it'll happen again no matter how I try to avoid it. It's inevitable, right?

Stop it. I snap at myself, taking a deep breath. *Just focus on the road. You're fine. Stop unnecessarily freaking yourself out.*

My paranoia is somewhat eased when I make it to the library

unscathed, park the car and slump to the ground. Fearing Lucifer would get angry with me for stalling, I manage to compose myself quickly and close the car door, locking it with slight difficulty.

I turn around and flinch when I come face to face with Lucifer. He gestures towards the library and vanishes, but I can still sense his presence surrounding me. I stumble inside and approach the receptionist, feebly asking to sign up for a library card. Unease itches under my skin, and I can't help but glance all around me as the woman prints out my card.

"Honey," She whispers, meeting my gaze. I turn to her. "Are you okay?

"Yes. Yes, I-I am."

"Is there someone coming after you? You look like you've seen a ghost." I could burst into laughter, but I don't since I no longer have the energy to. "No, no, seriously, I'm fine."

She reaches over the desk and grabs my hand. "I can have 9-1-1 dialled in less than a second. You tell me, and I'll get the cops here in under a minute. I can help you."

No, you really can't, I want to say. Instead, I bite my tongue and nod, relishing in the warmth of the contact. A part of me doesn't want her to let go; the gesture is just so caring and genuine. "Thank you, seriously, but I'm fine. It's just... my-my brother recently passed away, and I'm still grieving."

She nods sympathetically and backs off. I sigh in relief; I don't even want to imagine what Lucifer would do if she wouldn't let it drop, and I can't let there be any more casualties on my behalf. Not after Mom and now Oscar too...

She hands me the card, and I thank her quietly before wandering around, searching for books about the Garden Of Eden. I immediately approach the 'Religion' section and start scanning the shelves. My vision swims, likely from malnutrition and sleep deprivation, but I shake it off and keep looking. I can't afford to disappoint Lucifer when he can still hurt so many people to keep me focused.

I find three books all about the possible locations of Paradise, and, assuming they'll appease Lucifer, I check them out and shove them in my book bag as I leave the library.

As soon as I start jogging towards the parking lot, it feels like everything catches up to me, and I'm hit with a sudden wave of lightheadedness that makes my consciousness flicker in and out. The next thing I know, I've collapsed on the ground, my face pressed uncomfortably against a pile of snow. It's cold, and I can feel the wet, thick slush beneath me, but I'm too drowsy to care until Lucifer reminds me why I should.

My ears are ringing, and I feel like I'm underwater as I come to. The first thing I realize is that someone is yelling in my ear as my consciousness returns.

'Get up,' Lucifer's voice is terrifyingly low and aggressive. My limbs go numb, and I whine, scared but tired at the same time. 'Get up. *Right. Now.*'

"Whoa, hey, are you okay?"

Warm hands rest on my back, and I instinctively tense but roll over. I blink sluggishly up at the man standing there, looking down at me with concern and fear. Wait a second, is that… Nolan?

"Maggie? Are you okay? Can you hear me?"

I nod slowly and squeeze my eyes shut, trying to blink away my bleariness. Gentle hands are on my arm, and I don't fight back as I'm lifted into a sitting position. I'm so fatigued that I can't even feel the snow beneath me anymore. "What happened? Do you need an ambulance?"

I shake my head. "No, no, I'm… I'm okay. Just… had a faint

spell there."

He looks unconvinced but nods. "Can I help you home or something? You don't look well."

I shake my head. Somehow I can feel Lucifer's anger burning me up. Sweat trickles down my forehead despite the frigidity. "N-no, no, I'm good. My car is just over there—" I point to the parking lot, "—so I'm okay. I'll manage. But thanks anyway."

"You sure?"

'Get up.' Lucifer hisses. 'Go to your car and go home.'

I nod a little bit too quickly. "Yeah, yeah. I'm sure." I force myself onto my feet and disregard the way I sway. Nolan mirrors my movements, getting to his feet to hold me still. In a split-second decision, I know what I have to do.

"You have to run," I whisper in his ear. "I know it sounds crazy, but Lucifer was controlling you, and now he's using me. Save yourself before it's too late."

I push myself away from Nolan and focus on putting one foot in front of the other as I leave without looking back.

–TWENTY-FOUR–

The Concept of Life

y head is pounding, and I can distantly hear Lucifer screaming at me as I stumble to my car. I don't have enough energy to focus on his words as I use all of it that remains just to make it to the vehicle.

I make a beeline for it. My vision swims, and my legs buckle with every step, a thick sickness churning in my gut, but I don't dare stop.

It takes me longer than I'd like to admit to settle in the driver's seat with the way I fumble with the keys like a character in a horror movie who's about to be murdered (God, I wish). Finally, I unlock the car and collapse inside, closing my eyes while catching my breath.

'Are you even listening to me?' Lucifer seethes. I flinch and open my eyes to find him standing in the doorway, glowering in rage. 'How dare you ignore me? You are nothing compared to me. Do you even understand what powers I possess? I could kill you in an instant.'

"I may as well be dead with the way I'm living now!" I snap back. "I'm done with this, with *all of this*. I cannot TAKE IT ANYMORE!" I yell, rage burning up inside me. I don't even have the sense of mind to consider what I'm saying to Lucifer, too overwhelmed by my fury. "LOOK AT WHAT YOU'RE DOING TO ME. I DON'T EVEN CARE WHAT YOU DO ANYMORE! DO ME A FAVOUR AND KILL ME. I DON'T GIVE A *FUCK!*"

The sight of Lucifer's shocked expression makes me smile as I slam the door shut in his face before turning on the car and speeding out of the parking lot. My vision is blurry, and I feel like I could pass out at any given moment, but I don't stop. As much as my common sense screams at me not to be driving when I'm so clearly out of it, all I want to do is go home, and by God, *nothing* is getting in the way of that at this point.

I could've called a cab, called Dad, or taken the bus home, but instead, I risked everything. Why?

Because I don't care, I genuinely don't care.

I *want* to die.

I crank the radio, and "The Other Side Of Paradise" by *Glass Animals* blasts from the speakers as an unsettling stillness drapes over me. The air feels thick and syrupy as time slows down. The hairs on the back of my neck stand up, and my gut tells me too late that something is seriously wrong.

Déjà vu solidifies in every inch of my body as the familiar sensation of a car colliding into mine settles over the deceitfully calm atmosphere.

The fact that it's such a familiar situation unnerves me as I lay at the brink of consciousness, trapped within my car. One second I'm swaying my head to the music, and the next—complete devastation.

I smile and close my eyes. *Just what I wanted.*

I cling to consciousness, my whole body encased in a fiery agony that strips me of my strength. I crack an eye open and look up to see Lucifer grinning at me through the window.

'How's that?' He spits.

I have just enough energy to raise my right arm and flip him off. He snarls and disappears in a blink. Immediately, I drop my arm, exhausted. All I can do is lay there, trapped, blinking sluggishly as I fight to stay awake. Wait, why am I fighting to stay awake? I don't even know anymore. It would be so easy just to fall asleep and never wake up…

I can feel the cuts littered across my face alongside the steady spurt of blood gushing from my side, where my body is pinned to the car. My left arm is wedged to my side, and I can't move it; it aches worse than anything I've ever experienced and had I the energy, I would've been screaming in pain. But it just dies in my sore throat with a gurgle of hot blood.

An icy stillness spreads rapidly over my body. My ribs feel like they're straining against my midsection, and my lungs throb with each laborious inhale. I can barely fight the exhaustion weighing me down; I'm just too tired to stay awake. And I have no reason to, so why should I?

My mind screams at me to stay awake and call 9-1-1, or even Dad, but exhaustion prevails, and my eyes roll back into my head as I slump forward, unconscious.

I drift in and out. I know I'm not awake by the hazy weightless sensation that overtakes me, but I can still hear a steady beeping and am aware enough to know that I'm at least somewhat coherent.

Someone clears their throat, but the sound is garbled as if underwater.

"M-Maggie?" Dad's voice cracks, and my heart breaks. Oh, right. *That's* why I stayed. "Maggie? C-can you hear me?"

Like every nightmare I've had where my lips are sewn shut, I can't speak; I can't open my mouth or produce any sort of sound from my aching throat. I remain still and half-asleep, unable to speak or move in any way besides an uncontrollable twitch in pain now and again.

"I hope you can hear me," He sniffs. "'Cause this would be r-real awkward if you couldn't." He giggles joylessly, and I wish I could do the same. I only realize he's holding my hand when he releases it long enough to give me something. "I-I thought you might appreciate a friend so... so it doesn't feel so scary and unfamiliar."

He carefully lifts my right arm and tucks something underneath it. It's soft and feels like...

Bearley.

He gently lays my hand on top of the bear's stomach and grabs it once more, gently rubbing circles over the bandages with his thumb. "I love you, Maggie. I love you so *so* much and... and I'm so sorry it had to end like this." He pauses. "Why'd you leave the house? Why didn't you ask me to drive you somewhere? What the *hell* were you doing out in the world all alone like that?"

I wish I could tell him everything. I wish I could cry into his shoulder and confess to him everything that's been going on with me, but I can't, and it's too late now.

Dad sobs louder this time. "Why..." He mutters over and over, voice wet with misery. "Not you too... *not you too...*" He chokes on his words but recovers quickly. "Maggie, honey, please... you can't leave me too... you just can't... I need someone left. I can't... I can't lose my little girl. I just can't... You've gotta do this for me. You have to get better. You just have to!

Please, Maggie… You're everything I have left..."

Misery fills my throat like a balloon inflating, but it almost immediately morphs into a fiery explosion of agony. I want to cough, but I can't. Everything hurts, especially my heart right now. How could I have been so stupid? How could I let this happen? I wasn't thinking, and now Dad's left to suffer. I can't imagine how he'll deal with this. Mom's dead, Oscar's dead, and now I'm dying and leaving him completely alone.

Pain follows me like the promise of suffering, and there's nothing I can do to rid myself of it. Death permeates my very existence like the rancid stench of burning flesh.

Dad squeezes my hand, leaning in close. I feel his tears dampen my hospital gown. "Everything's okay. You… you're okay. I love you so much, baby. If… if you can't make it—" He falters. "Do something for me, would you? Please, say hi to Ala and Os for me, would you? Tell them that I… that I love them and miss them so much. And that… that I'll be okay. And—"

An electric jolt suddenly pierces my mind and body. Like before, I have no control over the way my body seizes and spasms aggressively or the shockwaves that course through me. It hurts so badly, and a wrecked sob shakes me to my core, but I swallow down the rest, allowing the spasms to ripple through me like tiny bolts of electricity striking at random.

I take one final gulp of air and feel myself drifting away, my whole body stiffening as the pain melts from my system. It's bliss; it's peaceful and welcomed. My body sinks back against the bed, and I feel my heartbeat grow quieter and quieter. The last thing I hear is a steady beep piercing the air.

Finally.

-TWENTY-FIVE-

Rebirth

ilence. The room is pitch black.

Through squinting eyes, the outline of the walls is barely visible, their perspective constantly shifting the longer they're gazed upon. It isn't clear whether or not the walls *do*, in fact, end—with the inky texture of the atmosphere, it could be either and would be impossible to tell.

It's a desolate place full of nothing. The gentle pad of feet against the floor is what disrupts the uneasy silence, the sound bouncing off the walls like a church bell as a soft and dim light shines on one side of the room, exposing its surroundings. The walls no longer appear black, as the illuminating light brandishes alabastrine walls. With it, the room is substantially less menacing and feels more like a vivid, new dream, yet one that becomes foggy the more and more you try to focus on it. It's the calm before the storm, coming to bring an artificial sense of peace before havoc is wrought.

A figure begins to form after stepping out from the darkness, frail like a newborn baby. First, her feet and legs appear as though an invisible mould is filled with a liquid-esque substance. Slowly but surely, her torso and arms materialize, then her neck and lastly, her head.

Unbothered by her sudden creation, she takes careful steps, the room travelling with her. Her pace is slow and steady, and the room becomes brighter and brighter the further she walks.

I don't question where I am or why I'm here as I mindlessly wander the dark room.

I stop only when I see something a few steps away from me. We stand in silence for a few moments before they elongate their arm, beckoning me forward. I'm hesitant to oblige but inevitably approach and stop just in front of them. They close their eyes, and I look down to see a near-blinding light emitting from beneath their clothes, a string of which runs down their arm through a vein, glowing brighter than the rest as it reaches their hand. The vein splits off to each finger until their palm and fingertips all glow with a brilliant blue light. I'm given no time to react before they gently place their hand on the side of my head, and a sensation like I've never felt before hits me.

It's as though their fingers adhere to my forehead as the energy flows through me in two currents; one that streams to my chest where it begins to collect in my upper torso and the other that accumulates in my head.

A sudden pressure distends beneath the skin of my shoulder blades before splitting into two wide apertures spanning from the small of my back up to my shoulder blades. I glance over my shoulder just in time to see two brilliant cerulean wings extend from the fissures with a glossy sheen. They slowly materialize from their transparent state into thick umber wings, simultaneous with a similar split that pierces my temples.

From my very scalp emerges two thick horns that slowly grow

and curl towards one another until connecting into a wide ring that blinds me with a harsh white glare. Tears gather in my eyes from the burn until the light clears enough to provide me with a newfound means of sight alongside a subdued warmth and comfort. I blink moisture from my eyes and take a moment to adjust my equilibrium from the newfound weight of the horns and my wings.

The figure pulls their hand away from me, and the absence of touch is what brings me back to reality. They approach me, producing a gold robe and lightweight armour they delicately secure around my body. They fasten the attached length of the cord around my neck before repeating the process with the twine cinched around my waist, allowing my wings to move without restraint.

I absentmindedly fish a hand in my right pocket, feeling a small round object within. I pull it from the folds and stare at it for a few moments, surveying the gold carvings spanning across its surface. *Conversion Clock,* my mind produces. I stare at the device as I take in the new information I suddenly seem to possess, confused and bewildered.

I look back up and shove the device into my pocket. The figure from before is gone, replaced by faint white light spilling into the distance. It's so benign that I almost miss it, but when I see it, I concentrate on it and approach cautiously.

Bathed in the light is an old wooden rocking chair supporting a teddy bear atop it. I stare at the plushie and lean into the beam, casting a shadow across the chair, and the cream-coloured stuffed animal, his fur splattered with various tints complemented by the long red ribbon tied loosely around its neck. The thing that stands out most is the army commendation medal attached to the bear's chest—the gold surface brandishing an eagle with wings spread, the green fabric of the award almost enveloping him.

I reach out and pull the bear towards me, surveying it closely. Holding it gingerly, I bring him up to my face, his forehead just barely grazing my lips as I absentmindedly press my fingers into his paw. It was something I didn't even realize I did, nor expected it to do anything, certainly not trigger a voice from the bear's paw that says, *"I love you, Maggie. You're my little angel."*

The words unlock something within me, releasing a dam whose contents seep into my very being. As soon as the words register in my mind, a warm feeling washes away everything else in my body with years worth of memories that hit me in a fraction of a second. My entire life flashes before my eyes and my senses are overwhelmed with the presence of new colours, colours I hadn't been able to process before now. My whole world is overturned; there's so much I've been missing all my life.

I stumble from the ray of light and grip Bearley with trembling hands as fresh tears burst from my eyes. I look down, overwhelmed by the memories resurfacing so suddenly, and I stagger backward, losing my footing.

I tumble harshly onto the floor, lifting my trembling body to stand uneasily as I stare forward blankly, protectively clutching Bearley to my chest.

I lift my head from where it's buried against Bearley's and startle upon seeing an unfamiliar figure approach me. My eyes widen when I feel the palpable energy radiating off them, and I stare at God through blurry vision. Their gaze feels as though it's burning me as they stand there, mighty and potent, and say, *'You, Magda Mercy, have been Reversed.'*

-TWENTY-SIX-

Everything Will Fall Into Place

he second I blink, I'm engulfed in the darkness once more.

I drop Bearley, startled by the sudden emptiness, and can do little besides watch in abject horror as he disappears mid-air, leaving me well and truly alone.

"H-hello?" My voice quivers as I speak. "A-Az?" Desperation overtakes me as I scour the vast room for any indication of another presence, to no avail. "Hello? God? GOD?"

Like the snap of a tree branch, something shatters within me. A sudden surge of memories overwhelms me again, but this time they aren't my own, but Az's from their conception.

I see Az and Ona's generation at the beginning of time, not as a family but not so much as strangers either. Az watched Ona nurture Earth from its infancy, watched their attempts to actualize a sustainable earth by creating the other planets in our Solar System. Ona threads our world into existence and tethers their Grace to the core of the Earth—The Crux, my mind supplies—therefore binding themselves to the Earth, prohibiting any means of destroying them without destroying, too, the Earth.

I see Ona peel the surface of the Earth into two to create a shadow of the real world as their domain; Paradise, they name it, somewhere inaccessible without either god's Grace to perforate—*That's* why no one knows where Paradise is. It's not somewhere *on* Earth; it *is* Earth, just another dimension of it, like Heaven for angels—I see the creation of Adam and Eve, created immortal as Ona's first human prototypes to be their defenders and the leaders of humanity. I watch as Az seeks to create Heaven but instead creates Hell, abandoning it when they realize what it became before developing Heaven—the first glimpse of which I get leaves me speechless.

Pathways criss-cross around the open area, bright white icy floors with golden waves trapped amidst it. White clouds lay in uneven textures, creating pillowy hills around the pathways resembling grass. There's a faint blue outline streaking across the sky in a triangular dome shape as if the canopy of Heaven itself. The ceiling resembles the tall and elegant roof of a church—ovular and round where various other structures stand tall beneath, many of which contrasting angels roam around to and fro.

Ona is the first to take on a human-like form between Az and themselves. Their irises flash a kaleidoscope of all the colours of the rainbow while the whites of their eyes capture a universe within. Their face is almost ordinary save for the subtle beauty throughout their features; smooth, unblemished pearly skin (except for the constellation of black moles and freckles scattered across every inch of their form; an inverted galaxy), natural thick eyebrows, pursed plump lips, and a wide, upturned nose. Their hair flows in an iridescent waterfall down their shoulders, black with the same galaxy gleaming in the tufts as their eyes. A dark green cloak is draped across their head, the material adorned with intricate purple designs.

It's then that Az takes their respective form—dark skin, gleaming eyes, a kind smile, and neat black curls—and approaches Ona on Earth.

'Have you no will of your own?' Ona's voice is thick with regality and contempt as they speak. *'You* dare *create your abode upon my own and intrude upon my creation?'*

Az shakes their head. *'That is not my intention, Ona. Your abilities exceed my own; I am unable to create the expanse you can—I must settle where there already is existence if that is what you will allow.'*

Ona laughs. *'You have built your haven already, without considering the intrusion upon my domain. I am the superior here. Have you forgotten already?'* Ona glances down at their humans as they momentarily glisten with a blue sheen. Az looks on in confusion before Ona continues. *'There is no coexistence that can happen between us, Az. You and I both know this. Let our creations battle on our behalf to decide the worthy Creator, the God of this realm.'*

Az resigns themselves, and I watch as millions upon millions of angels emerge from Heaven and into a merciless war with the equivalent millions of humans. It takes a few seconds for Az to realize what the blue sheen signified:

One by one, Az's angels are turning to stone mid-battle.

Panic is evident in their expression as more and more angels' fall. None of Ona's humans have yet to face any harm. A raging battle ensues, and I barely notice Lucifer devising his rebellion with Ona. It's bloody, and soon, many humans begin to fall, the unavoidable casualties of such a war. While Az pleads with Ona to stop after witnessing millions of angels' murder, Ona barely bats an eye when a human falls.

'Ona!' Az shouts when another angel is petrified. The only angels remaining are Lucifer and his associates. *'How can you remain so uncaring while your offspring fall?'*

Ona shrugs. *'They are my warriors and do as I say. They are nothing more.'*

To Ona, we—humans—are nothing more than pawns of power for their manipulation. We were created to serve and die for them—something that doesn't matter because, to Ona, we are expendable.

'I plead mercy, Ona; I submit. End this bloodshed.'

Ona smiles deviously. *'Just as I anticipated, you—'*

The distant sound of the earth splitting open interrupts the god mid-sentence. Lucifer, his demons, and Ona all turn to face the entrance of Hell that looms below, where the traitorous angels plummet before the earth reseals itself and the air stills once more.

Ona barely has time to turn around when Az appears and plunges their fist into their chest, ripping a small blue fragment of Ona's Grace out in one swift movement. Before long, Az has Ona's wrists bound with the newly-fashioned shackles and says, *'Humans should not exist to die for your causes. You do not create life to control how it exists.'*

Ona's visibly speechless as the scene in my head shifts.

Well. That is so *not* how Lucifer told me things transpired.

New memories come to light, and I see a dozen or so angels standing amidst the vastness of Heaven, one in particular almost cast aside.

'Laramie—' Az barks, to which the angel straightens her posture, *'—shall be your angelic name.'* She looks up and nods firmly. The sudden realization hits me that this memory is from the beginning of angels' existence after the war with Ona— more specifically, the creation of Laramie.

This, *this* is Laramie.

Not only that but Laramie… Laramie's a *she*.

Ever since Lucifer, he's painted such a distorted picture of who Laramie is in my head. He made me associate her with my suffering and pain, evil and torment. But that's just what Lucifer represents; I have yet to understand who the real Laramie is; all I know of her is from the lies I'd been tricked into believing.

The memory shifts to Laramie hovering on Earth staring in fascination at… me. It shifts again, and I'm shown Laramie in Heaven standing in the presence of an angel, and although it's a scene from the past, I can feel the anger radiating from them.

The scene plays out like I'm fast-forwarding a movie in my head; Laramie begs the angel—Razael—to help me before Razael reveals it was all a trial to test angels' preparedness for emotions. I see Laramie's wings stripped and halo broken. I watch the Powers drag her to The Passage before casting her from her only home, and I see Laramie fall.

Scene after scene flashes in my head like a complete recollection of my life since Laramie began watching over me. I watch as she rejects Lucifer's offer to be a demon and saves me from Nolan, and I watch as she slowly deteriorates while defending me. I see Lucifer intervening to ruin my life, controlling Nolan into assaulting me, killing Mom, causing my accident, and hurting my family beyond repair.

I see Laramie embrace me, and I subconsciously wrap my arms around myself where the angel had wrapped hers as the pieces fall into place. Laramie had hugged me, had reached out, and tenderly brushed against my cheek before her body became stone.

The memories fade away as I'm left with the haunting image of Laramie's stone-coated body burning into my mind.

I stand in stunned silence and stare blankly at the darkness in front of me. I can barely stand the dread permeating my body, not with my heightened emotions dragging me down. I can barely move, and all I can focus on is how unnecessary Laramie's death was, how unnecessary all of what she and I had to endure was.

When I blink, I find myself lying on a cot. I startle from the sudden environmental shift and look up to see Az sitting at the foot of the bed, smiling softly as they regard me.

I look around, realizing that the room is identical to my bedroom. All I can do is let out an appreciative hum as I momentarily pretend that I'm still alive and that everyone I love is okay.

'My child...' Az begins quietly. *'I apologize for the pain inflicted upon both you and Laramie. The Authoritarian Razael was assigned to Laramie, one of the many I assumed to oversee task regulation. I don't have time to regulate every small incident here in Heaven; therefore, I was unaware of what a mess all of this had become until it was too late and Laramie had withered from existence. This should not have been allowed to happen, and I relay my deepest condolences for what transpired beyond my understanding.'*

I can't meet Az's eyes. I look away and hesitate, feeling just as vulnerable as I did the day I was admitted to the hospital after my first accident. Exhaustion overtakes me, whether from the strenuous mental field trip I just took or from being, oh I don't know, *Repersed* (reincarnated) I can't determine.

"Where... where were you when Oscar was forced to enlist?" My voice is wobbly and weak, but a sudden burst of anger provides me with the confidence I need. "Where were you when Lucifer was meddling with the conscience of a human to... to make him... where were you when my mom died? When Oscar k-killed himself and I attempted? Or when Lucifer fucking blackmailed me into doing his bidding while all I did was pray for death? When I was laying in that hospital bed fucking *dying.*

"My whole family was being slaughtered one-by-one, and you didn't care. You didn't do anything. And not just for me, but for everyone else—us, humans, people of Earth. You didn't care when my whole life went to shit, or even when it ended."

Az's silence provides me ample time to think through what I've said. Scared and embarrassed, I realize how stupid it was to yell at the *literal God,* and I lower my gaze, bracing myself for their rebuke; maybe they'll banish me just as Razael banished Laramie, and I'll have ruined my last chance of saving myself.

'I understand your anger,' Az says, rising to their feet. *'I will allow you time to rest. When you feel better, we shall discuss further how to continue.'*

I watch Az take one last look at me before leaving, their form dispersing into Heaven the second they vacate the room. It's unsettling, the suddenness of their absence when they leave the room. It feels as though one second I'm bathed in the warmth of the sun itself, and the next, I'm cast in the icy depths of the deepest, darkest ocean.

Turning away from where Az just stood, I catch a glimpse of my reflection in the mirror on the far wall. Since I've not yet seen myself as an Angel, the dissimilarities are appalling, especially to see myself in another body and lack recognition of it. I can't see my own eyes through the glow radiating from those *things* that protrude from my head. My skin is unnaturally smooth and unblemished, and my features are different; they're perfectly symmetrical. I still look somewhat like I did, enough to know whom I'm supposed to look like yet altered to the point where I still look like a stranger.

I've never felt confident with my appearance—this should be a dream come true—but it's not. Instead, it's become my worst nightmare; looking in the mirror and seeing a stranger staring right back at me.

I tug on my stupidly perfect brown hair, the presence of my halo halting me from ripping at my scalp. *Well, there goes that plan.*

I feel like every physical flaw has been extracted from my system, leaving me as this perfect cookie-cutter rendition of myself. As uplifting as it should feel to be "perfect," instead, it's just… it feels wrong—so very *wrong*.

I fall back against the blankets, staring at the unmarked skin of my forearm, the previously scarred skin clear in my mind if I close my eyes. I can even see the blood oozing from the cuts I made not even twenty-four hours ago. But when I open my eyes again, the skin is completely unmarred, the way it should have been.

"Start over…" A spark of hope ignites within me. I let my arm fall flat against my chest, but the longer I lay there, the more I feel deeply disturbed. I can't seem to identify why until I realize I can't feel my pulse. My chest is just hollow. I can't even feel the rise and fall of my breathing because I'm not. I'm not breathing; angels don't breathe, *I'm not breathing*—

What am I anymore? I feel inhuman, but worse than that, I feel like a *monster*, even though the real monsters, *demons*, are the ones with a heart and lungs.

I force my thoughts back to Laramie and what she did for me—how she saved me all because she was an angel gifted with emotions who fell in love with a human, with *me*. A part of me still doesn't believe that an angel fell in love with me and ended up turning to stone by her own volition.

The amount of pain Laramie must have felt on my behalf, the sacrifices she made for me…

Suddenly it's all too easy to look back on my life and put the pieces together. The things that seemed too unreal to happen, how lucky I'd be in times of peril, as frequent as they were upon Laramie's presence. Even if only for the short amount of time Laramie followed me, it was still enough. It was *something*.

My brain produces thoughts. Feelings. Memories. All of which plague my mind and keep my subconscious occupied.

And yet, all I want to do now is sleep.

Forever.

...Peacefully.

TWENTY-SEVEN

Reunification

ou're unwell.'

Az's sudden presence startles me; my eyes snap open, and I roll over to see them looking down at me, their expression worried and scrutinizing. I awkwardly pull myself into a sitting position and hang my head, unable to meet their gaze. *'Whatever is the matter?'*

"I-I can't… be like this," I gesture to myself, sighing as I struggle to find the right words. "I'm not me. I'm someone else. Too perfect. It's just… it's wrong." I impulsively scratch my arms where my scars used to be.

'I had assumed you would prefer this version of yourself. However, if it is your preference to appear as you did when human, I will restore you to your desired state.'

They tentatively approach me, and I have to suppress the urge to flinch back when they reach for my forehead. Their middle and pointer fingers press against my head, and I tense as a wave of familiarity sweeps over me before they pull away. I expectantly turn to the mirror and feel tears building behind my eyes at the sight of whom I used to be before. I never expected to be relieved when looking at myself in a mirror to see the permanent pimples covering my face, but I am.

Glancing down at my arms proves saddening, however, when I see the scars crisscrossing my skin once again, some fresh and some old. It's poetic in a way; no matter how much I grow and mature, I can never escape my past. My scars are a part of who I am and what I've overcome to be where I am today.

The sudden need to see Laramie concentrates beneath my skin as an itch. The need to see her, to say goodbye, closure to move on.

I tell Az, and they nod as though they anticipated I'd ask. *'If that is what you feel is right for you, we shall go to visit Laramie's statue on Earth. I will do all in my power to aid your mental recovery, for I have seen what pain your mortal life entailed, and I regret that the banishment of Laramie caused more.'*

Somehow, I can tell they mean what they're saying, which satisfies me more than I'd expected.

I rise and follow close behind Az upon leaving the replica of my bedroom, briskly strolling across a golden pathway that leads through Heaven towards The Passage. All the angels around us part and stare at Az, telling me it's not often the god takes on a mortal form. I simply fall in line and try to hide behind Az, intimidated by all the eyes on me. I try telling myself they're looking at Az, but I can't help but worry they're all looking at me.

I lean into Az, subconsciously using them as a shield like I've done before with Oscar.

Oh. God. *Oscar.*

Curiosity latches onto me and doesn't let go. I hurry to catch up with Az, quickening my pace, so we're walking alongside one another. When I weakly tug on their arm, they immediately stop and turn to face me. I almost flinch at the abruptness. *'Yes?'*

"May I ask what happened to... Oscar? My brother?"

'I hoped you'd ask. Your brother is fine. He's been Repersed.'

For a few moments, I'm entirely speechless. Before now, I'd accepted that the next time I'd see Oscar is in death. Hell, now that I'm an angel, I thought it'd be even less likely that I'd ever get to see him again. But… now I'm being told that I can.

The need to see him, to hug my little brother, and tell him how much I love him overwhelms me. The only thing that stops me from completely overturning the entirety of Heaven to find him is knowing just how vast it is while I have no idea where Oscar may be, the possibilities are quite literally endless.

"Why? Not that I'm complaining, of course."

'For you, child. After learning what became of Laramie and upon my discovery of your brother's death, I knew what had to be done as a form of recompense. It was by pure chance that you passed away shortly after he did. Well, by Lucifer's interference, that is.'

I grimace at the bitter reminder of Lucifer, my hands tightening scarcely. "He's here? And he's okay?"

'Yes. Go and find him. I expect you have much you need to say.'

I fail to thank Az, too preoccupied with thoughts of Oscar as I stumble into the crowd of angels.

In any other instance, I'd feel suffocated to the point of a panic attack right then and there, but my determination to find Oscar doesn't let me consider stopping as I shove my way through the angels and crane my neck around. There's a surprising amount of them that resemble Oscar, which only exacerbates my frustration the more and more I think I've found Oscar only to turn the being around and realize it's decidedly not him.

Too consumed by my crusade, I accidentally sprint into someone at top speed. My wings manage to stop me from falling, somehow regaining my balance, and when I look up, it's Oscar who's standing in front of me.

"M-Maggie?" His eyes widen when they meet mine, staring at me in complete disbelief, relief and abject horror. "Maggie? I-is that you?"

Hearing Oscar say my name mitigates any worry I'd had that I wouldn't be able to find him or that maybe Az was lying and Oscar wasn't here. But they weren't, and Oscar's here.

"O-Ossy?" I can't stop myself from weeping like a baby as I bodycheck him in a hug just like I did the day he came home on his leave. I hold him as though I'll never get a chance to again, with all the strength I can muster from my newfound angelic status.

Oscar's shoulders start trembling, and I can feel his face scrunched up where it's pressed into my shoulder. I don't bother holding back, either, as I allow myself to sob, pulling him as close as humanly (or would it now be angelically?) possible.

"I-I'm so happy to see you," He sniffs, his voice muffled as he clings to my robe. He chokes out a gut-wrenching cry as his words slur together into barely audible ramblings of, "I'm sorry."

Nothing can compare to this moment, in both pure joy and despair. It resembles all those instances where Oscar would return from the military, even if only for a month, and surprise me, just like he did this past time. Only now it's a relief that I get to see him again after coming to terms with the fact that he was finally gone for good. I almost don't believe he's actually here in my arms, and I would do everything in my power to make sure it stays that way.

We cry in each other's company for a good few minutes before I even consider letting go. When I finally do, I struggle to, not only because I got to hug my dead brother but also because we're entangled in a near bone-crushing hug. As I pull away, I wipe away the tears staining my cheeks while Oscar glances down after a moment. His expression immediately drops, eyes as unchangeable as the ocean itself falling still and morose. Upon following his gaze, I realize I'm brandishing the fresh cuts criss-crossing my arm to him. Instinctively, I shove my arm behind my back, but it's too late.

"Mags..." His voice is hollow and gravelly, and I can feel the disappointment oozing from his tone. "Show me."

I hesitate for a few seconds before slowly bringing my arm back out in front of me. I cringe at the raw skin split all across my inner forearm, and Oscar looks at me with the utmost sorrow and regret. "Maggie, I..." He gently grasps my arm as though afraid to hurt me and grimaces. "Jesus, Mags... What happened?"

"It's... kind of a long story."

He smirks. "Well, it's a good thing you have a literal eternity to tell me." The smile he prompts from me is small, but it's a smile nonetheless.

I explain everything beginning with Laramie and her influence on our lives. Oscar gets angrier and angrier the more he learns, and I don't blame him one bit since I, too, grow more and more irate with Lucifer the more I relay.

"That demented bastard" Is the first thing he says when I finish my explanation; I can't help but laugh. "You always know just what to say, Ossy."

He smiles sadly. "So... Laramie, huh? Guess she chose the wrong sibling to fall for."

I roll my eyes, but I can't seem to find it in me to genuinely be annoyed with the idiot after everything that's transpired. "Actually, what this means is we've finally proven who the superior sibling is by an entirely unbiased celestial appraiser. So, hah."

Indignant, Oscar shakes his head. "Nuh-uh!"

"Strong argument there, Ossy."

When he laughs, I grin, my chest overwhelmed with joy, an emotion I'd almost forgotten what it feels like until now.

The placidity is stripped from me when I remember what I'm supposed to be doing with Az. As much as I don't want to leave Oscar ever again, Laramie's statue calls me to settle something within myself that can't wait.

"Listen, Os, I, uh, I've gotta go. Az-er, God and I are going to Earth so that I can see Laramie's statue."

He nods. "Would you mind checking in on Dad if you're already heading that way? I can't imagine how he's fairing all on his own."

"I'll make sure to check in on him. Speaking of which, he says hi, and told me to tell you he loves and misses you so much. And that it'll be okay."

"Why would Dad tell you to tell me that? How'd he know we'd see each other?"

"It was while I was on my deathbed. He prefaced it by saying, if I happen to see you or... or Mom."

Oscar's expression falls, and he nods. "Oh."

"Sorry, Os, but I have to go. I'll see you when I come back. I love you."

He pulls me into one final hug before we part ways. "I love you too, Mags. I'll be right here when you get back."

As physically painful as it is to leave Oscar, I dolefully return to Az, falling into step beside them with my vision trained on the floor.

We proceed towards The Passage in a much-needed peaceful silence. I look up, suddenly, to see The Fulfillment Room just ahead of us. Az makes no move to stop, but I can't help my hesitation to take in the Seraphim and Elders congregating within. Seeing the Seraphim standing in front of me feels unreal, especially the wings that frame the halos over their heads, the ones that blanket their lower legs and feet and the last that span almost double their size, a bright titian-gold, warm and sunny, like the spirits of a blazing campfire.

Turning to the Elders, I'm visibly taken aback. They don't look even remotely like angels; I can barely even comprehend their appearance, constant orbs of shifting energy with rings crisscrossing one another in a hypnotic swirl that makes me dizzy.

I quickly catch up with Az and recognize the faint outline of The Passage ahead, its familiarity provoking some form of excitement within my chest that beckons me forward.

Besides a Power standing guard in front of the rift, the area around us is barren. His eyes widen as he recognizes Az's presence and straightens, defensively wielding his blade in anticipation of an attack, not from us but from anyone defiant enough to try.

'God,' says the Power as Az stops before him.

'Step aside,' Az commands.

He nods and steps aside. Az approaches The Passage and raises their hand towards the abyss until it rests flat against it. I watch, transfixed, as their hand begins to melt, blue beams of power consumed by the vortex.

Heaven rumbles softly before the murkiness clears and the circular opening finally reveals the sky beyond. Az hums in approval as their hand melts in reverse until materializing back to normal. They tug their hand away from the portal and turn sharply towards the Power; a silent understanding passes between them.

'Are you ready?' Az asks, approaching the entrance.

I nod, turning back to the sky in front of me as I stretch my back and experimentally spread my wings behind me. It's a sensation I can't quite put into words, something that feels both natural and unnatural at the same time.

Az stares straight ahead as two massive brown wings spread from their back ten times wider and taller than mine, their razor-sharp feathers, unlike the birdlike softness of mine.

We slowly approach The Passage, and I barely comprehend Az's presence beside me as I confidently cross the threshold.

TWENTY-EIGHT

Make It All Stop

pon finally arriving at Dad's house, I look down on it from afar with unease. The only visible light from outside is the one in the kitchen and dining room, and it almost feels as though the house knows Mom, Oscar, and I are gone with the dark cloud that looms over it.

I come to a slow stop in front of the living room windows. I carefully peer through them, given a clear view of Dad standing in the kitchen on the phone, his back facing me as he leans against the kitchen counter, hunched over like he's given up, and by his dishevelled state, he may just have.

My eyes brim with tears, and I slowly enter the house. Dad's conversation grows louder with each tentative step I take.

"Um, yes, okay. I suppose that should be fine," He says tiredly, running a hand through his hair. "She never expressed a preference for either because… well, because of her age. Neither of us were prepared nor expected her… death. Yeah. Mhm. Thank you. Okay, that should be good. If she were still here, I think she'd appreciate being buried next to… to her brother. Okay, okay, yes, thank you. Bye." Dad rushes to hang up the phone, bracing himself against the counter with his hands. He hangs his head as he slowly begins to cry, his shoulders shaking with the force of his sobs.

"Dad..." I manage, taking a few small steps towards him. I fumble with my hands as I stare at the back of his head, beyond worried and upset. He weeps as though he's in physical pain, and my brain screams at me to hug him just as I did with Oscar, but Az grabs my shoulder before I have a chance to make a move to do so.

When it dawns on me that I physically can't touch nor comfort Dad, the realization that this is what Laramie was forced to endure after being banished unites me more with my guardian angel than I've felt since discovering her presence.

Tears pour down my face as I stare at Dad and his puffy, bloodshot eyes. His face is worn and aged like I'm seeing him in ten or fifteen years, yet in reality, it's been mere hours since I saw him last.

The house is a mess. Papers are scattered across the dining table; the kitchen counter is covered with unpacked groceries, and the sink is filled with dirty dishes. The furniture has been moved around slightly; the couch has a pillow and blanket on it, and I realize it's where Dad's been sleeping instead of his—and previously Mom's—bed. Cardboard boxes labelled 'Maggie' take up all the space in front of the television.

I wish I could do something, *anything* to ease Dad's anguish. Even just tell him Oscar, and I are okay. I was the one who left him all alone; who went driving, reckless and uncaring about whatever happened. I was an idiot, and now Dad has to suffer the consequences of my stupidity.

"Is... is there anything at all I—or you can do for him?" I plead to Az. "Anything at all? Even just... just guarantee that he'll be okay."

Az considers my request before approaching Dad. Upon initial contact, his fingertips glow with white-gold-blue energy that amalgamates into Dad's forehead, and once he pulls away, Dad lowers his hands from his face and wipes his tears away. His body is still wracked with trembling, but it's beginning to lessen as his cries become sniffles and a sad smile spreads across his face. He takes a deep breath and staggers to the couch, where he begins to settle, half-heartedly pulling the blanket over his legs and waist. Closing his eyes, he rests his head on the pillow, and I watch his breathing deepen until he falls fast asleep.

Landing on a gravel path just behind Az, I let my wings fold behind me before surveying our surroundings for Laramie's statue. I turn to the apartment building, and before Az can even so much as glance in my direction, I take off towards the site, wandering around in search of the statue. Turning to the back of the building, I come to find a group of construction workers having a discussion during their final break of the night as the sun begins to set.

"What even was it?" A bald, middle-aged man with a bushy beard and square-shaped face says, the oldest of the three. "And how long has it been here?"

"Beats me," The brunette-dyed-blonde responds, similarly muscular with tattoos covering her body. "I couldn't care less, though. It's been here for, what, a couple of weeks? And no one claimed it. I mean, it *was* on government property, and it wasn't registered under anyone. That part's weird enough, but I don't blame whoever did it for destroying it."

"I don't know..." The last one responds, a young girl with

dark skin and spirally hair. Semi-rounded glasses sit perched atop her nose, and she has a distinct passion in her eyes that everyone else appears to lack. "I liked it. I mean, we may not know where it came from or why it kind of just appeared here, but I think it's cool. I hate that it got trashed. I would've loved to bring that thing back to my apartment! It could be a relic, I mean, who *knows* when it could've been sculpted."

"You just like it 'cause you're an art geek," The woman jokes. "It's okay. You're not a *total* nerd."

"Ha ha ha," The girl responds, monotone. "Very funny."

"I just think it's creepy," The old man says. "It was made of stone, but it was so gruesome."

"Yeah, that's the point," The girl states. "It's telling a story of pain and misery, loss and love."

"How'd you get love from *that*? Come on, Vaya, you're smarter than that. It was a bloodied chick! Where on *Earth* did you get love from?"

"It was the eyes," Vaya retorts with a glare. "The way her arm was outstretched as if reaching for something or someone." She mimics what she's explaining by extending an arm.

Laramie. They're describing Laramie and what she looked like after her banishment. Bloodied, sad, a gruesome scene indeed. It's her, definitely her. Wait—what else did they say about it? Destroyed it?

I narrow my eyes. As I begin to approach the workers, I can feel Az behind me, their hand clasped over my shoulder. I shrug it off and continue towards the group.

"Who even likes sculptures anymore?" The woman says. "We're not in the seventeen hundreds anymore; we don't need to take a freaking chunk of rock and turn it into some old-ass Greek tragedy!"

"One, sculptures aren't limited to stone and philosophers," Vaya corrects, adjusting her glasses. "And two, it was skillfully crafted by whoever created it. It was *so* realistic. Do you know how hard it is to make stone look *smooth*? And whoever made it did a damn good job. You try chiselling a smooth texture onto a piece of stone. It ain't easy."

The woman just shrugs in response.

"Oh, whatever," the old man snarls. "Just shut up already. It's not that deep, *Juliet*. I, on the other hand, am happy it was torn apart. It's just a useless piece of junk, anyways."

Scowling, I stride forward and slam my fist against the side of the building. The foundation begins to shatter like glass, the pressure rippling towards the workers. They don't have time to understand what's happening before two sharp pieces of rock suddenly burst behind the man and the older woman. The only indication that anything hit them is their slight stagger before going completely still. That's when I see the blood that trickles down the side of the building and gushes from their backs. Two small pieces of stone protrude from their chests, puncturing them through their hearts.

The girl flinches when she hears the stone split, and her eyes widen in horror when she sees the workers' lifeless expressions; their bodies held upright only by the stone that penetrates their bodies.

She stares wildly at them as her eyes flash with fear and confusion. She glances in my direction and somehow catches a glimpse of me for a split second, her eyes widening as they focus directly on mine.

The broken stone vanishes in the blink of an eye, and the workers shrivel to the ground, no longer suspended upright or brandishing any wounds or blood as though never there. Despite every sign that leads to the conclusion that they're alive and what happened was just some sort of hallucination, one thing's for certain.

They're dead.

I carefully walk past the girl, aware but uncaring of Az following behind me, and angrily turn the corner. I stop abruptly in my tracks when I come face to face with the very thing I prayed I wouldn't have to see; a pile of rubble next to a half-submerged stone head—Laramie's head.

I'm surrounded by debris from Laramie's destroyed statue, and I fall to my knees. My wings involuntarily wrap around my shoulders as if to shelter me from the world. I can hear Az grunt as they, too, see the Virtue's crushed remains.

Az places a tentative hand on my exposed shoulder as the rain starts to pour. I flinch away from them and instead make my way to Laramie's morbid decapitation, collapsing in front of it.

With trembling hands, I grasp Laramie's head, cupping her cheeks and tenderly stroking along her hairline, staring into her glassy eyes.

I don't realize how bad it's raining until the stone beneath my hands becomes drenched in rainwater. I just wrap my wings around the debris around me, attempting to protect it—to protect *her*—from further harm. My clothes cling to my clammy skin, but all I can focus on is Laramie's broken form beneath me.

A sudden burst of lightning ignites in the distance, and the flash illuminates Laramie's face through my feathers. It glows white as dark shadows cast across her features, making her look dead and decaying. I drop the stone head with a yelp, scrambling away from it as I sob, unable to hear or feel Az beyond the deafening ringing in my ears.

My mind begins to go numb as Az tries to pull me to my feet, but I struggle, thrashing and shouting against their grip. They easily pin my arms to my waist and fumble with their words in an attempt to calm me down, but I don't listen. I don't stop squirming, fighting to be free. Something instinctual ignites my need to free myself. Horrified, I realize it's because of Nolan. No, not Nolan. *Lucifer.*

I scream furiously at Lucifer and the world. My voice is shrill and carries all my passion to the sky before dissolving into the foul air. Exhausted, I go limp upon realizing how pointless it is to struggle. Az gently presses their fingers to my hairline before a wave of heaviness envelopes me, and I pass out.

-TWENTY-NINE-

My Condolences

'm trembling as I scramble to recognize where I am. Az strides through the doorway almost a second later and carefully approaches me on the bed, tentatively sitting at the foot of it.

I don't meet their gaze, too ashamed as I squeeze my eyes shut. "I'm… I'm sorry. I'm so, *so* sorry."

I look down, dropping my hands into my lap as I stare at my palms. I'll never be able to forgive myself for this. How can I when I've killed? When I've unlawfully shed blood of another while mourning my loved one's bloodshed in the first place? I'm nothing but a hypocrite, and I deserve the pain I've endured.

'The revelation of Laramie's desecrated statue was quite a shock.' Az says, snapping me from my self-deprecating thoughts. *'Would you be interested in visiting her Grace in The Rooms? While I cannot reverse the state of her decomposition, perhaps you may find closure by seeing her soul.'*

I've got nothing else left to lose.

I nod, peeling the blankets away from me as I rise and follow Az. They lead me down a narrow path towards a small building with one sealed entrance, and all they have to do is lay their palm flat against it, and the door clicks open. They usher me inside what appears to be an ordinary room, beige walls covered with various designs alongside a vast emptiness.

Az reaches forward and, as if submerged within water, their hand disappears into the air. A ripple emanates from their wrist as they swipe their hand, revealing a seemingly endless pitch-black corridor past the severed entryway.

I stare at the now open corridor, its darkness eclipsing my sight. Still, I plunge into it with no regard for where I am, pausing long enough for my eyes to adjust to the millions upon millions—maybe even billions—of glass-like ebony rooms, each containing a single body lying unmoving in paralysis upon a thick, flat glassy slab, strikingly similar to a morgue.

I stare in awe at the first body to my left, only to realize it's nothing but a pale outline of the deceased's features and clothing. Unnerved and desperate to find Laramie, I start down the hallway, glancing into every room for my angel.

Almost twenty minutes of futile searching goes by. Still, I refuse to give up, concentrating intently to find even only a remote resemblance of Laramie that may lead me in her direction.

It takes longer than I'd like to admit until I stumble upon Laramie's room—upon peering into a room to my left, the sight of a bloody wing suspended on the far wall is what catches my attention. I backtrack, staring in horror at the severed appendages dangling on the wall.

Upon closer inspection, the room is empty, yet I know that this is Laramie's room with a burning certainty. The only difference between this one and the others is the vacant slab in the center and the grisly wings nailed to the wall.

I'm vaguely aware of Az standing in the doorway behind me. I turn to them in confusion. "Where is she?"

A shrill shriek interrupts them before they have a chance to respond, preceding a plethora of deafening screams that fill the air.

When the wings on the wall begin eviscerating, I instinctively lunge towards them, watching as the paper-like strips glide into my cupped hands only to turn to dust. "Is this supposed to happen?"

As if in response to my question, the same wall that held Laramie's wings begins to glow a bright red, and everything goes startlingly quiet before the surface erupts in a swarm of arms.

I scramble back as a figure steps through a fluid fissure while the fists hammer behind, never faltering for even a split second.

When the figure steps over the threshold, he's illuminated by an unidentified beam of light. He stalks forward slowly yet with a deranged twitch as he smirks triumphantly, his eyes possessing a sinister undercurrent. The smell of rotting corpses takes me back to Lucifer, and it's at that moment that I realize why it's so familiar—whenever Nolan attacked me, its smell hung in the air.

Horrifying flashbacks rear their ugly heads. Dread and the urge to run festers deep within me. I can't help the way my knees nearly buckle from the scent alone, as an intense trembling overwhelms me.

Behind me, Az whispers so softly that I can barely hear him, *'Lucifer.'*

Epilogue

aya Abioye's eyes widen comically at the grisly sight of her colleagues' corpses pinned against the building they were leaning against mere seconds ago.

Standing in front of the bodies of Jeff Scaff and Cady Allen siphons every ounce of strength she possesses. She stumbles back a few steps before she locks in place, staring idly at the scene ahead. No matter where she looks, the blood and the horror of the lifeless bodies are cemented behind her closed lids.

The bodies are suspended by a piece of stone that impales them through their back, the tip of which just barely protrudes where their hearts dwell inside. Blood pours from the gaping wounds and streams onto the building behind them, so much blood that it looks like a scene straight out of a horror movie—the grotesque splatters of stark red droplets staining the snow beneath them.

Their legs lifelessly dangle like inanimate objects, and Vaya watches as their knees buckle before they collapse under their own weight motionlessly.

Vaya can only stare at the bodies, the all-encompassing fear of what happened beginning to cut off her air supply. *This isn't real. This isn't real; it can't be real. I'm dreaming, come on, Vaya wake up, wake up, Vaya, WAKE UP, Vaya!*

She's terrified and confused, so, *so* confused. There's way too much blood, and somehow, they were impaled by something sharp, but… what? And how?

She nervously glances around and stiffens when she sees something in front of her—no, not some*thing,* some*one.*

Looming over the limp corpses of her colleagues stands a girl with angry eyes and… and *wings.* Although olive wings spread behind her, she looks almost demonic with the malicious snarl spread across her face.

As soon as Vaya blinks, she's gone. The girl seems to have just vanished, and the air returns to its suffocating fog within less than a second.

Turning back to Cady and Jeff, Vaya stumbles away from them when the final realization that, *holy shit, I'm standing less than five feet away from the corpses of my coworkers whom I just watched die* hits her. She stares, transfixed in a blanket of revulsion, eyes wide and face drained of colour as she desperately attempts to control her rapid breathing. *In, out. In, out. In*—

From her vantage point, Vaya can see the bodies no longer exhibit any physical injuries. The blood previously drenching them is gone, somehow, and any indication of a stab wound—or any damage for that matter—has vanished as if never there. She miserably claws at her hair and whirls around, scanning the nearly abandoned construction site for any validation that she wasn't the only one who saw any of this, that someone else saw whatever just happened to prove she *isn't* going crazy.

Before she has enough time to properly assess the situation and coordinate herself (no matter how uncoordinated the whole situation is making her), Vaya feels a presence hovering over his shoulder before a warm and palpitating hand clamps down on her.

Her jaw goes slack before she can scream, and her eyes roll back in her head. Despite the hand holding onto her, she falls facedown through an invisible barrier before swinging back into a standing position. She pinwheels her arms out to regain her balance, blinking past nausea and delirium to make out the dark floor, walls, and ceiling that make her feel like she's being swallowed whole.

She pushes her glasses up on her nose and turns to see a small blue light shining in the distance. Desperate for anything to liberate her from whatever nightmare she's caught in, she sprints towards it, watching intently as it grows closer and closer.

Vaya realizes it's no bigger than her hand—smaller even—upon reaching the light source that floats level with her chest. Curious yet cautious, she tentatively elongates her arm, simultaneously flinching and screaming when, as if plunged into a pit of hardening cement, the globe of light traps her within its energy when contact is made.

She desperately tries to yank her hand from its keep with the combined strength of both hands, but it proves futile. The light intensifies like a ruptured star before seeping into Vaya's veins and enveloping her heart in a sheet of ice. The overwhelming sensation perseveres until it's no longer a ball of light but fully absorbed within the girl's body.

As soon as her hand is freed, Vaya pulls it away, the force of which sends her tumbling to the floor. She squeezes her eyes shut and braces for the impact as she plummets to the ground and falls through the floor again.

The first thing she feels is the numbing cold that seeps into her bones upon coming to. Gasping, her body spasms as she lifts her heavy head off the cold, wet ground, glasses muddled with water droplets from the snow. She blinks and looks up to see at least four officers kneeling around her, one staring at her with his brows furrowed and hand planted on the small of her back.

A spark ignites in her head, a dizzying yet comforting presence within her begins to buzz around her skull, fighting to be freed. Rain begins to pour, and confused and fearful eyes dart from officer to officer.

"Hey, you awake?" An officer's hands reflexively reach towards his holster when he notices Vaya awakening, his voice harsh and bellowing. She overlooks the shine of his lapel in the dim light that reads Sergeant Pearson, and before he can consider saying anything else, her hands shoot into the air, and she forces herself to nod. She sags against the ground, disregarding the snow soaking her clothes and dampening her body or the water trickling into her shoes.

Pearson stares at her, fist hovering over his holster as he glances back at the unmoving bodies.

It's at that moment that Vaya realizes she's collapsed across the legs of one of the bodies. She yelps and inadvertently throws herself into the officer's chest before launching herself back against the building wall, cowering against it. She ignores the moisture obscuring her glasses in favour of not making any sudden moves.

The cold is painful against her skin, but Vaya doesn't move, even as her arms shake from being raised above her head. Fearful glassy eyes aimlessly stare off into the distance as though she sees through everyone and everything, blank and semi-coherent.

"Hey, Pearson," Shouts one of the officers. "They're dead, no pulse, but there's no physical wound."

"You all right?" Pearson asks, his expression firm and intimidating. Vaya nods slowly, stalling her movements so they don't mistake it for anything that might threaten them. "Get up."

She immediately scrambles to her feet, palms cold and almost numb as she shoves them onto the icy ground to push herself up. She shakily gets onto her feet, arms hovering in the air. "You can lower your hands now."

She lets her arms drop to her sides, limbs suddenly heavy, and takes her glasses off, wiping them on her wet shirt before returning them to the bridge of her nose. She tries to avert her gaze to the ground beneath her as she listens to the rhythmic shuffling of the officers surveying the scene. She can vaguely make out Pearson's lips moving, but everything she hears is muted, her ears stuffed full of cotton. She's so dizzy and disoriented that she doesn't notice when she starts swaying, knees wobbling and about to buckle. She's dangerously sick to her stomach, and had she been the tiniest bit nauseous, she would have vomited then and there.

She snaps out of her thoughts when she feels the officer from before—Pearson—roughly grab her arm, dragging her to one of the nearby police cars.

She watches in a daze as he yanks open the door to the back of the cop car. She compliantly allows herself to be maneuvered into the backseat, and only then does she realize how numb and tired her legs are. Releasing a deep breath, she lets her eyes flutter shut as she focuses on the sergeant's voice.

"All right, girl. Let's start with your full name, address, and a couple of telephone numbers where I can reach you if I need to in the future."

As much as Vaya doesn't want to give up her information to these police officers, the fact that they know she didn't kill her coworkers—since there were no physical injuries—relaxes her, even if only slightly.

Taking a deep breath, Vaya gulps before answering. "Vaya Abioye, um, V-A-Y-A A-B-I-O-Y-E. I live at Forest Bank, a-apartment six-ten." She recites her cell number and her roommates, stuttering and sniffing as she wills herself not to cry, at least not in front of the sergeant.

"Okay. Now tell me exactly what you saw. Don't leave any details out."

Glossary

An·gel (Third Triad)

/ānjəl/

1. A spiritual being who acts as an attendant, agent, or messenger of God.
2. Classification of angels; lowest order of celestial beings.

An·gel·ic Choir

/an'jelik kwī(ə)r/

Hierarchy of angels in Heaven ranked by importance.

A·pos·tate

/ə'pä'stāt/

An angel who betrays their community; disloyal; traitor.

Arch·an·gel (Third Triad)

/ärk,ānjəl/

Classification of angels; entrusted with tasks within Heaven.

Au·thor·i·tar·i·an (First Sphere)

/ə,THôrə'terēən/

Classification of angels; disciplinarians, regulates the inner workings of Heaven.

Az

/əz/

The creator of Heaven and angels; God.

Choir·en

/kwī(ə)rən/

Fellowship of angels, denomination of "brethren."

Con·ver·sion Clock

/kən'vərZHən kläk/

A celestial device that translates human time in Angelic terms.

Do·min·ion (Second Triad)

/də'minyən/

Classification of angels; regulates the duties of lower angels.

El·der (First Triad)

/eldər/

Classification of angels; living symbols of God's justice and authority.

El·ys·pi·enne [el-ees-b-n]

/ə'lēz'pē'ən/

A weapon forged by God that can sever any surface.

God·spi·ttle

/gäd'spidl/

A derogatory term; an obsequious or overly deferential person.

Grace

/grās/

The blood of angels that administers celestial abilities.

Light·lapse

/līt'laps/

The time in the evening when the sun disappears or daylight fades.

Light·lift

/līt'lift/

The time in the morning when the sun appears or full daylight arrives.

Me·da·en

/mēdāən/

Twelve o'clock in the day; midday.

O·na

/ōnə/

The creator of the universe, Earth, and humans.

Par·a·dise

/'perə,dīs/

Also known as "The Garden Of Eden," the abode of Ona.

Post·mede

/pōst'mēd/

The middle of the day; noon.

Pow·er (Second Triad)

/'pou(ə)r/

Classification of angels; supervises angels' affairs.

Pre·mede

/pri'mēd/

The period of time between sunrise to noon.

Re·perse

/rēpərs/

The rebirth of a human soul in a celestial body.

Scr·ibe (Third Triad)

/skrīb/

Classification of angels; monitors of Earth who control what knowledge Humans possess of Heaven and God's existence.

Ser·a·phim (First Triad)

/'serəfim/

Classification of angels; God's attendants who oversee their throne.

Still·fall [stillfawl]

/still'fôl/

The period of time between sunset to sunrise.

The A·then·ae·um

/THə ˌaTHə'nēəm/

A book repository in Heaven that contains all worldly and otherworldly expertise.

The Crux

/THə krəks/

The dense central region and inner part of the Earth.

The Dawn (of Creation)

/THə dön/

The rapid expansion of matter; the origin of the universe.

The Pass·age

/THə 'pasij/

The portal that separates Heaven's and Earth's domains.

The Rooms

/THə rooms/

A division of Heaven of the good after death, where human and angel souls not deemed for Hell reside.

The Switch

/THə swiCH/

A condition of body and mind that recurs for several hours every night and day, in which Angels supervise humanity.

Vir·tue (Second Triad)

/ˈvərCHōo/

Classification of angels; embarks upon Earth to dole out signs and miracles.

Whyn·thal

/ˈwinTHôl/

Angelic term for "Winter."

Acknowledgements

Myself, L. D. Lewis, Elaine Broughton, Elizabeth Shumovich, Martha Welshman, Amelia Welshman, Jennica Comley, Natalie Flach, Lucy Webster, Ria Das, Mackenzie Brown, Maeve Wheaton, Kenya Mailloux, Elizabeth Kritzer, Abigail Ellis, Samantha Humphrey, Madeline Mortimer, Marguerite Cuddy, Mr. & Mrs. N. N. Light, Karen Haefling, Samantha Hodge, Laurie Craig, Bonnie Welshman, Paige Gumaer, Katelyn Van Veen, Mikeal Tyler, and You.

© Mackenzie Brown

A. L. SLADE is the 17-year-old author of "The Bloodshed of the Betrayed", the first book in the anticipated series, "The Mercy Chronicles". Slade brings this skillfully adapted tale to life with her endless creativity and descriptive story-telling as her hopes to enlighten readers and portray young authors in a bright and intelligent way is the backbone of her writing career. She currently lives surrounded by friends and family in Stratford, Ontario, Canada.

Printed in Great Britain
by Amazon

83531663R00150